The Prince, the Princess and the Dark Horse

The Prince, the Princess and the Dark Horse

LIZBETH ROANE

The characters and events in this book are a creation of the author's imagination and fictional. Any resemblance to persons or events past or present is completely coincidental.

Editor: Sharon Honeycutt
Cover design: KarrieRoss.com
Formatting: Ajao Ifeoluwa

First Edition Printing 2020

Dedicated

to my husband, Scott, who has spent far
too many evenings looking at the top
of my head as I was hunched over my computer.
Thank you, honey!

Table of Contents

One

Habsburg Empire, 1752

Olivia brushed her hair a few more strokes and headed out of the dressing room, ready for bed. The doors to the balcony were still open, and Olivia stood before them, debating. The spring evening was pleasant, but it was early in the season. Although the moon and the stars were bright in the sky, it would get chilly during the night, and she would have to get up and close the doors. As much as she cherished looking out at the brilliant night sky, she hated to get up shivering and run to close the doors.

Suddenly, a hand clamped over her mouth and pulled her back into a solid, muscled chest, taking Olivia completely off guard. She had not heard him approach. Who was this man? How had he gotten into her room? And did he know who she was? Olivia was startled but not afraid; she had been expecting something like this for a long time. Why, though, did he not just kill her?

"Be quiet and do as you are told, Princess, and I might let you live."

Olivia could see the moonlight shining on the metal of the knife that had been raised to the level of her chin. Even without the knife, she would have been helpless to do anything against him. His chest felt rock-hard against her back, and his shirt sleeves were folded up, displaying the strong muscles in his arms as he held the knife and her against him.

"Do you understand me, Princess?" The voice was in her ear, and she felt his breath on her cheek.

The word "princess" was full of disdain.

She could only bob her head slightly, yes. He removed his hand, but quickly replaced it with a cloth across her mouth, pulling it so tight that she had no choice but to open her mouth, the cloth threatening to cut through the sides of her mouth. One hand remained on the ends of the tied cloth over her mouth while the other grabbed the back of her dressing gown and jerked her towards the bed. Olivia stumbled and pitched forward, but her hands shot out and kept her from falling onto the bed. She knew it would not be in her best interest to fall onto the bed; she would not make it easy for him if he had thoughts of violating her before he killed her.

He pulled her upright. "Get the clothing out of the bag."

Noticing a traveling bag on the bed, Olivia reached for it, removing a dirndl and apron—servant clothing, but they smelled clean. Olivia sought her mind to understand why this man was doing this. Did he have to kill her in another place? He could well be done with it here and gone without such a concern. He must have another intention as well, but what, she could not fathom.

"Put it on."

Olivia hesitated and was rewarded with another harsh pull on her nightdress that brought her back against his chest again.

"Put it on,—now!"

Olivia slipped the nightdress off her shoulders but held it up with her upper arms until she was ready to pull the dirndl down over her head. This was the best she could do to guard her dignity. Next, she placed the apron around her waist and tied it in the back. Once that was done, he grabbed her wrists and bound them together, then he pushed her back into the dressing room and sat her upon the settee. He plowed through her footwear until he found a pair of low walking boots and placed them on her feet. Pulling a scarf from the peg, he tied it, securing her hair.

With a hand clenched around her upper arm, he pulled her up and guided her back into the bedroom where he retrieved the bag that had held the clothes. The knife reappeared. Slipping behind her, he held it to her throat, and she felt the cold steel against her collarbone. She knew he was taking her somewhere, somewhere far enough to need footwear. If he were just taking her outside, it would have been a waste of time to find the walking boots, not to mention the noise they could create compared to her bare feet. But this man seemed to have no concern for time.

"Not a sound, Princess, not one sound."

He opened the bedroom door, pushed her out into the hallway, and pointed her to the back stairway. All was quiet for the night. Her mother had retired early, as usual, and most of the servants had left for the day, not to return until dawn. They went down the servant stair and out through the summer kitchen, then walked through the herb garden towards the stables. If Olivia was to raise an alarm, it would have to be here, but only some of the older servants stayed on the estate, and Olivia was sure their windows were closed. Shouting would only anger him and would most likely not rouse anyone that could actually help her.

Passing through the door in the garden wall, they came to a horse standing untethered just outside the wall. When they approached, the horse fell in and walked quietly along behind him. He untied her wrists and brought them in front, tying them again, the process happening so quickly that Olivia had not a chance to break away had she even had the thought.

He stayed the horse, then pulled Olivia behind him as he walked up the sloping wall. He turned and mounted the horse, then pulled Olivia onto the horse in front of him. Olivia immediately started to sway as the horse moved, and she feared she would fall off. She had never been astride a horse and did not know how to gain her balance. Just as she righted herself in one direction, the horse swayed in the other.

He pulled her back tightly against him and wrapped his arms around her. "Relax against me and move with the horse."

Olivia had no idea how to do either of those things, but he held onto her tightly and slowly the horse started to walk. After a few minutes she felt like she was moving with the horse instead of against it. They rode slowly for an hour, then left the road and headed over fields, then finally down along a stream. He told her he would untie her mouth if she was quiet, and she nodded her head, yes; the cloth was wearing into her skin.

He said not a word as they rode, still holding her tightly against him with both arms, the horse barely needing direction; it seemed to know where this man wanted to go. They rode for what seemed like several more hours until he stopped near some large boulders. Olivia knew not where they were. She had never been this far from the estate, but she knew the stream that ran through the lands of the estate wound in every direction.

As he helped Olivia from the horse, her legs were so numb that she almost fell to the ground. He caught her, though, and helped her to sit on a rock before taking the horse to drink from the stream. Leaving the horse to eat, he produced a skin of watered wine and, after untying her wrists, gave it to her to drink. They sat in silence for a few minutes until Olivia asked permission to step around to the other side of the rocks for a moment of privacy.

"Why are you doing this?" she asked, coming back to where he sat. She could not keep the question to herself any longer.

As they had been riding, Olivia had little else to do except think. It was not a robbery; this man had not touched any of the valuables in the house. This was not a rape; this man had not touched her. If he was to kill her, why take such a concern as this? Whatever his purpose, it was well planned. This man had not stopped to think; his next move was already decided. Everything was well-thought-out and prepared for; nothing was left to chance. There was a purpose for this, but Olivia could not reason why anyone would have need of her.

"Your father is holding someone I want back very much. He has not been willing to talk, negotiate, or reason with me. I will trade his precious daughter for my brother."

"And if he will not listen to you?"

"I will inform him that I will kill you."

"You may as well kill me now. My father cares not what happens to me. He will tell you to kill me."

"Why would your father have such little care for you?"

"Because I am a woman. I am not his heir, and I am no use to him."

"But daughters can be sold—for land, money, alliances—especially beautiful daughters."

"Surely you can see that I am well past the fashionable age of marriage. My father has no desire to concern himself with a marriage for me."

At eighteen, Olivia would be considered an old maid and had long given up hope for a family of her own. She would live a life of solitude as her mother had done. No one had much use for a female that was an embarrassment to her family. Her life would not be long; her father would never allow the possibility of his secrets to be told ... but at least the curse would die when Olivia did.

"I do not believe you, Princess. You say what I would expect anyone to say that wishes to escape the predicament in which you find yourself. I have no pity for you. I will not let you go because you have squeezed a few tears from your eyes. Your father may be hard with you, but I am sure his mind will change when he sees a knife to your throat."

"You have been ill-advised," she told him, "My father has never set eyes upon me. I doubt he will even believe it is me. Either way, he will not care."

As they sat in silence for a few minutes, she knew there could be no good outcome for her from this. She could only pray that her death came swiftly. She would die, and she did not fear it; she only hoped to escape prolonged pain. What good would crying or screaming do? The outcome would be the same—although she did hope this man would be able to rescue his brother. Olivia had little doubt that his brother was not a villain, but rather a victim of her father.

"He has never seen you?"

"Within an hour of the egregious sin of giving birth to a daughter, my mother was ordered from my father's house and commanded never to return again. My mother went back to her parents. My father paid the church for a divorce from my mother, and her parents placed her in the country, out of their sight and out of their minds."

Olivia had never spoken these things to another person, though she had spent a lifetime gleaning these tidbits of her early life. It was not the sort of thing that was supposed to be discussed, but the servants passed gossip and sometimes were unaware of where little ears happened to be. Although she had known these things for a very long time, she had an ease of mind now that she had told another person. She would have to pay for a sin she never committed, but now she felt that someone would know that she had been alive, even if she would never really live a life.

"If you were to release me, I could not go back. My mother's parents would not take me back. I have left the estate with a man—willing or not—and so I am no longer clean. They need little more of an embarrassment. The church will not take me. I am a bastard as my father divorced my mother. I have been expecting my father to send someone to kill me all my life, and I thought you were the one. There is no point in burdening yourself with me. You will travel with more ease without me. It would reason for you to kill me now. This is a pretty spot. It is more than most have as their final sight."

Thorne could not believe the words coming from this woman's mouth, but looking into her face, he knew that she told the truth. The prince had always maintained that his first two wives died in childbirth. His third wife, recently wed, was expecting a child. His second wife died at court in Vienna, as did the child. Most thought the child from the first wife had died as well, but a few had said, no, the child was alive. The child had been sent to be raised properly by her mother's parents.

The prince was known to be an extremely ambitious man, mayhaps the most ambitious in the empire. Many said that the prince was hiding his daughter and that she would emerge to marry mayhaps the next archduke or the king of a neighboring empire. One needed allies outside this empire as well as inside. And when Thorne had seen the prince's daughter in the garden of the country estate, it was obvious that she was a woman of uncommon beauty. The prince would have the pick of grooms for his daughter.

But Olivia had said that her mother had been alive after giving birth, and Thorne did not doubt that the prince had paid for a divorce. Although it was strictly against the church, a divorce could be had for the right price. Thorne felt the weight of everything Olivia had said. She would be dead, and she would be dead soon. The question was, by whose hand? If Thorne followed through with his plan, the prince would have her killed to keep his secret quiet. If he took her back to the estate, her grandparents would turn her away, and she would be forced to wander the streets, where she would find no kindness. The church would not allow her in either; the knowledge of a divorce would shine a light on the sin of the church while calling the child a sinful being.

He had spent so much time planning and researching this plot, but the outcome hinged on Thorne's belief that the prince would want his beloved daughter safe and sound. Thorne had never considered that the prince would want his daughter dead. Thorne looked over at Olivia's beautiful, calm face, but all he saw was the face of his sweet Auria. His heart gave a painful squeeze, thinking about Auria being in the dire situation in which Thorne had put Olivia. Would she look at her future with the clarity and peace that Olivia did?

He would take Olivia home with him. His mother would know what to do; she was far more clever in this type of situation than Thorne or Chance, for whom his fear escalated. The prince was indeed a cold-hearted man, capable of doing anything to see his aspirations come to fruition. This was a small matter with Chance, but it was escalating into a battle of wills. And thus far the prince could only be satisfied by winning not only each battle, but the entire war into which this disagreement was intensifying.

Both Thorne and Chance had traveled to Bruneck to enjoy the spring festivals. Thorne had grown bored and restless with the revelries and headed back home, but Chance had stayed to compete in the archery competitions, which Chance was favored to win. After soundly trouncing his competition, Chance too had headed home, stopping at a hamlet for a repast and to shelter for the night. While awaiting his evening meal and enjoying a few pints, a man entered the inn and became quite agitated by the sight of Chance.

During the night the prince's men came and took Chance, by some considerable force, and locked him in the prison at the prince's castle, accusing him of seducing the wife of a guest of the prince's. Chance had insisted he never touched the man's wife, but the woman gave testimony with certainty that it was Chance. Thorne knew full well that his brother was innocent. Chance was married to Margarette, whom he loved to distraction. Thorne knew his brother would never touch another woman, and certainly not another man's wife. Chance was a man of honor.

Thorne, however, was not, and now his twin sat in a prison cell accused of a crime that he had not committed. In truth, though, the woman never mentioned to Thorne that she had a husband until the man came crashing into the room. Thorne had been lucky to escape with only a sore ankle from his jump from the balcony. He could have been leaving with his head under his arm.

He had planned to have the Dark Horse take Olivia to her father and make the trade. If Thorne did it himself, he would likely join his brother in the prison cell with nothing to gain from it. If the deal could not be done, then the Dark Horse could kill Olivia. No one doubted that the Dark Horse would kill her. He was known for all manner of deeds, benevolent as well as evil, whichever suited his whim—and his purse—although all knew the Dark Horse had no need of coin, was high because that suited his whims as well.

No one knew the identity of the Dark Horse. It was said that he was indeed the angel referred to by St. John as the Dark Horse of the Apocalypse. All feared him, and none dared to cross him. If one required the services of the Dark Horse, all one must do was to put out the intent. The Dark Horse would come to you, in his time, and agree to the deed ... or cut out the tongue of the requestor. One did not coquet with the Dark Horse. The stories of his deeds went back generations and generations. One had little choice but to believe him the angel bearing the scales of justice.

Thorne turned his horse towards home; there was no need to tryst with the Dark Horse now. Olivia had been fully cooperative, and he saw no need to bind and gag her again. They traveled until the wee hours of the night as clouds moved in and slowed their progress. When they came to the remains of an old house by the river, Thorne decided to stop. They would pass the rest of the night there and cross the river in the morning.

Two

livia had no real fear of this man, something she had realized even back in her room. Although at times his voice was harsh, he did not radiate any true malevolence. She had no idea what this man planned to do with her now, but that really did not concern her. He had planned all things well before now; she was sure he would make a new plan. Olivia was simply unsure she would be part of his plan.

As he laid out his cloak to rest upon, he looked at Olivia. He had spent so many hours looking at her, he knew her well by now. From afar, her beauty was stunning; up close, it was almost unbelievable. She was slightly taller than most women, only a hand span shorter than Thorne's six-foot frame, and she was much thinner. Her hair was the color of early summer honey with a touch of white, as if the clouds had dripped from the sky. Her mother, whom Thorne had thought her grandmother, was not an unpleasant-looking woman, but the prince was not blessed with even a sparkle of joy for the eyes. His daughter, however, had a face that must have been intended for an angel.

In most of the surrounding countries and empires, beauty was appreciated, but it was not what made a woman valuable. Here, though, beauty was prized. If the prince had taken Olivia to court in Vienna, every man would have been on his knees begging for her hand, but the prince had chosen not to claim this treasure that had been given to him. Mayhaps after he saw her beauty, the prince would change his mind, but there was still the problem of her age.

It was common to arrange the union while the issues were still infants. If the mother was pleasant to the eye, it was believed the daughter would be as well. The marriage would then take place when the female physically became a woman. Thorne had no interest in wedding or bedding children; he preferred a woman at least Olivia's age. But fashion was what it was, and Olivia was too old for the current marriage market.

It took Thorne almost an hour to talk Olivia into sleeping on the cloak with him, underneath another cloak for warmth. He had never made that many promises to all the women he had known, let alone one, but Thorne did not want Olivia to mention to his mother that he had not treated her with the respect her position required. He was twenty-seven years old, and there were some aspects of his life that he did not want open for discussion with his mother. Consequently, Thorne had promised to keep his back to her, his hands completely to himself, not to snore, and not to steal the covering cloak all for himself—and he could never tell another soul that they had reclined anywhere near each other. Thorne thought mayhaps he had even promised to deny this happened to God himself.

Thorne never promised, however, not to bind Olivia to him. In truth, she had never brought it up in all her demands. So when Thorne tied their wrists and ankles together, he could honestly reply that he was not violating any of the promises he had made to her. Thorne did not trust Olivia—he would not trust anyone in circumstances such as this. He did not want her running off on her own. Her current predicament was his fault, and if she ran off, he would have to go after her. Something told him that he had only seen a glimmer of the strength this woman had, but inner strength and discernment were not the same. Running off would not be in her best interest, but that did not mean she would not try.

Thorne lay on his side, trying to sleep, as the fragrance of some wildflower drifted towards him from Olivia. He had been smelling it since he grabbed her in her room. It was a very subtle fragrance, not like the strong fragrance that women preferred, and Thorne rather liked it. One day Thorne had watched Olivia walk two hours to a field where she slowly and carefully picked specific flowers for hours, stopping only for a quick drink, until the sun had started to slip from the sky. Then she had walked the two hours back to the estate with the flowers tied up in a bed cloth, a bundle almost as big as she on her back. Thorne wondered if this scent came from one of those flowers.

For almost two weeks, Thorne had watched her for hours and hours, every day. He needed to know who was in the house and the usual daily flow of the estate, and he discovered that Olivia was not a pampered princess. She worked in the herb garden and helped with the daily chores. It was not uncommon to see her playing with the servants' children or reading to them. She also played the pianoforte and read in the evenings. Unlike fashionable women, her hair was usually down, bound at the back with a scarf. She wore work clothing during the day and bathed and changed before dining with her mother. Otherwise, Thorne had rarely seen her mother out and about the estate.

He had enjoyed watching her, far more than he should have. He was scouting, but he told himself that there was no reason he could not enjoy scouting. After watching her, though, he knew he would never be able to kill her; he would leave that for the Dark Horse to do. But as he lay there, he realized he would miss the subtle, flowery scent of her. It was comforting and alluring at the same time, smelling of clean spring air and warm sunlight, of making love in a field of flowers. He drifted off to sleep thinking of making love to Olivia in her field of flowers.

"Damn ... damn ... damn." The thought marched through his mind as he headed home, unsure who he was angrier with, Olivia or himself. When he had awakened in the morning, Olivia was gone. An expert tracker, he had searched for her for two days, but he found no sign of her—no hair in a bush, no broken twigs. It was as though she had vanished into the air.

"The prince has sent word that he will meet with you concerning Chance," his mother informed him as she came in to dine.

He had been back only an hour—enough time to bathe and change before coming to the evening meal. Neither Margarette nor Auria had come to dine, which was not a good sign. Thorne had little doubt that his mother intended to use this time to impress upon Thorne that he needed to get this matter settled with the prince and get Chance home.

"This situation is not good for Margarette's delicate condition," his mother said without looking up from her soup, but Thorne knew a reply was expected.

"I have no desire to concern her unduly."

"And Auria should be focused on the wedding. We have delayed it as long as possible."

"There is no reason she cannot make arrangements for the wedding."

"She is worried that you will not be here. She can hardly wed without you here!" his mother responded, her voice rising in volume. Thorne wished he could thwart her anger, but he had nothing to say to placate her.

"I thought this matter was settled," she said.

"I was wrong."

His mother's eyes bore into him, and her eyebrows shot up nearly to her hairline. If this had not been such an important matter, Thorne would have laughed at the sight. He did not worry about his brother in the prince's prison cell; Thorne knew Chance was hardy. But he had to remind himself that although his mother had mentioned only Margarette and Auria, it was her son in prison. Her connection with Chance was different from Thorne's, but no less of a connection. He could not tell his mother that he felt no distress about Chance though. If his twin were in trouble, he would know; no matter the miles between them, he would know.

"The prince's daughter is not alive?"

"Oh, she is well alive, but the prince has no desire to claim her."

"Is there something wrong with her?"

"Not that I could find. In truth, she is very beautiful and intelligent. But his first wife did not die in childbirth."

Now his mother's face registered shock, and Thorne knew the rest of the story would shock her more, but he had to finish it now.

"The prince divorced his first wife."

"Divorced her? How? Why?"

"He did not want a daughter," Thorne said. "He wanted an heir."

"But you said she was beautiful ..."

"He has never seen her. He no doubt wants the knowledge of his divorce to stay hidden."

"The church should never have let him remarry."

"I am sure that can be bought as well."

"So you never took the girl?"

"Yes, I did."

"But, Thorne, her family will not want her back."

"She mentioned that."

"Where is she? You did not just leave her in the woods?"

"She ran off."

"What do you mean, 'she ran off'?"

"We—or rather, I—decided to wait until morn to cross the river. In the morning she was gone." His mother's lips pursed, ready to interject. "Wait! Before you say more, I searched for her for two days, but I could find no sign of her."

"I must go to the chapel and pray for her." His mother rose from the table.

Thorne knew that his mother had a kind, loving heart, but he also knew that the old ways had not died. His mother would pray for Olivia, but she was also praying that Olivia did not rain down a curse upon the family for what Thorne did. Thorne had not a care concerning a curse, but he did worry about Olivia out there and alone. He needed to put her out of his mind; he needed to concentrate on Chance. He would leave to speak with the prince first thing in the morning.

Thorne was escorted into the prince's drawing room by several well-armed men. The prince was far more important than Thorne and had armed men all about the residence. Thorne saw these men exchange looks when he presented himself. No doubt they had seen Chance and realized the two were twins. He noted the look in their eyes; superstition had not been kind to identical twins.

Two more armed guards preceded the prince into the room. Thorne wondered if the man feared walking the halls of his own home, but he knew the guard was meant to impress upon others his esteem. Thorne attempted to put a properly contrite look upon his face, but the prince looked upon Thorne but a moment.

"Seize him!"

The guards grabbed Thorne, and another came forward to relieve him of his blade. Thorne wondered if the prince had been able to appraise the true culprit, or if he was punishing Thorne for his lack of respect—for not cowering to the prince during their negotiations for Chance's release.

"Do you believe me a fool? You sentenced your brother to prison for your crime. I will not deal well with either of you. Your brother could have said he had a twin, but I am not surprised by the deception of twins. Is their evilness not known?"

The guards threw Thorne to the floor and searched him for other weapons, a process that included several punches and sharp kicks, although Thorne put up no quarrel with the prince's men. Thorne knew that he should be mindful of his life and future, but he could only think that the prince was Olivia's father. He had seen the prince, at a distance, and even from afar his ugliness was obvious. Thorne knew nothing of the man's character, except he was ambitious at any cost, but Thorne searched for anything the prince had passed to his daughter ... and found nothing.

The armed men dragged him down numerous hallways and finally took him down several flights of stairs. There was little light, but Thorne could see that the prince had many prison cells, and all were full. He was taken to the last cell and thrown in with enough force to send him painfully into the stone wall. As the blackness in front of his eyes fought to take over, Thorne noticed movement from his left side.

"Shall I embrace you or kill you?"

"Kill me. I would rather die by your hand than the prince's. At least you have reason to kill me."

"How is Margarette?"

"She is well in body, but poor in spirit. I have promised to bring you home to her."

"Have you a plan for this?"

"Not at this moment in time, no."

As the fog cleared in his head and his eyes adjusted to the light, Thorne could see that Chance looked well. He did not look like he had been starved, and he was fairly clean. In truth, he barely looked like he had been imprisoned for almost six weeks. His dark-brown hair had grown down below his shoulders—longer than Thorne's and longer than fashionable. His lower face was slightly darkened; he had shaved in the last few days, and although his clothes were not his own, they were clean a few days ago.

Thorne had Chance tell him everything about the ancestral home of the prince. Summer would be upon them soon, and the prince would not travel to court until fall. Thorne had no desire to wait until then to find out if they would be released or taken to court to be sentenced by the archduchess. Thorne knew the archduchess faced threats from many sides and doubted she would have patience for this matter. In truth, she was a very pious monarch, and adultery would not stand well with her. Either way, Thorne did not feel his chances to walk away a free man were in his favor.

Over the next two weeks Thorne gained no new information that would help them escape the castle. Three times a day they were taken to the servants' kitchen and served decent meals. Thorne noted that he and Chance were the only prisoners given this deference. Because they were taken through the servants' area of the castle and the journey was short, Thorne was not able to get a clear understanding of the castle.

Every three to four days they were allowed to bathe, and they were shaven and given fresh clothing. For the average prisoner, it was not bad at all, but to another prince, it was more than a slight affront—which Thorne was sure it was meant to be. Well-practiced and comfortable in conversing with all stations of society, any attempts Thorne made to speak with the guards were met with stone-cold silence.

There was no word from the prince; he was allowing the brothers to sit and stew. As time went on, Thorne thought about using his knowledge about the prince's divorce as a blackmail tool, but that could also come back to hurt Thorne and, even worse, Chance. Thorne could not, even for a brief moment, allow himself to forget that Chance was an innocent victim in this circumstance. No longer were they two young, reckless brothers on an adventure; Chance had a pregnant wife and another child at home. If they were killed, it would leave all Carinthia open as fodder for the swine to fight over. Thus far, all his attempts to resolve this matter had ended poorly; he could not afford another mishap.

Thorne did not think that the prince was a complete fool. If Thorne uttered any word about the prince's divorce, the prince would march them off to Vienna. The archduchess's religious views were a double-edged sword: they would work in Thorne's favor regarding the prince's divorce but hurt Thorne in his crime of adultery as she wrestled with that herself—her husband had several mistresses. Thorne could see no opportune outcome for him and Chance should this matter be brought before the archduchess; he needed to bring this to a resolution before fall.

They needed to escape. Thorne was sure that the matter would be quietly dropped if they managed that feat. The prince could not chase Thorne and Chance to Carinthia without a greater charge. Could his witness be sure which brother was indeed to blame? And without a doubt the prince would not want to be publicly humiliated by admitting the brothers had escaped from his prison.

Unfortunately, absolutely no opportunity presented itself.

It was Wednesday, and the priest would be coming to hear their confession. Thorne had little new to say to the priest, so he would confess his sinful anger with the prince again, although he spent his nights full of thoughts and desires for the prince's daughter, a sin to which he had not verbally confessed. He was in a prison cell for his one-time act with the wife of the prince's guest; the irony did not escape Thorne, though he saw no reason to share it with the prince. Thorne knew the castle priest would have no choice but to report such a thing to the prince, even if the information had been gleaned from a private confession.

Thorne spent the evening saying penance for his thoughts concerning the prince, although Thorne felt justified in his anger. He did not say penance for his thoughts about Olivia; he could not imagine any man not having the same thoughts of her. In truth, how could God create such a vision of beauty and expect a man to have nothing but pure thoughts? On Saturday night the priest came and gave a homily to all the prisoners and then came cell to cell to give Communion. This evening the priest came in with another brother who kept his head down and his cowl covering his face. As the priest started to give Chance Communion, the brother moved towards Thorne.

"Take this chisel. There is a grate under the cot. Remove the grate. It is large enough for you to crawl into. Head south. It will empty into the drainage from the kitchen. Follow the flow, and it will lead to a lake. The Dark Horse will be there waiting for you. You must leave tonight. The lock on the grate across the sewage tunnel has been broken, but you must leave before it has been found."

"Olivia!" Thorne exclaimed in amazement when he recognized her voice. "What are you doing here?"

"Shh, take the chisel." Her hand came out of the sleeve of the robe, and Thorne could see that her skin was dry, cracked, and bleeding.

"Your hand ..." How could this princess have the hands of the lowest servant?

"I work in the kitchen." Olivia had no idea why she was giving this man this information.

She had just mere moments to compose herself once she stepped into the cell. Her nerves were jumbled enough—this was the greatest risk she had ever taken in her life—but as soon as Olivia walked into the cell, she recognized this man. The priest had warned Olivia that the two men were identical twins and she would not be able to tell one from the other. The priest could not. But Olivia had no difficulty seeing the difference between the brothers. It soothed her nerves (and yet was more unnerving) that the priest had gone to the one brother and she would have to speak with this man.

Thorne could not believe his ears. She was a scullery maid. "Does your father know?"

"No, you must keep silent."

"Come with us."

"I cannot."

When Thorne reached out and grabbed her hand, she winced in pain, and he withdrew his. There was blood on his palm.

"Please come with us." Thorne was in no position to compel her; he could only plead with her.

"No, I cannot." She placed the chisel in his bloody palm and turned to rush out of the cell before he could say more.

Three

Thorne had been aware of the grate, and he had almost decided that although they had no idea where it led, it would be their pathway to escape. When the guards retired for the night, Thorne and Chance worked to free the grate from the vent. It was a tight squeeze, but the two men were able to get their frames into the stone passage. Thorne led the way in absolute darkness, trusting that the passage did not just drop off, and slowly they made their way to the sewage tunnel. It took several hours to get through the tunnel, and more than once Thorne wondered if they had headed in the wrong direction.

The stench that preceded the next tunnel assured the two brothers that they were indeed heading in the proper direction. Both Thorne and Chance had to clamp their jaws shut to prevent the violent physical reaction they had to the smell. The sewage water from the kitchen was knee-deep, and a rancid layer of grease lay on top of it as thick as a fist. They still had no light, and Thorne and Chance had to trust that they were indeed following the flow of the sickening ooze. The sludge gave no feel of flow; it just felt stagnant. They traveled again for several hours with just their tracking skills to lead them in the proper direction.

The lock on the gate was broken, but the gate was rusted in place. At least they finally had some moonlight to guide their movements, and they were able to breathe fresh air. Using small stones, Thorne and Chance worked on the melded spots on the gate. The toll of their night was starting to be made known— their muscles were sore, blood ran from wounds, and the men were parched.

Plunging into the lake, they swam away from the castle to the shore. Thorne thought it blissful to wash the rancid grease off his body, but his muscles groaned as he worked his way to the shore. Both men were excellent swimmers, but Thorne noted that it took them far longer than it normally would have to swim the small distance. Once out of the water, Thorne and Chance stood still, allowing their eyes and ears to gain purchase.

When they heard the soft whinny of horses, they headed that way, but circled about and approached with caution until they had a clear view of the sole rider and the two other horses. Few words were exchanged as Thorne and Chance mounted and followed the Dark Horse into the night, but Thorne kept looking back at the castle. He did not want to leave Olivia. It was his fault that her hands were bleeding. He could not go back to his comfortable life while she was scrubbing floors and dishes.

Thorne reined in his horse. "I have to go back."

"Thorne, are you mad? Why would you face the prince again?" Chance could not understand why his brother would willingly walk into death.

"I cannot leave her."

"Who?"

"Olivia."

"The prince's daughter. She brought the chisel to your cell with the priest." The Dark Horse gave Chance an idea of what was on Thorne's mind.

Chance had not been able to hear many of the words Thorne had exchanged with the brother in their cell, and Thorne had not mentioned anything to Chance until the guards left for the night. Even then, their words were few; their concern was with leaving. Chance had heard the brother say, "I cannot," and was shocked by the thought that the brother was a woman. He had the thought that mayhaps this was the woman that was the cause of their imprisonment and that she had come to right the wrong to which she had been party. But now Chance was more confused than ever.

He had no idea that the prince had a daughter—and one that was not just a child—and Chance had seen the blood on Thorne's hand, knowing it had come from the woman's hand. But if this woman was the prince's daughter, why would she have bloody, painful hands? And why would she risk her father's wrath, assisting with their escape?

"I will meet up with you later."

But the Dark Horse moved to block Thorne's way. "She is not your concern."

"I cannot leave her to work in the kitchen. She is a princess and does not belong there. It is my fault that she is."

"She made her choice when she ran from you."

"I will not leave her."

Chance looked at his brother with astonishment. Who was this man? Even without knowing all that had happened, Chance could see that the Dark Horse made a fair argument. Normally it was Thorne who could look at things with a fair eye. He was the brother that had always been willing to embrace the reasonable and the logical without the burden of his emotions interfering—not to mention that one did not argue with the Dark Horse, most notably after the Dark Horse had saved their lives. But Chance recognized the look on Thorne's face. Not only did he intend to argue with the Dark Horse, Thorne intended to win.

"I will go with you." If Thorne was willing to cross the Dark Horse, then Chance would stand at his brother's side.

"No. This is something that Thorne needs do. Your wife has need of you now." The Dark Horse had moved out of Thorne's way to block Chance.

"The problem is not the accident of her birth." Thorne looked sharply at the Dark Horse for his words.

The Dark Horse turned and brought Chance's horse around with him. In just a few seconds Thorne could not see or hear his brother or the Dark Horse, so he turned to find a place to spend the night. At first light he would begin to find a way to get Olivia out of her father's castle, with or without her permission. She did not belong there. She was not a servant. She deserved to be picking flowers in a field with the sun shining down on her. As Thorne drifted off to sleep between two boulders, he could see Olivia picking flowers in her field.

As Chance and the Dark Horse traveled home, Chance gave thought to the last few minutes he had spent with his brother. They had been together for almost three weeks in a prison cell, and nothing seemed amiss with Thorne. But the last words he had heard from his brother made Chance wonder if indeed that was his brother. Something in Thorne had changed, something having to do with this woman, and that confused Chance the most. Women had no lasting effect on Thorne, until now.

The words of the Dark Horse also echoed in his ears. The Dark Horse was telling Thorne something significant, but Chance was at a loss as to what. Thorne had some past with this woman, but it was a past about which Chance had never been told, a past he had not seen. Chance was not surprised that his brother had spoken; he had felt Thorne's unease as they rode from the prince's. Then there was the matter of the prince's daughter's bleeding hands; Chance could find no logic among these facts.

If the prince was ready to have their heads for Thorne's interest in the wife of a guest, then he would surely separate Thorne's head from his body for his interest in his daughter. But Chance had never heard of a daughter. Both he and Thorne had gone to court with Auria, and their knowledge of the great families of the empire was vast. There was much here that Chance would need to know if he were to understand Thorne's thoughts.

Thorne watched for her for a fortnight and saw not a sign of her, even after ensconcing himself inside the castle walls. He had spent several days watching the kitchens while shoveling manure on the herb gardens, but there was no glimpse of her. He dared not risk going inside the castle itself, though he had spoken to several of the stable servants and the gamekeeper, none of whom seemed to have taken notice of a newer maid in the kitchen.

There was also little talk about the escape of the prisoners. A stable boy had made one comment concerning the prince's anger about the prisoners, but a look from another stable boy silenced him. Thorne was amazed how many armed men were scattered throughout the castle grounds. It would be of no difficulty for the prince to seize another duchy with the number of able bodies available to him. Thorne watched as the men were given daily instruction and training. The prince's army was well ready.

Thorne had to admit that he had been bested by the woman again. He could not stay at the prince's castle indefinitely. He had responsibilities at home. Auria, no doubt, was beside herself about the wedding. He could not keep her waiting forever. He needed to head home and put Olivia out of his mind, but she had been the center of his life for over a month now. Thorne knew she was not going to just evaporate from his thoughts; he had tried that already.

Rain loomed on the horizon, and the sky was as dark as Thorne's thoughts as he turned his horse towards home. He did not relish the long ride with nothing but his dark thoughts as he remembered his failure yet again. At least Chance was home with his wife. Thorne tried to think of some uplifting thought about the wedding, but he had to admit he had none. He was not looking forward to it, though he would put a smile on his face, act happy, and play the part for Auria. She deserved to be a happy, blushing bride. Thorne would not ruin a day that Auria had been dreaming of all her life.

Two horses were tethered ahead, but Thorne knew there were more than just the two of them, just off the road. He could leave the road now and travel through the trees, avoiding the possible trap, but Thorne was feeling more reckless than not. Thieves on the road were not uncommon, but he was still on the prince's land. The gall of the thieves surprised Thorne, and the prince would not take to having others causing terror on his lands. Thorne would not be riding into the melee a babe; the prince had been gracious enough to replace the blade he had taken from Thorne. In truth, the prince had been overly—

though unconsciously—gracious. The devil of having so many armed men about was that the men could lose their arms so easily, and none had suspected the servant covered in manure.

Before Thorne was too noticeable to the party ahead on the road, he placed several small blades within a momentary reach and a larger blade on the opposite side of the horse where it would be difficult to see. This would put it far from his preferred hand, but Thorne was equally proficient with the blade in either hand. As he approached, Thorne continued on as though he had not a concern. The men were standing in a slight depression on the side of the road. Thorne caught a flash of a bare leg—a female bare leg—in the depression.

This was not what Thorne had first thought it to be. He thought to continue on, as he had no stomach for this pastime. The men were dressed in the clothing of the privileged, and the horses were of fair quality, but not the best. Thorne had thought that these men were guests of the prince's. Only a fool would attempt such a thing on the prince's lands otherwise. Had this been on his lands, he would be thrashing the men now, but he was not on his lands. He had no concern with this.

"You can have her when I am through, but you will have to wait for a while," the bigger man said as he struggled for his breath.

The men were not young, nor were they in a sporting

state. One was much larger than the other, and both were endeavoring to control their labored breathing. Two women lay upon the ground with their arms tied behind them and dirty rags stuffed into their mouths. It was obvious that the women had made the men work for their prize. Both women looked up to Thorne, beseeching him with their eyes to help them. The younger woman was very young and not pleasant to the eye in the least, but the big man had concern only for the other woman.

Thorne shifted nervously on his horse, pulling slightly on the bit and agitating the horse, who moved closer to the men so that he was well visible to them. Pulling his cloak tighter around him, Thorne pulled the hood of his cloak lower on his face as he searched the surrounding terrain with quick, furtive eyes. His change of countenance was not lost on the two men.

"No, no! I want none of this! Do not tell him I was here!" Thorne pulled the bit even more, and his mount started to trample and stomp. The men's horses now felt the distress of Thorne's horse and started to tromp as well.

Thorne toiled to bring his mount under control. "Come about, horse. We must be away before he finds us here!"

Thorne's horse turned one way and then the other, seemingly opposite Thorne's commands. The other horses were pulling on their tethers and fearful cries escaped from them.

The air was charged with fear, and the smaller man now had rivulets of sweat pouring down his face. He looked from Thorne to the horses to the bigger man and then back to Thorne again, his grave concern etched into every line on his face. The bigger man had fear on his face, but he was not ready to allow the fear to seize him as it had the younger man.

"Who? Who do you fear?" The smaller man was holding the older of the women to the ground by the shoulders, but his grasp was relenting. His voice shook with fear as he spoke.

"I will not be part of this. I must be away! Heed me, horse!" Thorne's fear had given way to mortal terror. The battle for control of the horse continued without a true victor.

Tears streamed from the younger woman's eyes as both women struggled with their bonds and tried to roll away. One of the horses broke free and reared, but did not take off.

"Brother, we should go." The smaller man got up and rushed to the bigger man, who was obviously torn. He could feel the fear, but every time he looked at the older of the women, he forgot his fear.

"The Dark Horse!" The volume of Thorne's voice rose, as did his fear.

At the utterance of the angel's name, the smaller man stepped behind the bigger man to hide. He scanned the countryside, hoping to spy the object of his fear before the Dark Horse saw him. Thorne's horse reared, and the cries from all the horses filled the air.

"Is he here?" The words were quietly spoken, as if the speaker feared that the sound would inflame the Dark Horse even more, but they were spoken at just the briefest moment of silence, which made the voice sound thunderous.

"That one!" Thorne pointed to the older woman. "She is favored by the Dark Horse. They say she is an angel as well, her beauty mystifying. To think of touching her is blasphemy! The Dark Horse must burn the man with covetous thoughts of her from the inside to the out!"

Thorne's voice held the group spellbound. Complete panic overtook the two men, and they grappled over each other to get to their horses. As they mounted, Thorne finally gained control of his horse and took off at a full gallop in the direction he had come. As he rounded the bend in the road, he slowed his horse and steered it off the road to a thick crop of trees. He knew he would not have to wait long; the men had good reason to fear. The Dark Horse would have no mercy with them should he appear.

His horse had performed perfectly. Stephan, his huntsman, could find no benefit in having a horse uncontrollable by fear. He could not offer Thorne any advice. But Thorne never intended that his horse would be uncontrollable; he intended to completely control the beast's movements and reactions, although it appeared to others that the horse was out of control. Stephan had thought him mad when Thorne had explained the hand commands he was to teach his horse, but many thought Thorne's ideas were mad.

In a few moments Thorne heard two horses thunder past his hiding place. He waited only a moment more before heading back to where the two women lay upon the ground. He attended to the younger woman first; she had nearly choked on the dirty rag in her mouth as she sobbed in fear. Thorne then turned to attend the other woman while the younger fled across the road and into the forest. Thorne called for her to come back, but her stride did not slow. He loosened the other woman's bonds and helped her to her feet.

"Are you well, Olivia? Need I bring them to task for touching you, Princess?"

Olivia dropped her head, her cheeks flushed with color. She had no want to discuss such a personal, sensitive issue with this man. She shook her head no.

"I am without harm."

Four

"We have to go after Anna. She cannot run about the forest alone. She could get hurt." Olivia started across the road, but Thorne's grasp of iron took her upper arm and stopped her short.

"I will not let my eyes off you again, Princess. You have proven to be harder to find than the Holy Grail."

Thorne whistled for his horse, and it came about. He bent and laced his hands to assist her onto the animal.

"I am not comfortable astride a horse."

It was true—or mostly true. She had been astride only once, with this man, and although she had readily conquered the rhythm of the horse, her body closely pressed against this man made her very, very, uncomfortable. Her traitorous body longed to be close to this man again, but Olivia wanted not to be ruled by her traitorous body. The look upon his face, however, told her that he would not relent, so she placed her foot in his hands.

When Olivia was seated, Thorne mounted the horse.

"Lean back against me, and follow my lead. You must learn to trust me. I will not let anything happen to you."

He had leaned close to her ear and quietly spoken those words, and she felt his breath on her neck and shoulder. Although it was a mere instruction, the moment was very intimate to both of them. Thorne immediately reacted to her body so close to his, and Olivia was struck with a delicious wave that swept over her body—a wonderful feeling that was new to her. Recently she had glimpses of this feeling, but now she experienced it in full measure. Her instinct told her it was desire, and every time it had come on her, it had been connected to this man.

Why could this man not leave her? They had no business together—that had already been decided—yet he continued to control her life, not only by day, but by night as well. Olivia wished she could say that she was sorry that this man had taken her from her home; she should feel that way, but she did not. She was born to a doomed life, though Olivia did not feel that her life was any more doomed than most. Others decided what she could or could not do, as well as what she could or could not be. Was that not the fate of most?

People could have or not have, depending on their birth. They could marry or not, depending on their circumstances. Their daily toil would be decided before they were knee-high, and those decisions were made by others. Olivia had no quarrel with her fate. She would accept it—whatever it was—without complaint. To do otherwise would only cause her misery at her own hand.

But she had been restless of late. For what, she could not say. To what purpose, she could not say. But she felt that it was time. She could no longer glean from her current life, and she felt she no longer gave anything in her current life. She was merely being—no more, no less. It was time for her fate. It was time to begin. Then this man stole into her room.

Thorne was not prepared for the way his body reacted to Olivia. It was true that he had been without company for an extreme measure, but this was not an uncommon practice for him. Thorne was particular about the company he kept, and he was not accustomed to his body acting like a common billy goat. It was her scent. When he had bent to give her instruction, he had expected the wildflower scent that infused his dreams, but besides the smell of the common soap provided at the castle, there was a teasing of Olivia.

Thorne had never noticed the scent of a woman before, only the concoctions they slathered on for fashion or to mask the lack of a frequent bathing ritual. The essence of wildflowers drifted through his dreams every night as his thoughts were only of Olivia. Thorne had come to believe that the wildflowers were some aphrodisiac. He had associated the alluring scent with Olivia and thus dreamed of her. But it was not the fragrance of the flowers that captivated him; it was the bouquet of Olivia herself—although in truth, the wildflowers complemented her in a pleasing way that the prince's common soap could not match.

Thorne admonished himself to keep his mind directed. He would take Olivia home and allow his mother to decide what to do with her. It was not Thorne's place to make that decision, nor could he be trusted to do so. He knew she would be sent away; Father Adolphus would find a place for her. She was educated; mayhaps she would be employed as a tutor in Bohemia. But her beauty would be noticed, and Thorne knew she would be the victim of uninvited advances anywhere she went—just as she had today—and Thorne would not be there to save her.

Though they searched the forest, they did not find Anna. As the sun started to dip in the sky, Thorne told Olivia that they had to trust that Anna was safe at her destination, and Thorne turned his horse towards home. They would travel through the night since Thorne could not trust Olivia. She had slipped away from him whilst he slept once; he would not be fooled by her again. He had considered that if he lay with his arms around her and bound her wrists together and then to him, that it might be possible. In truth, however, Thorne knew that if she was in his arms, he would never be able to sleep.

The ride was slow during the night. Thorne kept alert for any sign of danger; robbers and thieves preferred the cloak of darkness. His horse was well trained and needed little from him, and it was also alert for anything that was not as it should be. Keeping a tight hold on Olivia, he told her to sleep, and she drifted for short periods of time. As Olivia dozed with her head on his shoulder, Thorne found himself looking down at her beautiful face more often than he cared to count. While Thorne enjoyed the sight of a beautiful woman, as a man would, he was drawn to gaze upon Olivia as if he had no choice.

They arrived at the castle mid-morning and were greeted by Chance and Auria. As Thorne well knew, his mother had not yet left her rooms; she would not make an appearance until the midday meal. Auria readily took care of Olivia. As Thorne headed for his rooms, he heard Auria telling Olivia that she would have a bath placed for her and find her suitable clothing. Olivia had a bag she had made from fabric scraps that contained a change of clothing, but it was only her servant clothing. It would be an affront for Olivia to present herself to the serene highness attired in that.

Auria selected a day gown from her wedding wardrobe that would not make a concern for Olivia's slim build and her greater height. Grabbing some slippers, she headed for Olivia's room. Auria had not spent more than a few minutes with Olivia, but she believed that Chance was right. Olivia was the one, the one for whom they had been searching. If Auria had a doubt, was not Olivia here? Was this not a sign from God that their prayers had been answered? They would not have to send the Dark Horse to find her. But time was quick, and there was much to be done. The wedding was fast approaching.

Thorne escaped to his rooms for a bath before meeting with his mother at the midday meal. He had concerns about his mother meeting Olivia. No matter how many times Thorne told himself that it was no longer his concern, his anxiety would not abate. His hope was that the matter of Olivia would be decided and he could release the concern from his mind. He hoped to spend the afternoon sleeping, something he done little of as late.

"Princely Grace, we must have words." His valet Johann was laying out fresh clothing.

"Tonight, after dining we will talk." Thorne was almost out of his clothes and watching steam rise from the bath. He thought nothing ever looked as wonderful as that bath.

"No, my prince, we must speak as soon as possible."

Thorne knew whatever it was would not be good. "After I meet with my mother."

"Yes, of course," Johann replied. "We will ride with Stephan this afternoon."

Thorne looked at his close and trusted friend, but Johann's face remained impassive. This was not just a bad matter; this was a disastrous matter.

"Should I drown myself in my bath?" Thorne already knew the answer.

"You may wish to." Johann stepped out to give the prince some privacy.

Olivia looked much the princess in the gown Auria had provided. There was a regal air about her. Her beauty was magnified by her attire, but there was also a humbleness that tempered her. The serene highness was much impressed with the woman presented to her, and Anja was not quickly impressed. Although she had chosen the provincial country life, Anja had been bred to be the matriarch of a great ruling house. The aristocrat lived in the country, but she was still a woman who could walk into court and be completely at home.

Anja had been promised to marry the heir of one of the great houses of Croatia, but her intended died in a hunting accident. Again, she was promised to marry, this time abroad, and again her intended passed. No new promise had been made for her before her father's death, and Anja informed her mother that this was a sign from God. So against convention, Anja chose her own husband. She married late, at sixteen, and she married a completely unambitious, mostly forgotten prince. Anja knew, however, after meeting Tobias that he was an unrecognized jewel.

Anja had withdrawn from the arrogant, pompous fools at court that played at ruling. They spoke of social justice and change, but did nothing but line their pockets and turn their eyes from threats both outside and inside the empire. There would always be wolves in the dark, ready to strike when they smelled weakness. Their only hope was in their people—strong, healthy, happy, educated people—whose allegiance was to their families and their homes. A prince must lead by serving, not destroy his people with demanding service.

Anja concentrated on her husband, her children, and her people. Being forgotten in the distant country was often a gift. Their people were strong, and they thrived. Instead of listening to conversations about social change at court, Anja implemented it in Carinthia. Her children were sought throughout the empire and beyond for marriage, but Anja insisted that her children choose their own paths. And had not her children done well? Peter, the son of Chance, her first to marry, would one day rule one of the largest houses of Hungary. Margarette's brother, the heir, was sickly and had not married, nor did he show any interest in marrying. Yes, all had done well, except Thorne.

"I will speak with Father Adolphus about how we may best serve the princess." The proclamation from the serene highness had been made.

Thorne cringed at the words, but he knew he could not speak. He had thought that once Olivia had been passed to his mother, he would be able to put his concerns to rest, but now he felt his concerns were only beginning. He would spend a lifetime wondering what he had forced upon her head and wishing he could save her from it.

"I am grateful for your kindness, Serene Highness," Olivia said and looked down at her hands in her lap. As she raised her head, she opened her mouth to try to convince the serene highness to let her find her own circumstances, just as she had tried to persuade Thorne to let her go her own way. He had refused to listen to her, so she would raise her plea with the serene highness; mayhaps she would understand.

Thorne cringed even more. Olivia was going to say something that would not please the serene highness; he could feel it in his bones. He wanted to jump across the table and clap his hands over her mouth. The serene highness would never agree to allow Olivia to walk out of the castle going her own way. Could Olivia not see that no one would allow that? She was a princess; she could not wander the countryside alone!

Chance looked to the serene highness and said, "Mother." Thorne's eyes were still intent on Olivia, so Chance turned to the princess. "Forgive my intrusion, Princess." Turning once more to his mother, he added, "As Margarette is close to her time, mayhaps the princess could stay and help with the wedding."

Now Thorne had to restrain himself from jumping across the table and cuffing his twin. What thoughts could Chance have? The last thing Thorne needed was Olivia spending time with Auria. Thorne wrestled with keeping his thoughts about Olivia to himself. What if Auria knew his thoughts? She would make his life hell, not only in this world, but in the next as well! Thorne had dreaded this wedding, and though he knew he had been party to the delay more than once, he was ready for it to be over with. He would be a man and keep his feelings to himself, but he did not need Olivia involved in this.

"That is wise counsel. I understand the princess is not ready for travel. I am correct?" The serene highness looked to Auria, who nodded her head "yes" at the question.

"Mayhaps it would be best for her to stay with us while her wardrobe is prepared." Anja liked the idea the more she thought on it. "It is decided then. Princess, you shall stay with us until after the wedding."

Anja sat back and watched the reactions. Chance and Auria exchanged a triumphant glance. Ahh, there was a coup as Anja had expected. Thorne looked murderous. But why? Was this not his making? Should he not be pleased that the sweet princess would be cared for? The sweet princess herself looked vexed. And why? Should she not be pleased that she would not be whisked away without proper preparation? Anja would let this play out. Sometimes it was best to let others think one had no concern for the situation.

Thorne had left much out of Olivia's story because his mother need not know all the details. Now, however, Thorne had best keep Olivia quiet and away from Auria. Busy—that was what Olivia needed to be, busy. As Thorne was leaving the dining room, he suggested to his mother that Olivia could oversee the guest rooms. His mother thought the guest wing just needed airing and freshening, but Thorne knew differently. The guest wing was a mess. It was just what Olivia needed to keep her busy.

She looked out the window of her room before preparing to rest for the afternoon and saw three riders heading out at a leisurely pace. No one at the castle gave them concern. No one noticed how much alike the three men were, save one. Olivia mused that the three were the same height, weight, age, and coloring. It was almost impossible to tell them apart from the back.

The prince, the valet, and the huntsman rode until Stephan reined up at the side of the stream. The men allowed the horses to drink and taste the fauna while they gathered to talk, far from where any ears would be about. The three men were often in each other's company, and should anyone see them speaking, they would not have concern.

"Princely Grace, while you were gone, two men were killed by the Dark Horse. A man in Sankt Michael for not repaying a debt and a man in Seeboden for beating his wife." Johann knew that Thorne would be shocked by the news.

Thorne could not believe what he was hearing. "You are without doubt?"

"I saw the fresh graves and spoke with the grieving."

Stephan understood his friend's thoughts. He knew that Thorne did not doubt what his friends were reporting to him; the difficulty lay in believing that this could be.

"As Father Frederico?"

"Of course."

"We cannot allow this. The Dark Horse must be stopped—and quickly—before another befalls this anarchy. We must kill the Dark Horse."

Johann and Stephan nodded in agreement. They knew this would be Thorne's decision. They also knew that this would be no easy task. It must be done properly. There was much to consider, but it also must be done soon. The Dark Horse could not just kill without clear reason, and Stephan was not convinced there was a clear reason for these men to die. The man accused of not paying a debt was not known to borrow, and the widow of the man accused of beating his wife had married again before the man was cold in the ground. There were murmurings that the woman and her new husband had been lovers for some time.

Five

The difference between her father's castle and Thorne's was the difference between day and night. Both were large, impressive structures, but while her father's had been ostentatious, she found Thorne's to be beauteous but comfortable as well. Her father's castle was to admire; Thorne's was a castle to live in. Although the furnishings were far more well-appointed than at her grandparents' country estate, Olivia found Thorne's castle to be just as much a home.

Olivia had spent the morning walking through the guest wing; people would be arriving to stay in less than a month. Two young girls from the village had been brought in to air and freshen the rooms, but the rooms were completely uninhabitable. She spoke with the aging housekeeper, Elena, and even with the help that she was requesting, Olivia would be working from sunup to sundown to get the guest wing ready for the wedding.

It was obvious that someone had taken care to pack up the rooms, but Olivia had little idea where to look for everything. She would start with the cabinets in the rooms, but she dared not hope that her search would be that easy. She would need direction from the housekeeper, as searching the entire castle would take her months, and she did not have months to prepare before the wedding guests began arriving from all over the empire.

She found the basins and pitchers and various other articles for the rooms in the chest of drawers, but no linens. Everything would have to be washed and dried—bed linens, bathing linens, and curtains for the thirty-five suites on each of the two floors for the guests—and this did not account for the two floors of servant quarters that must be prepared as well. She needed to find the linens and find them soon. It was apparent that the guest wing had not been used for at least a decade, and Olivia feared many of the linens may need to be replaced.

Olivia did look forward to the time she would have to plan her next move whilst she was away from the distraction of the wedding plans. She did not doubt that Father Adolphus would try to find a suitable situation, but Olivia was not trusting enough to leave her life in anyone's hands. She must find a better solution than she had at her father's castle. Olivia did not have a concern for backbreaking work, but she did not want to continue to do the same.

She doubted that there was a soul that walked the earth

that wanted to spend their time scrubbing dishes, pots and pans, or the floors, especially whilst trying to stay out of the path of the cook's angry stick, which would be applied to her back or fingers to remind her that no matter how hard or how quickly she worked, it was never pleasing. Olivia found no shame in honest hard work. Her argument was with the other duties she was expected to perform.

The activities that happened at night in the women's room at first shocked Olivia, but then she looked at the nightly frivolity as an education regarding what transpired between a man and a woman. As no one expected Olivia to marry, there had been no discussion with her about the intimacy between a man and a woman. She, of course, had some notion from the animals on her grandparents' estate, but that little prepared her for what she was to learn at her father's castle.

Olivia received an education that she doubted any other princess had ever received.

What happened mere inches from her, often on the same mattress ... she could not help but see and hear the deed known as "making love." Her vantage point gave her a colorful under-standing of the male body and how the male and female bodies fit together. She also gained valuable awareness of playfulness between lovers.

When Olivia was informed that she would warm the

bed of the prince's guest, however, Olivia found argument, and another maid offered to take Olivia's place. The maid found the guest pleasing, and she thought he would give her coin for her time and talents. Olivia knew, though, she could not always count on fortune to help her avoid these tasks, and when she heard that the prince himself—her father—found her of interest, she knew she must leave, and soon. She would die by her own hand without concern for the eternal damnation of her soul before she would allow any attention from the prince.

When Olivia tried to leave, however, she found that she was in debt to the prince, owing him the worth of her board. She had never heard of such an arrangement; the servants were not charged for their meals at her grandparents' estate. So she stopped taking as many meals as she could spare and used her two hours of leisure time each week to collect nuts, roots, and berries to eat. Unfortunately, she was not able to collect much as she had to walk quite a distance to get off the prince's lands. It would not do to be caught stealing from the prince.

And that was where the Dark Horse found her. He enlisted her assistance in helping two men in the prison cells escape. The priest would allow her to come with him, but he would not do the deed himself. The Dark Horse gave her coin to cover her debt with the prince. She knew she was helping a prince from Carinthia, but she did not know that she had met this man before. When she stepped into the cell, she immediately recognized the man who had taken her from her home.

She had no idea who he was when he stole into her bedchamber, and she had no idea of his name until the priest told her after they left the cell. She had heard some of the maids speak of these men; many feared them because they were identical twins, but just as many found them pleasing, especially the one. He had a wicked glint in his eye that caused the maids to swoon. Olivia had seen this look in the man's eye, but it was when he was having jest at her expense, as he did when Olivia made her demands when they were to sleep in the ruins of the house when he first took her from her home.

Olivia requested four more girls to assist her, preferably older than the very young maidens that had already been provided. She also requested the use of two stronger young men. It was a shock, but nonetheless it pleased Olivia that the housekeeper had been instructed by the prince to give Olivia anything she wanted. The housekeeper would send someone to town today to find the girls who would be ready on the morrow, but Olivia did not have the luxury of waiting.

As she went searching from room to room, she tried to think of a means for her future. She needed to use this time. She would be prepared, and when she walked out into the world, it would be a quest of her own. Thorne may have been the one to start her on this journey, but Olivia had long decided she would be the one to decide what road she would choose. She would not have a concern that she was using Thorne's roof and food; he owed her that, at the least.

As the sun started to rise, Olivia headed for the chapel where Father Adolphus would be having morning prayer. In her few days at the castle, only Margarette had attended morning prayers with regularity. The castle was well-appointed with a double chapel for Sunday Mass or holiday Mass, situated just inside the gate where those of the town had access. In the eastern corner of the residence was a smaller chapel for morning prayers or vespers, and the Chapel of Our Lady for personal prayer. Upon entering, one may ascend a half flight of stair to the smaller chapel or descend to the Chapel of Our Lady.

All the mattresses would have to be replaced, lest the guests would sleep with nests of mice. Olivia headed for the stables; the housekeeper had directed her to find stable boys that would help her with whatever she required. Her dirndl had been cleaned and returned to her, and with nothing but the gown that Auria had given to her, she wore the servant clothing now. Olivia entered the stable and requested to speak with the stable master. She was waiting for the man when her gaze was drawn to another part of the stable. Thorne was speaking with another man, and unfortunately, Thorne saw her and his face registered his displeasure.

He was readily on her. "What are you doing here, Princess?" He towered over her, his hands on his hips, giving her a look that could wither the hardiest of weeds.

Thorne called to a man that was putting hay into stalls. He gave the man instructions about the mattresses and then proceeded to grab Olivia by the wrist and drag her back into the main house. She had scarcely been able to keep up with his long stride, and after the third turn, she was completely lost. She asked him to slow down to allow her to gain her feet, but his only reply was to send a very dark, very angry look in her direction.

He stopped outside the door of her room. "Mayhaps you could change into something more appropriate, Princess."

"The only other clothing I have is the dress that Auria gave to me. It is not more appropriate, Prince. I have been working in the guest rooms. I believe it was your request that I care for the guest wing."

As the last word left her lips, he grabbed her by the wrist again, taking her once more at breakneck speed throughout the castle. Olivia was not sure what floor she was on, or if she was in the family, guest, or servant section of the castle. As confused as she was, it was possible that they could have left the castle and the country and now were half the way across the world. But Thorne would not tell her where they were going, nor would he tell her why.

Finally Thorne opened a door and dragged Olivia through it. Women of various ages were seated at a table in the center of the room, and bolts of cloth, spools of thread, pins and needles, lace and fur covered every surface. All the women looked at Thorne with confusion and then hastily started to rise as they recognized him.

"Stay as you are. The princess must have a complete wardrobe as quickly as possible."

With that proclamation the prince left the room while the women continued to stare at Olivia, their confusion obvious. Where was the princess of whom the prince spoke? Olivia explained that she had been separated from her wardrobe, and the dawn of understanding rolled across the room. Two women jumped to their feet and commenced to measure Olivia in every way possible. This continued for near an hour until Olivia insisted that she had an appointment concerning the wedding and had to leave. The women insisted that Olivia return at first light to start dress fittings.

"I cannot! There is too much to do before the wedding.

Is there not another that can stand in my stead?" Olivia looked around the room, but there was not one that was the same size.

Then three girls came in carrying more bolts of fabric, and the last girl looked to have the same frame as Olivia. The woman, Pia, was measured, and she was indeed very close to the same size as Olivia. With the current fashion, it was not necessary that the girl be exactly the size of the princess. Olivia explained that she would be working to prepare the guest rooms. The dresses she needed first were clothing she could wear while she was working. The women looked one to another. They were not sure what Olivia was saying—a princess ... work?

Olivia bathed and changed for the evening meal, putting on the dress that Auria had given to her, which she had worn each evening now. This did not bother Olivia, but she was sure this was not according to the fashion of the ladies of the castle. The serene highness had inquired about her dress fittings the eve before; fortunately, Thorne had spoken to his mother, and the subject was dropped. Olivia had no desire to be indebted to the prince, but there was little she could say.

Although she would rather have a light meal in the kitchen or in her room, Olivia was expected to make an appearance. She hoped Thorne would not be in a foul mood or that he would just leave her be; he seemed to be in a foul mood every time he was in her presence. However, Olivia need only put up with him for a few minutes when they spoke in the morning, at the evening meal, and in the drawing room until Olivia could escape for the night.

The serene highness and Auria dominated the conversation with plans for the wedding. Olivia listened to the ladies talk and prayed that the next course would be the final course of the meal. Thorne and Chance discussed crops and livestock, and Margarette was quiet throughout the meal. Olivia rarely felt so out of place. She actually felt more comfortable scrubbing dishes or beating rugs; she had no gift for senseless words.

Thorne, Johann, and Stephan took turns riding the empire, searching for the Dark Horse, although Thorne did not spend as much time taking part in the search as he had to stay close to the castle to be ready for the wedding festivities. He had taken to going to the guest wing every morn that he was home, telling himself that he was making sure that Olivia was behaving and that he wanted to be assured that all was prepared for the guests. She was always up early and working when no one else had yet risen, and Thorne enjoyed the few minutes they would speak of nothing consequential.

Olivia had not a moment to spare, and she attacked the

task of the guest wing as she did all others, with her full measure. She could not be pleased with just doing an undertaking well; it must be beyond reproach, and she sought to glean as much as she was able. She worked exceedingly well with those who had been set to prepare the guest wing, and she gave clear directions and was available to hear complaint and suggestion alike. She inspired her small assemblage in a manner that the housekeeper had been unable to do. Her effort was not of notice to the serene highness, who was distracted with wedding concerns, but it was of notice to all the staff of the house and to Thorne.

In the drawing room after the evening meal, Auria took possession of Olivia's time. Just one year younger than Olivia, the younger princess set out to learn as much as possible about Olivia. Just as earnestly as Auria fired questions at Olivia about herself, Olivia deftly turned the questions back on the subject of Auria or some other topic the women had touched upon, such as a favored Greek tragedy playwright. Thorne kept as close an eye on this as he was able without it being of notice to Auria, who would surely wish to know why Thorne had care.

Olivia most often was the first to turn in for the night, citing morning prayer as the reason for her early leave. For an hour before she retired, she would play the pianoforte. Thorne knew this was her habit back at her grandparents' estate. Olivia played very well and completely became absorbed in the music, and Thorne wondered if she was aware of the others in the room or if she had run off to a land where music was the only language spoken.

Late one afternoon, as Olivia arrived in her room to bathe and change for the evening meal, she noticed several new dresses had been placed in her room. Each dress was a work of art, the mixture of colors and textures exquisite. Day after day more dresses appeared in her room. Olivia had noticed how well dressed the ladies of the castle were, but she had no belief that she would need such an extensive wardrobe wherever Father Adolphus found for her to go. She could not say this, however; she was a guest, and she was without doubt that the prince would not take her comment with good humor.

Six

It was the last day of known peace before the guests would start to arrive. The main meal had been at mid-day after the morning Mass, and most of the household had retired to their rooms to enjoy a rest on the Sabbath, though Thorne was only growing more restless the closer the date came to the wedding. He soon would have to concern himself with a household of guests, and the situation with the Dark Horse had not been brought to a conclusion. In addition to all of this, Olivia would soon be leaving. He would have no peace until he knew that she was well cared for; he felt sure it was his guilt that needed to be consoled.

Thorne decided to take an afternoon ride and headed for the stables. Looking across the field, he saw a blonde woman with a sewn bag, made of scraps, walking up the hill. His pace quickened, and he prepared his horse swiftly, heading out of the stable at almost a full gallop, grateful that no one was about to be trampled.

"Damn!" he muttered under his breath. He had taken his

eyes off her for but a moment, and she was trying to flee.

Olivia heard the horse, but paid it no mind until it was almost upon her. As she turned, Thorne brought the horse up short and dismounted in one movement. In two steps he was upon her.

"Where do you think you are going?" For one to say he was angry would be to say a mountain is but a slight hill.

"To gather herbs. Father Adolphus thought I would find what I need near the lake. He indicated it was this way." Olivia could not understand why this man was always angry. He had a good, comfortable life, yet he was always dissatisfied—mostly with her.

"I will take you." Thorne turned and whistled for his horse.

"You need not burden yourself."

Olivia had no desire to go anywhere near this man when he was of a foul mood, as it rarely ended well for her. She had also hoped to use this afternoon to gain a better understanding of the landscape. With Thorne about, Olivia could not be free to explore any trails or paths she may find.

"I assure you, Princess, it is no burden. I know these lands well. I can be of service to you," Thorne said, struggling to be cordial. Why could Olivia not accept his help? Must she do everything on her own, in her own way?

"Know you herbs?" Olivia had doubt he would be well educated in what she needed.

"I know many of the flowers and plants of this area, and what I do not know, you can teach me."

Olivia knew she would not be able to persuade this man to leave her be. She wanted not to get on the horse with him again; she did not want to be that close to him. She enjoyed his arms around her too much. Thorne threaded his hands to assist her to mount, and Olivia resigned herself to riding with him.

Thorne pulled himself upon the horse as if the horse was a mere extension of himself. He gave little instruction, allowing the reins to lie across the back of the beast, yet the horse knew where to go. They rode at a fairly slow pace, Thorne holding on to Olivia with both arms. The two had done this enough that Olivia knew to relax against Thorne, to follow him and allow the horse its lead.

It was a short ride to the lake, but it would have taken Olivia a few hours to walk. She had to admit (but only in her own mind) that had she spent all her time walking, she would not have had time to hunt for the herbs she needed. Thorne dismounted and helped Olivia down. She had taken her hair down after Mass and tied it in the back with a scarf. Thorne much preferred her this way; it made her look natural and free.

He was able to point out three of the five plants that she sought. They carefully collected what Olivia needed and then commenced a search for the remaining herbs. Sitting on a felled tree, they drank some watered wine.

"For what do you need the herbs?" Thorne knew these were not cooking herbs, and he thought that they were not for fragrance, but he could not think why Olivia would need these herbs.

"To make a balm for Pia."

"Who is Pia?"

"The seamstress's daughter. She is only twenty, but her joints are as swollen and painful as an old woman's. She has had this affliction for many years. Elena, the housekeeper, has tried many mixtures, but with no help. This is a mixture that is most often used on large animals, such as horses, but I know of a woman that used it with great relief."

"Where did you learn this?"

"From the housekeeper at my grandparents' estate, but I also learned much about caring for animals from the men at the stables. I know how to birth a cow and a sheep. I have been told how to birth a child, but I have not had an occasion to see thus. I can treat most matter of wounds and ailments."

"This is not the usual education for a princess."

"I am not the usual princess, as you well know. I assure you my Latin and Greek are without question, and I am able to do all manner of numbers. I have a book with all the herbs listed and many of the mixtures. I may as well fill my time with something of worth, as I have to fill my time with something."

Thorne could think of no reply. Her words were true. After an hour of searching, they found the last few herbs she required. The horse walked back slowly to the castle as the two spoke of local greenery and vegetation. Olivia enjoyed talking to this man. He spoke to her like she was an intelligent adult, although when he was of a foul mood, he spoke to her as if she were a mischievous child. Thorne was sorry when they arrived at the castle; he had enjoyed the afternoon with Olivia. He could not go to the kitchen as she made the preparation; others would see and wonder why he was tarrying there.

Olivia brought an armload of table linens into the ballroom. There were but a few days remaining until the wedding, and most of the guests had arrived. The castle was bursting at the seams with people, and the servants worked nearly around the clock to attend to all their needs. Olivia was generally expected to attend the evening meal and to assist in entertaining the guests. This moment, she had need of a needle and thread, and she knew she could find these in the laundry; no one would have concern for her being there. So after preparing for the evening meal, she headed to the laundry, taking the table linens with her to help the overworked servants.

She laid the armload of linens over one of the tables in the ballroom. The chairs had already been covered with silk and a silk banner had been draped over the railing of the musician's balcony. The ballroom would have tables set up around the edges of the room, and the doors would be open with more tables set up around the gardens. Olivia hurried back across the room and glanced back at the balcony. The silk banner was not hanging properly. The draping was not pleasing to the eye.

Walking back from whence she came, Olivia looked up at the balcony. It looked better from this side of the room, but it still was not a pleasant sight. The musicians were coming from Vienna and were considered to be as excellent as one could want. Olivia knew that the guests would be looking up at the balcony first as the bride and groom entered the ballroom and then at the musicians. It would not be agreeable with the serene highness if the draping was not done properly.

A ladder—well tall enough to reach the balcony—leaned against the wall next to one of the windows that reached to the high ceiling. It was a slight struggle for Olivia to move the ladder, but she was able to do the task on her own, positioning it to fix the drape starting in the middle. Satisfied the middle section was correct, Olivia moved the ladder to the right and quickly situated that draping in a pleasing way. She moved the ladder to the left and repeated the process. Olivia then walked across the ballroom to check the whole of the draping, but the left side still was not pleasing.

She knew she would be a bit later than usual to the meal. She was usually prompt to a fault, but she still had time to fix the draping so that the serene highness would be pleased. When she could almost reach where the problem was with the draping, she dabbled with the idea of moving the ladder, but she would only need to stretch to the fold for but a moment. As she reached out her arm, the ladder swayed before it clamored to the floor.

Olivia grabbed the balustrade when the ladder swayed, hoping to right it, but as the ladder fell, she was left hanging. Her grip was tight, for the moment. The fall would be too great; if she let go, she would, without doubt, be seriously injured. She would have to think of a way to go up. Olivia knew she could not pull her body up with just her hands, and the silk banner was only pinned in place; it would be of no use to her. There would be no one in this part of the house to hear her call out, and her hands were starting to complain at the weight.

"It is always of great interest where I will find you, Princess." Thorne quickly strode over to the ladder. "Hold tightly."

"I have little choice to do otherwise." Olivia was grateful to be saved from this unfortunate circumstance, but she would rather have been saved by Satan than by this man.

She felt his arm encircle her waist just as her hands started to cramp with pain. Thorne pulled her tightly against him and slowly descended the ladder. Once on the floor, however, Thorne did not release her, and Olivia turned towards him, her annoyance obvious on her face. Thorne trapped her between himself and the ladder, and her hand itched to slap him. How dare he stand so familiarly with her!

"What were you doing?" Now that she was safely on the floor, Thorne was furious with her.

"I was fixing the banner." Olivia looked him straight in the eye. She would not cower to his anger.

"You should have called for one of the servants." Thorne was near ready to shake some sense into her; Olivia obviously could not see the folly in what she had done.

"I should have moved the ladder, I willingly admit, but I am capable of fixing the banner myself. I need not bother others." Olivia just wanted him to let her go on to the meal. It was a simple mistake, surely not something to be such a concern.

"You could have been killed!" Thorne's temper was rising. The woman could not admit to making an egregious error in judgment.

"I believe you had planned to kill me. I was simply saving you the concern."

Olivia could not believe that he had any true concern for her welfare, he most certainly did not wish to disturb his guests with her death. Olivia pushed at his chest to free herself; there was no reason to continue this pointless conversation and upset the serene highness by being late.

Thorne could not let Olivia continue on to the dining room. This was his home; she would do what he said, and she would do it without question. Thorne placed a finger under her chin and forced her to look at him. Olivia did not like standing so closely to this man. Her traitorous body was responding to his—her breath felt short, and her heart was pounding. She had no concern for any other man, only this man, and he disturbed her dreams every night. Could he not leave her in peace?

Their noses were but an inch from each other. Although Thorne was acutely aware of a woman pressed so tightly against his body, with her face so close to his, all he could think about was how much he wanted only her, only Olivia. He could feel her breath on his cheek, he could smell her wildflower scent, and he wanted to taste her lips. Thorne pulled her to him and slowly his lips sought hers. He felt like he was diving into a pool of pleasure. Pleasure was not untested by Thorne; he had known pleasure in many arms. This was different though; this was a pure pleasure he had never known, and he wanted more—much, much more.

Olivia did not consciously decide to indulge in this moment of ecstasy. Her traitorous body made the decision for her; it would not be denied this. Her sensibility, however, saved her from this scandalous moment. She pushed him firmly and was able to escape his entrapment.

"Thorne, you should not—"

"Do you not wish to say 'we' should not? Your lips did not flee from mine." His shoulder was reclining on the ladder, his arms folded, one leg crossed the other, and his eye had a wicked glint.

Olivia looked at this insolent man. "I suppose it is not unthought that any woman would care to know of a kiss at least once in her life." She would not allow him to paint her the strumpet.

Thorne could not believe that she had not ever known a kiss. Men would ride across the empire for just one kiss from a woman as beautiful as she.

"I thought—"

"When men are concerned for their desires and making

unwanted advances, they do not care for a gentle kiss." She had cut him off; she had no care for what he would say.

Thorne dropped his head and bit his tongue. This woman had not taken the same road as other gentlewomen. She had not been promised in marriage, she had not attended the festivities of court. He could not think of her as he would think of a woman like Auria. Had she not been on the ground as a pair of thugs planned to take from her what only should be offered? Although he was well acquainted with her previous life, what he saw before him was a princess—and quite possibly the most beautiful princess in all the empire.

He let her walk off. He should not have allowed himself that moment with her. She was untouchable, to him and to all other men, even though many of the guests (mayhaps even all the male guests) had asked after her. She was introduced as a cousin of the serene highness's family. She was not given a title, and she was given her mother's surname, a name with many branches to the family. Interest had been feverish; she was requested as a riding partner, a partner in board games, and to host the afternoon lawn games. But the serene highness had kept Olivia with the younger children, and the children loved their nursemaid.

Olivia strode quickly from the ballroom, lest the prince come out of his reverie. Since coming to the castle, she had heard tales of the prince's skirt chasing. He stayed away from anyone near the castle though, as he had a refined palette with his taste in women. Regardless, his exploits were well-known. Was that not why he and Chance were in her father's prison?

Thorne was not ruled by his head, nor even his heart, but by another part. From her experience with men, Olivia was of the belief that all men were ruled by the same. Thorne should not be thinking of his own pleasures; he should have his mind on Auria, the wedding, and the wedding guests. Olivia had wondered why any woman would want to have thoughts of a man. Their eyes would always wander, and if given a chance, they would wander as well. There was no sensibility in having care for someone who would not have care in return. A man would only mean a heart full of pain and eyes full of tears.

Seven

Olivia endured the wedding festivities with outward good humor. The Mass droned on for hours, many of the guests using the opportunity for introspection with an itinerant snore, but when the parish had given in too far to the sin of slothfulness, the call to kneel would come from heaven through Father Adolphus. The bride and groom struggled as the guests, but they had to stand as the Latin monotone flowed throughout the double chapel.

At the wedding feast, Olivia was seated with Father Adolphus, a man given to contemplation who required little of Olivia. The courses of the wedding feast were endless, and Olivia, eating but a bite of each course, could not imagine who could consume such a larder in entirety. The toasts were infinite. Even with her watered wine her head was fuzzed; those who swilled their glasses would surely be stricken in the morn.

As the guests wandered to the ballroom, Olivia slipped to the basement laundry where no one would be. A feast and instrumental festivities were provided in the courtyard for the people of the village and those that worked at the castle. She found her clothing in which she had come to the castle lying to the side on a table and hid the clothing under her dress, using the servant stair to steal away to her room. The needle and thread she had acquired afore were hidden in a drawer. She laid the clothing on the divan and looked at the damaged fabric.

Thorne watched as Olivia slipped out of the crowd moving towards the ballroom. He went to the ballroom and waited as the bride and groom were announced to the guests. The serene highness was seated properly and receiving her guests. Thorne looked about the room for Olivia; had she needed a moment, she would have joined the guests by now. He knew she had withdrawn from the festivities. He did not have question that the day may have been a trial for her—to sit through the wedding of another when she would never have one—but he also had concern that she may have something else on her mind.

Thorne rapped upon the door, having little doubt she had gone to her room. "Olivia! Olivia!" He had not wanted to make a scene; family and guests alike might step to their rooms to freshen before the evening festivities. He knocked again. "Olivia, open this door!"

Olivia froze. Mayhaps he would move on if he thought she was not in her room. There was no other way for her to get out of the room except to go through the window, a drop too far to bear. There was no place for her to hide; she hoped he would not try to look in the room. She removed herself without notice from the celebration—or so was her belief—why would he have concern?

Thorne turned the knob, but the door was locked. "Olivia, open this door or I will thrash it down!"

Olivia knew she was trapped. Hopefully he would not be so bold as to enter the room. She knew Thorne had no concern with entering her bedchamber without her consent, but she hoped that the guests would restrain his true nature. Going to the door, she released the lock.

"I am indisposed. I must change my dress. There is a drop of wine …" Before she could finish, Thorne had pushed the door open and strode into her room.

He slammed the door and stood with his hands on his hips, looking at her from head to bare toes. "I see nothing wrong with your appearance, but you may wish to put your slippers back on." He reached to grab her arm and drag her from the room when his eye came upon the clothing on the divan.

He strode over to the clothing, dragging her behind him. "What are these doing here?" He held the clothing up to her, an accusing look upon his face.

Olivia opened her mouth to reply, but her tongue found no words. He threw the clothing on the floor and turned on Olivia as a bear on its prey.

"You are not leaving."

"I am most able to care for myself." Olivia raised her chin.

"Need I remind you of the circumstances in which I found you on your father's land?"

"I intend to carry a knife and I will not be inclined to forgive such transgressions so easily." Olivia was sure he would see that she had learned from her previous folly and would do well.

As the words left her mouth, Thorne lunged at her, taking her down onto the bed. His body captured hers beneath, and his hands found her wrists. Stretching her arms above her head, he took both delicate wrists in one of his hands, sliding the other beneath her dress to her underclothes and slowly pulling them down.

A shadow of shock crossed her face. She was not astounded that the men on the road had looked upon her and Anna with such little regard, but Olivia was wont to credit Thorne with more prudence. Fear gripped her. This castle was his—he may do as he will, and Olivia had little recourse to stop him.

"No, Thorne, I beg you."

"You cannot be watchful for yourself. Had you a knife, it would be at your throat. There is little you can do—save kill a man—to keep him from powering over you. I do not tell you for my purpose; I tell you this for your welfare. You may have the heart of a bear, but you have the frame of a woman. An unusually pleasant woman."

His hand released her undergarments, but with the touch of a feather caressed her leg as he withdrew it from under her dress. He released her wrists and rested on his elbows above her, looking into a face more beautiful than any man could imagine. He rested his forehead against hers and allowed his eyes to rest, drinking in the scent of her wildflowers. In his mind's eye he saw her in the field of wildflowers, her hair barely bound with a scarf, tendrils dusting her cheeks flushed by the sun, the wind swirling her dress around her legs.

The field was where she belonged. She would not be like the caged bird she was forced to be, desperate to flee the bars that held her from the freedom she needed to survive. She was created to be free, but her freedom would come at a cost that Thorne was not willing to pay. She would tempt predators far beyond their ability to resist. Thorne felt overwhelming guilt for taking her from the safety of her grandparents' estate, but was she not a caged bird there as well?

Thorne could not tarry here. The castle, his home, was full of gentry from across Carinthia, all Austria, the duchies and counties, and well beyond. Olivia's own father had been invited, but Thorne could not say he was sorry the prince had not shown. He needed to attend to his guests; he could not leave that for the serene highness alone, though Thorne was most assured that there was never a place he wanted to be more than here with Olivia. His mind and soul were at peace when he was with her, even when he wanted to thrash her in anger.

He should spend his last time that he had with Auria. The younger sibling, almost half his age, was more of a daughter to him than a sister.

Auria had chosen her own husband, and she had chosen well. Grego was the heir of a great house of the Duchy of Styria. He had been promised to marry as a child, but she had died. The house had tried to promise for Auria, but the serene highness would not allow it; Auria must choose her own. Through the negotiations Grego and Auria had become acquainted, and several years later Grego had asked for her hand, having proven he would cherish Auria as her family had done.

With great regret, Thorne got up from the bed, gathering

Olivia's servant clothing. "I will burn these myself, and I will set a guard on you. You are not to leave the castle."

Thorne put his hand out to assist Olivia, turning his back as she straightened her skirts, then he helped her as she took a few pins from her hair and repaired the locks that had escaped. Thorne considered taking all the pins out, allowing her hair to flow freely. He was of the mind that it was as God intended Olivia to look, with her hair dancing in the wind.

After checking the hallway for stray guests, he pulled Olivia along with him and steered her towards the ballroom. He would not make the same mistake yet again; he would keep her within arm's reach until a guard had been placed on her. Their time away from the guests went unnoticed, except for Chance. He had seen Thorne head towards the family rooms with anger on his brow and purpose in his step, and Chance was not surprised when Thorne emerged again among the guests with his hand at the small of the princess's back.

Olivia felt as though she was a horse being directed by the prince, but instead of bit and rein, his hand to her back turned her this way and that. Thorne seemed to be intent on introducing her to every guest that had come but was not staying at the castle. Olivia committed every name, title, and from whence the guest had come to memory. Tonight she would add these members of the gentry to her growing list of the aristocracy that she had met.

Almost every man in attendance asked for the honor of a dance with Olivia, but Thorne allowed her to dance with only a few elderly gentleman, and one dance only. By midnight Olivia's feet begged for rest, but she would not give Thorne the satisfaction of claiming her to be weak by asking to sit a few moments. He seemed to have a mind to test her patience, and Olivia was determined not to complain. She smiled and complimented her way around the room.

As the first colors of dawn crept across the land, the musicians played the final dance of the night, and Thorne took Olivia by the hand to the dance floor for a slow loure. He had taken to the floor only once, to dance with Auria. Many of the guests were dozing in their seats, no one wishing to leave before dawn. Snatches of conversation and drunken laughter floated across the room as two other couples took to the floor as well. Olivia would have preferred the floor to be full if she was to dance with Thorne. His behavior throughout the night—keeping Olivia by his side and his hand upon her back—was enough to keep the women's tongues busy.

The dance began, and Olivia allowed herself to float upon the notes and across the floor. As she dipped in front of Thorne, she could feel his breath on her shoulder and the heat of his body against her back. He was far too close and had bent his head to be even nearer her shoulder. Olivia's cheeks suffused with color at his daring intimacy. Her traitorous body felt his calling to hers and wanted to reply, but Olivia would not allow it. She could only hope that the guests had not noticed the moment.

The serene highness watched her son dance with the young princess. His behavior this night with her had been scandalous. Many a mother had congratulated Anja that Thorne had finally found a woman with whom he could settle down, and many had commented that Olivia was so much more regal, beautiful, and gracious than Katarina. The words had stung Anja, although she had not shown it; Katarina was her good friend.

As Olivia turned, Thorne's hand reached out, as gently as a light summer breeze, and caressed the length of her fingers as she passed afore him. Olivia's head dropped in embarrassment as she heard the sharp intake of breath from around the dance floor. The guests had noticed. When Olivia dared to look, she noted every eye in the room riveted to the intimate display between her and Thorne as they now danced alone.

Olivia dared not walk off the dance floor; she trusted not that Thorne would drag her back. She could only hope that Thorne would reconsider his bold intentions in front of the crowd, but that was not to be. He continued to dance far too close to her, his head or his lips as close to her shoulder, neck, cheek, or lips as they could be without touching. His hand brushed her hand or her arm, or slid slowly across her lower back. At the end of the dance, Olivia dropped low in a respectful curtsy as Thorne bowed, then took both her hands and brought her to stand.

Olivia kept her eyes down as she gathered her skirts. She could hear the guests murmuring, certain that Thorne's bold, familiar display was the topic. Without proper permission from the serene highness, Olivia left the ballroom and headed to her room as quickly as possible without running. Thorne acted as though nothing was amiss as he started his round of "goodnights" and "good-byes."

A male guard was placed outside Olivia's door each night, and a female servant was with Olivia every minute of the day; Thorne thought placing a male guard on her during the day would fuel gossip. In his distraction with the Dark Horse, he failed to give thought to the guests' new pastime—speculation about him and Olivia. Olivia was barraged with questions for which she had no answers. As the serene highness tried to quell any notion of an impending wedding between Thorne and Olivia, Auria fueled the gossipmongers. Chance was silent on the subject; he would merely raise his eyebrows and smile slightly.

Thorne would laugh and say that this was Auria's wedding celebration, and he had no announcement to make. Hoping to silence the tongues, Olivia had taken to staying in her room when she had no other duties, but the story changed to Thorne locking Olivia in her room to keep other men away from her. Olivia's departure to her room pleased and angered the serene highness. Anja felt that Olivia should do more to stop the gossip, but at least she was not a constant reminder of it. Olivia had no understanding why the serene highness had placed this all upon her shoulders when Thorne's actions had started the tongues.

A desperate plea had gone out to the Dark Horse, but his reply was very long in coming. He accepted the request—at an exorbitant price, even for the Dark Horse. Thorne and his men waited, but the Dark Horse did not appear to carry through with the bargain. Thorne had heard of this happening before. If he was to slay the Dark Horse, another proposal must be employed to draw the Dark Horse out.

Father Peter Simon came from town to counsel with Father Adolphus. A man's herd of sheep had been slaughtered by the Dark Horse for an unknown infraction. This could not continue. The Holy See would never allow this. The Dark Horse had always been an agent of righteousness, but now the Dark Horse struck without concern, for purposes unknown and unholy.

Father Adolphus was mindful of this. His needs were packed; the dispatch from the Holy See had arrived this morning. As soon as his greeting with Father Peter Simon was complete, he would leave for Vienna as commanded. The charge on the Dark Horse had always been upon the priest's shoulders at the prince's castle. He would be called to account for this, and he would be charged with the duty to right this.

Eight

Well into the small hours of the morn, Johann and Stephan carried Thorne, bleeding and injured, into the small Chapel of Our Lady, when few eyes would have seen the deed. The serene highness was alerted, and she made haste to the side of the bleeding man.

"Someone must care for him. Father Adolphus has been called to Vienna," Anja said, seeing her son covered in blood.

Precious few were skilled in caring for the sick and injured. Elena, the aging housekeeper, cared for the women of the castle, while Father Adolphus cared for the men. Should anything happen to either of them, there was no one to take their place.

"We will care for him," Stephan replied. This man was a brother to him; he would not let him perish.

"Neither of you have the skill, and both of you will be missed. You must see to the guests." The serene highness knew that this situation must be kept from all—from the staff and guests. Although the wedding was more than a month past, many guests would stay until the fall, then travel to Vienna for the winter court season.

"I will get Princess Olivia. She has good knowledge of herbs and healing. Thorne has told me thus. She is of the ability to birth animals." Johann turned to head up to the princess's room; morn would be upon them soon, and there was much to be done.

"She cannot care for him! That is not decent for a woman, a stranger, or a princess to do." The serene highness had never heard of such an absurd notion. She could not fathom this gentle-bred woman having this knowledge. And a woman could not care for Thorne; she would not allow such a thing.

"She has been confined to her room for long periods of time. The guests believe that she is ill and will not miss her. She has the instruction needed to save the prince's life." Without waiting for the serene highness to answer, Johann headed for Princess Olivia's room. He may be punished for his boldness, but he would take the lashings. He wanted nothing more than Thorne to live.

Olivia hastened to the chapel. Johann had told her little: someone had been shot and was in need of care. Father Adolphus was still in Vienna. Olivia would have questioned why someone from the village had not been summoned, but Johann was in grave concern for the injured man. Olivia requested that hot water and linens be brought and had appealed to Johann to bring the injured man to a room instead of the chapel, but Johann refused.

It was Thorne. His eyes were closed, and he was waxen in color. Olivia saw the blood on his shirt and with urgency cut the shirt from his chest. Others were about the room, but she paid them no mind, her thoughts only on Thorne. She scrubbed her hands in some of the warm water and cleansed Thorne's chest and shoulder, slowly working towards the wound.

"Help me. We must look for where the bullet has been released." Johann and Stephan rolled Thorne away from Olivia to let her look for the wound she was seeking.

When the men turned Thorne, he moaned with pain. Olivia stripped off the rest of his shirt but could not find a wound where the bullet had exited his body. She washed and dried his back and placed clean linens under him as the serene highness watched the young woman go about her healing. This was no pampered princess; this was a woman who had sought and learned knowledge that would not be considered prudent for a gentlewoman to know.

When Thorne was placed upon his back again, a pool had seeped from his wound. "We must stop this bleeding," Olivia said. "He has lost enough."

Olivia knew that one could lose a great quantity of blood without concern, but Thorne's color told her that this was dangerous bleeding. She called for a myriad of supplies; some the huntsman expected her to request, but many vexed his thoughts. This was not how Father Adolphus would treat the wound, but as a witness, Stephan had to admit that Father Adolphus saved only a fraction of the lives he was given to cure. Father Adolphus's gift was in the absolving of souls.

Olivia's mind was preoccupied with preparing to care for Thorne. She had seen this practiced, but only once and many years ago. Her memory replayed every step she had seen as she went about preparing the articles she had requested. Stephan sharpened the knives Olivia had selected. Johann brought her gin as she had asked for the strongest liquor in the castle. She put the cotton thread and linen strips into the gin and passed the needle and knives into the flame of the candle.

His eyes opened slowly to see Olivia beside him. It was dark, save for the candle next to the bed. Thorne could not remember where they were or to where they were traveling. There was a frown on Olivia's brow, and Thorne thought to see what was distressing the princess. As he started to rise, pain tore through his shoulder, arm, and chest. Thorne became alarmed—was Olivia harmed as well? His alarm brought him up, and he attempted to rise again until Olivia was there, telling him to rest.

"You have blood on your dress." Again Thorne worried that she had been harmed, but slowly the cloud over his thoughts dispatched, and he remembered the events of the night.

Olivia could see Thorne fighting with the confusion of his mind. "You should heed where you leave your blood."

Thorne looked at his shoulder. It was bleeding more than a flesh wound. But why was Olivia here? Did Stephan not send for Father Peter Simon? Thorne watched as Olivia held two knives in the flame of the candle until the color of the knife took the color of the flame. Was Olivia given to superstitions?

When she had prepared all her tools, she turned to Thorne, needing to gird him for what was about to happen. He had to be calm as possible; she would be asking him to be as still as a stone while she put him through hell.

"I have to remove the bullet and slow the bleeding. The pain will be like none you have ever known. It will be of greatest help for you to be as still as possible. I have gin here to help you with the pain." Olivia reached to pour some drink for Thorne, but he stayed her arm.

"Leave the liquor, Olivia. I will stay as you ask." Thorne did not trust a muddled mind; he knew he must do as she bid.

Thorne well knew that his life was in the hands of the woman he had threatened to kill. Should he lose his life, he would well deserve it. But he knew Olivia would never do such; he trusted her. Should he die, the face of an angel would be the last thing he saw on earth. Looking into her eyes, he saw not fear. Thorne nodded his head "yes."

She cleansed the wound with gin, and Thorne felt like fire was flowing into his body. Muscles twitched despite his resolve, but he did not move. To the three that stood helplessly aside, Thorne's sharp intake of breath was all the reaction they could see. Olivia quietly spoke to him, instructing him on the movements of her hands, telling him why she moved as she did and how long he must endure. Thorne thought only of her sweet voice; it kept him still when he wanted to bolt from the bed.

To all in the room it seemed as hours upon hours had passed since Olivia had asked Thorne if he was ready. In truth, it was almost an hour in passing. Her movements were sure and true and as gentle as she may be. She removed the bullet and sewed near to where the bleeding issued, slowing the flow. Olivia explained that she must leave part of the wound open, but bound it tightly with the help of Johann and Stephan. She washed the blood from Thorne's chest, and the two men stepped in to change the soiled linens at Olivia's request.

Dawn was starting to break. Olivia persuaded Thorne to take some gin so that he may sleep then went to her room and changed her dress, gathering what she thought she would need for the next few days. By the time she returned, Johann had removed Thorne's bloody clothes and redressed him. No one told Olivia she was to stay with Thorne; she knew she was the one that needed to care for him.

The serene highness pulled Stephan from the room into the chapel as Johann changed Thorne's clothing. "She cannot stay with him. I will not allow it! You must go for Father Peter Simon."

"You doubt she can care for him? Did you not see what she did?"

Stephan knew he was treading on thin ice as Johann had done earlier. He had full trust in Johann's decision to get Olivia, and after watching her remove the bullet, he was of the mind that Olivia would care for Thorne better than all others.

"She is a woman and a princess, even if she does not act as such!" said the serene highness.

"Thorne will allow no other to care for him. He will do as she says." Stephan knew that Thorne would do anything for

Olivia, even if Thorne did not know it.

"I will tell him to send her away!"

"He is your son, but do not distress him. We must do what will save his life. Only the five of us know. We can keep it such."

The serene highness went back into the small room to have Thorne tell Olivia that Father Peter Simon would care for him. Thorne's eyes were closed. Quietly he called for Olivia, and Johann told him that she would return but a moment. After a second he called out for her again. Olivia entered the room with a basket's worth of clothing. Thorne called for her, and she set the basket down and rushed to his side, taking the chair in which Johann had been sitting. Thorne reached for her hand, and Olivia put hers in his, smoothing his brow with her other hand, quietly calming him.

The serene highness left the small room, fearing what she saw was true—Thorne and Olivia were in love. Why else would he call for her? Why would she rush to his side? The serene highness was unsettled by this. This was not the woman she envisioned taking her place. This was not the woman who should be the mother of the next prince. When Thorne was well, she would tell him that Olivia must be sent away at once. He must see that she could not be his wife. And he must punish the valet and the huntsman. It would not be tolerated for them to speak to her in such a manner.

Thorne fell asleep on the bed, and Olivia moved to the large reading chair next to the window. She fell asleep as soon as she knew Thorne's breathing was deep and easy. They both slept soundly until Johann brought them a tray for breakfast. Johann attended to Thorne's needs and then withdrew, and Olivia assisted Thorne in taking breakfast. He ate little and would not have eaten that had Olivia not insisted. She checked his dressing, satisfied that he was not bleeding overly much.

He became gruff with her ministrations, and she went back to her chair after she offered him more gin for his distress. Thorne did not like taking liquor for pain, but again, Olivia insisted that it would be best for his welfare. As she curled up in the large chair, Thorne inquired as to how she had the knowledge to take the bullet from his shoulder. Olivia told him of the neighbor who had been accidentally shot while hunting and brought to their estate as it was closer than his own. She watched and assisted her grandparents' huntsman as he tended to the man. She had wanted to learn, and none opposed her assisting.

Thorne dreamed of Olivia while he slept. She was in the field of wildflowers, but now he walked by her side. They talked and laughed as she picked her flowers, and Thorne carried the load. He slept peacefully, his soul wanting to stay with Olivia and her wildflowers, but the pain in his shoulder wrenched him awake. Thorne lifted his head and saw Olivia sleeping in the chair, a slight smile on her lips. Was she dreaming of the field as well? Thorne attempted to reach for something to soothe his parched lips, but a moan of pain escaped him, awakening Olivia.

She rushed to his side. "You should call for me if you have a need."

"I am not a babe."

"Act not like one and allow me to help you." Olivia poured fresh water from the pitcher into the goblet and handed it to Thorne.

"I am tired of lying about here."

"It has been but a day."

"I have business I must attend to."

"And what would you have your guests think of your injury?"

Thorne answered her with a scowl.

"I understand not why you wish to hurt the Dark Horse."

"What do you know of this?"

"I heard your valet tell the serene highness that you were

shot by the Dark Horse. You were in search of the Dark Horse to kill him."

"Forget what you have heard. This is not your concern."

"The Dark Horse came to me to ask me to help free you from my father's prison. Is this how you repay him?"

"It is not as simple as it may appear."

"Then tell me—tell me so that I can understand."

"I told you, Olivia, it is not your concern."

"I am not a fool, unable to understand because I am a woman."

Thorne answered her with a laugh, which caused him great pain, and he held his breath to keep from moaning. He had grabbed her hand without knowing, and Olivia gently caressed his hand with hers. Slowly the pain started to wane, and Thorne was able to breathe again. Olivia did not withdraw her hand. Thorne had started to drift back to sleep; so little had taken so much out of him.

He woke as the sun slipped from the sky. Olivia was seated in the chair next to him, still holding his hand, but she had laid her head down on the pillow beside him. Thorne struggled with the idea of waking her. She had less sleep than he last night and through the day, and she had done much to exhaust her. If he did not wake her, she would have pain in her neck and back from her unnatural position. He did not want her to leave him, but she should not be seen reclining with him.

Johann and Stephan came with a tray of dinner for Olivia and Thorne. Olivia insisted that Thorne eat, and then she had the men help her unwrap his bandage. The wound was not bleeding overly much, and Olivia was satisfied with the look of it.

"I need to make a poultice to help it heal. I will need to gather the proper herbs and roots. Is there one who can show me where to find these?"

Olivia had not had enough time nor the freedom to explore the castle or the area just outside the castle walls. What she needed was common enough, but would be difficult to find in the dark, and she did not know where to look. Olivia left with Stephan while Johann saw to helping Thorne bathe and change. She was able to find everything she needed in the cook's garden. Few eyes would see them there; dinner was being served to the serene highness and the guests.

There was something very familiar about the huntsman. Olivia felt she knew him, but in another place. He spoke not directly to her, and she had barely been able to hear him when he spoke with Thorne—and then she was focused on what he was saying. Now she felt she would know from where she knew him if she heard his voice, but he remained mute.

When they returned to the small room off the Chapel of Our Lady, Thorne was seated in a chair. Olivia removed the linen cloth from his wound and placed the poultice near it; the juices would absorb into the wound as Thorne reposed. Thorne did not wish for the light in the room. The guests and servants would know that Father Adolphus was away, and Thorne did not want to invite prying eyes. He could not explain his infirmity as yet and planned to stay hidden until he regained more of his strength.

Olivia pressed some gin on him as he finally relented to go back to bed. The men had left, and Thorne's strength had rapidly declined. As much as it galled him, he had no choice but to allow Olivia to help him the few steps to bed. The pain was beastly, and Thorne had to hold his breath to bear it. As he did so, his head became fuzzy, his footing untrustworthy.

She was aware that Thorne was unnaturally limp mere seconds before he started to topple, and his injured shoulder would take the brunt of his fall. Thorne was too much of a burden for Olivia to hold; she could only hope to lessen the impact. Her only regard was to draw Thorne to her, and then she had to let the forces of nature determine their descent. Olivia fell with more of her body on the bed than off. Thorne's full measure landed on top of her, and she held tight lest he slip to the floor.

The fall jarred Thorne from the emptiness of his mind, but his thoughts swirled around his head like clouds. He lifted his head and opened his eyes to see Olivia beneath him. The pain in his shoulder thundered with each beat of his heart. He was drenched in sweat, and he fought to bring his thoughts into focus. Olivia was holding him so that he would not slip to the floor.

"Can you bear?" Thorne feared that he was too much; she would be hurt holding him.

"I will not loosen." Olivia held fast and contemplated how to get Thorne into bed.

After explaining her plan to Thorne, they rolled to the side, and Thorne's torso was fast onto the bed. Olivia sat up and lifted his legs into the bed. As she rose from the bed, his arm weakly grabbed hers. "Stay, if only for a while."

Olivia lay on the bed next to Thorne, gently brushing the wet hair from his forehead. His hand came up and captured hers, holding it fast as he brought it to rest over his heart. Olivia knew he had lost much blood, and the strain of healing had weakened him as well—far more than he knew. She had little doubt that it was hard for Thorne to be as powerless as a babe. The fragility of his body had caught him completely unaware, and although he had the scars to prove he was not untested at danger, he had not acknowledged the measure of his wound. Olivia doubted he had ever been weakened as he was now.

Olivia got up to spread the blanket over Thorne and turned to go to the chair, but Thorne's hand caught her and drew her back to the bed. She had no concern that he would compromise her in any way—he had not the strength to walk across the room—but she could not be on the bed with him when Johann came in the morning to see to Thorne's needs. She did not allow her thoughts to dwell on what Johann and Stephan thought of her staying in the same room as Thorne, and the serene highness would no doubt press Olivia's conduct on Father Adolphus when he returned.

Nine

When Thorne was able to care for himself, she would leave, though Olivia still had no clear plan where to go. She had thought to go to Vienna where she may find more agreeable arrangements. She had planned to take little of the wardrobe that Thorne had had made for her, but with nicer clothing she may find a situation that would suit her better. She had also thought to change her name and tell of a family and past that did not belong to her. She may even have a chance to find a husband and have the life of others if she was no longer her father's daughter.

Thorne did exactly as Olivia bade: he ate what and when she decreed; he strode, and he rested at her behest. In less than a week's time, he felt more like himself; his strength was returning. Olivia was well pleased with his healing; he had no sign of poisoning of the wound or the blood, and his pain was near as naught. Olivia had started making an appearance among the guests in the afternoon. The serene highness had suggested to the guests that Olivia had debilitating headaches, but still many of the guests thought that Thorne was keeping Olivia locked in her room. Others thought that Olivia had melancholy; it was believed that Thorne had gone to Vienna with Father Adolphus, and Olivia was heartbroken to be separated from him.

They settled into a comfortable routine, sleeping late until Johann brought them breakfast. They passed the rest of the morn reading, talking, or playing board games. Later in the morn Olivia would slip off to her room to bathe and change and then make an appearance among the ladies. While Olivia was gone, Johann would help Thorne bathe, shave, and dress, and then he would pick up the small room. Thorne was kept abreast of the goings-on in the castle and any rumors flying about, especially about the Dark Horse, though there had been no musings about him. Thorne wondered if he was dead. He knew he had wounded the man, but he had no thoughts that it had been a fatal blow.

The plan had not been without merit. An owner of a local public house had boasted that he heard that the Dark Horse had been contracted about a matter in a town just over the border in the Duchy of Carniola. In less than a day, the word was taken by a patron to Thorne, who rode through the night, with Johann and Stephan, to awaken the owner and find out as much as possible for very little coin. They were given the name of the man who had contracted the Dark Horse, and as the sun rose, they were on their way to him. It took some persuasion—and, regrettably, the threat of pain to the man's wife and children—but the needed knowledge was given. Thorne's men were masked and unknown to the man; Thorne did not fear retribution.

The Dark Horse was to kill a neighbor and his family. For several generations there had been enmity between the two families. Thorne had been shocked by how much the man had paid for the deed to be done—more than a year's wage. With only two days to wait, the three men had taken up positions around the family, and Thorne had taken the most dangerous position. He would not ask another; he felt it was his place to take the mortal position.

Johann and Stephan had taken the wife and children into a sheltered area and were not to leave them for any reason. Just before sunrise, the Dark Horse struck, setting fire to the area around the house and breaking through the door with a ram. He was well armed with several dueling pistols, primed and ready to shoot, in his belt. Thorne had pistols like this himself; they were new to fashion and very costly. Thorne had never heard that the Dark Horse used this type of weapon.

Thorne was not armed as such, but the pistols would have only one shot each. Thorne's ability with all manner of blades was without question, so he did not fear taking the Dark Horse to task in this uneven fight. The confrontation started with rapiers on both sides, Thorne keeping the Dark Horse on the defensive from the moment the blades were raised. After several minutes of thrusting and parrying, Thorne could see that the Dark Horse was tiring. Thorne had come to believe that the Dark Horse was much older and did not share Thorne's sporting figure.

With his blade, Thorne wounded the Dark Horse in the right shoulder. It was not a mortal wound, but it kept the Dark Horse from using his arm. As Thorne moved in for the capture, the Dark Horse pulled a pistol from his waistband with his left hand and shot Thorne from a distance that required great skill. Given that the pistols had been positioned to use with the right hand, Thorne had not thought the Dark Horse would be able to get to the pistol in time, nor did he think the Dark Horse would be that skilled with his left hand.

They had saved the man and his family, but the Dark Horse knew he was being hunted. When they heard no more of the Dark Horse, Thorne, Johann, and Stephan feared that he would not appear again. If the Dark Horse disappeared, the terrorizing threat to the empire would be gone ... for this time. No justice would be had for those who had been wronged, and the empire would forever fear the return of the Dark Horse, whose name would be forever tainted.

Thorne had not expected to long for Olivia while she was gone in the afternoons, but he did. Worse still, he kept track of the time, counting down the minutes to her return. Late in the evenings, when the sky was dark and no eyes would be looking from the castle windows, Thorne and Olivia would walk in the chapel garden, speaking little, both looking at the stars and enjoying the air of the night. Thorne had taken to placing his hand at the small of her back, hating to admit that it felt like it should be there.

Olivia was becoming too important to Thorne. He knew that it was dangerous to let her into his heart, but he feared she was there already. He had planned never to marry. He had considered it once, but that was not a matter of the heart; it was a matter of convenience for his loins. To consider marriage to Olivia was impossible—her father would never allow it, and she would want a normal life with a husband at her side and a home full of children. Thorne could never give her that.

Thorne sat in the chair by the only window in the small room. The sunlight was fading; the sky was an orange and yellow blaze. He was waiting and watching for Olivia, who was always punctual to the minute. In truth, Thorne did not need her to stay with him each day, and he certainly did not need her to sleep in the chair each night, though he would not suggest thus to her. He did not want to be without her, and their time together in the small room was near to the end.

This was all against Thorne's nature. He was not a man content to be idle. He was not a man content to leave his business unanswered. He was not a man content with just passing the day with a woman. And he was not a man that allowed himself to have tender thoughts for a woman other than Auria.

But Thorne was content locked up in this small room with Olivia. And he did have tender thoughts for her, although he had warned himself repeatedly that he must not have any concern for her.

When Thorne was healed, he would distance himself from her, and Thorne had little doubt that his thoughts of her would diminish. He was sure that she was no more than a passing fancy, someone who helped him while away his time spent caged like an animal. He dreamed of her at night simply because he was without female company. In a few weeks Thorne would look back at his concern and laugh at himself.

As the guests headed for the stair, retiring to their rooms

to dress for the evening meal, Olivia slipped into the kitchen and out through the summer kitchen to the courtyard, making her way to the entrance to the chapels. Fewer would notice her in the courtyard than if she took the route inside the castle, but in her rush she failed to notice that she was not alone this eve.

She felt him come up beside her, and Olivia stopped. It was Joseph, the son of a baron. During Thorne's absence, Joseph had intensified his attention towards her. She was seated next to him at the midday meal, and when Olivia changed her seating placard, the serene highness instructed her to sit next to Joseph. He sought her out as soon as she entered the drawing room and would not allow Olivia to speak with other guests.

She had stopped coming to the drawing room before the midday meal, but the serene highness informed Olivia that she would not allow her to be so rude to the guests, questioning the necessity of Olivia attending to Thorne in the evening. Surely he was well enough to care for himself? Olivia did not bring to the serene highness's attention the fact that she was still spending the nights in the chair in the small room.

Joseph was being far too forward; following her was inexcusable. Had Thorne's intimacy at the wedding given Joseph the notion that Olivia would be party to his behavior? Olivia knew not. She did know that Joseph had been more than a stone in her slipper, and she feared his intentions tonight were not honorable.

Olivia was of the thought that the serene highness was encouraging Joseph's affection for her, but she could not understand why. Why would she play the matchmaker for Joseph and Olivia?

When she told Thorne that his mother had suggested that she did not need to care for him any longer, Thorne became very angry. He told Olivia that she was not to concern herself with what his mother thought or said. Olivia was to continue with the routine they had established. Thorne said he would speak with his mother. Olivia had not told Thorne that she felt his mother was encouraging Joseph's pursuit of her. Olivia would not accuse the serene highness; she was a guest in this woman's home. It truly would be an insult for Olivia to suggest such.

Olivia also felt that it would anger Thorne, and she did not want to be a concern between the serene highness and her son. She felt she was being pushed from one direction and pulled by the other, but she need endure this for only a little while longer. Thorne would be about the guests soon, and Olivia would be able to leave.

"Olivia, where are you going? Are you not coming to

dine this eve?" Joseph had caught her by the upper arm, and although Olivia had stopped walking, Joseph had not released his hold on her.

There was nowhere she could possibly be headed except for the chapels. She wanted not to draw any attention to the chapels, but there was no other place she could claim to be headed. Had she not come so far, she could have claimed she was going to the herb garden for herbs for her fictitious headaches, but she had passed the gardens. To continue on would take her to the stables; that destination would not do, and the rooms on this side of the castle were mostly for the servants, where she would have no business.

"I am going to prayer for a few minutes. I fear a headache coming. It would be best for me to rest, but I missed morning prayer, and I wanted to take a moment to pray." Olivia had not missed morning prayer; there had been none since Father Adolphus left for Vienna, but none of the guests had noticed.

"I shall go with you to pray."

"Oh no, Joseph, we do not have a chaperone. We should not even be here speaking together. You must go back now." Olivia hoped he would heed her appeal without further discussion, but it was not to be.

"God will be our chaperone in the chapel."

"God is always my chaperone, but I would not want to disgrace the serene highness so. Please, Joseph, you must go back and dress to dine."

"No one needs know of this. It can be our little secret. Should there be a question, I assure you I would do what is honorable and marry you."

He had gotten closer to her as he spoke. Olivia had taken several steps backward to keep the distance between them and felt the three-foot wall of the pool surrounding the fountain—but not in time. The force of her step took her tumbling towards the pool.

Thorne sat and watched the exchange between Olivia and Joseph. Without conscious thought, he rose from the chair and started for the door before remembering where he was and why. Thorne forced himself to sit and stay in the little room, not wanting to watch Joseph advance on Olivia as though he was about to devour her. Should the situation become more threatening to Olivia, Thorne would leave the small room—and thrash his guest.

Thorne had known Joseph for almost as many years as they had been alive. Joseph's reputation was even worse than Thorne's, but where Thorne had high standards regarding the company he kept, Joseph was not as discerning. It was also said that Joseph would not take "no" for an answer. Thorne jumped to his feet as he saw Olivia start to tumble into the pool.

Joseph reached out and gathered Olivia into his arms, saving her from a plunge into the pool and pulling her close to him. His head bent to capture her lips, and his hands wandered to where they should not be. He would take her into the chapel for a quick tryst before he dined. She was an untitled cousin, so no one would have a concern. If there was a question, he would deny that he had been with her. He had no wish to marry so lowly; he would marry much later, and to a titled, rich family.

The sound of her hand upon his cheek was so loud it echoed in the courtyard. Thorne heard it in the small room. As Joseph's hand went instinctively to his cheek, Olivia abruptly pushed him in the chest with her full measure. Joseph went down onto the walkway with a thud, but Olivia did not stay to watch the result of her handiwork. She turned and ran into the chapels as quickly as she was able, hurrying to the far end of the Chapel of Our Lady to the door to the small room.

Thorne had the door open for her, and as she entered, he quietly closed the door and pushed the bolt into place. Olivia sat upon the bed with her hands over her mouth. She felt her heart beating so loudly that she feared Joseph would follow the pounding of it to where she sat. Her breath was ragged from running and from the burst of energy that had helped her escape.

Thorne came to the bed and guided Olivia to lie down, before joining her on the bed. A rose bush in front of the window would prevent Joseph from getting to the window to look in, but Thorne did not want Olivia visible at all. They heard Joseph come into the chapel and call Olivia's name, but he did not come near the door. Thorne heard the door just inside the outside entrance open and slam shut. Joseph had gone back into the castle using the inside passage.

Tears stung her eyes, spilling over despite her determination not to cry. It was not common for her to dissolve into this feminine pastime, but she was helpless to stop the tears. As she heard Thorne's words, the tears amassed. Joseph had a reputation for doing such. It was well-known throughout the empire that he forced himself on women; she need not feel that it was any fault of her own.

Did the serene highness know of this? Had the serene highness set this moment into motion by encouraging Joseph to chase after Olivia? Olivia could not share her painful thoughts with Thorne; she could not speak against his mother.

Olivia's tears had alarmed Thorne as she had faced more threatening situations with little disturbance. Thorne had to admit that she had been through so much in the last few months that she was more than entitled to this usual reaction.

Gathering her to him, Thorne held her, brushing the wayward curls out of her face, kissing her gently on the forehead, and murmuring comforting words to her. His heart was grieved; all this had happened to her because of his foolishness.

Thorne put a blanket over them and gathered her up in his arms again. He had insisted that she come to care for him, but this night he needed to care for her. When her crying slowly stopped, Thorne knew she had fallen asleep. He drifted off as well but never left her; she was with him in his dreams of the field of wildflowers.

A rooster crowed although the sun had not come near the horizon. Thorne rose and moved to the chair, awakening Olivia with his movement. She insisted on going to the chair, but Thorne went back to the bed, leaned down, and kissed her on the forehead.

"Go back to sleep. I will take the chair. You rest." He kissed her forehead again, and Olivia drifted back to sleep.

Johann looked to Thorne with a raised eyebrow at the sleeping arrangement then checked the chapel at Thorne's request. When no one was found, Olivia stepped out to the bathing room to attend to her needs, and Thorne gave instructions to Johann to give to Stephan. Johann looked at Thorne with both eyebrows raised.

Later that day, as Joseph went to his room to change for the evening meal, all thoughts of the moments with Olivia were long forgotten. He turned towards the bed and stopped abruptly, breaking out in a sweat as his heart began to race. He looked about for the culprit although he knew he was alone. Who could have done this? Who could have known?

The white silk pillow slips on his bed bore the message "Leave Her Alone," written in blood.

Ten

Who was the real Thorne? Was he the intelligent, charming man that debated philosophy with her, or the blustering ogre that ordered her about? When he was relaxed, he really was very handsome, but when he was angry, he was so infuriating she wanted to claw his eyes out. She did not want to admit it, but she treasured their time together. He made her smile, and he made her laugh and think and question. He made her happy—deliriously happy.

Olivia knew this was just a slice in time that would pass quickly. Their paths were never meant to cross, and soon they would diverge. Thorne would be a memory that would make her smile from time to time. She would enjoy his company for this time, but she would be gone as soon as she could get away. Olivia was sure that Thorne would forget to place a guard on her once he had healed. She had been so helpful to him—why would he have a concern with her?

For just more than a month Olivia and Thorne remained in their bubble in the small room off the Chapel of Our Lady.

Neither had a complaint of the other. Thorne was even fairly content with his infirmity, but Johann and Stephan could see what was happening. They discussed it much as it had great bearing on their lives. They knew that Thorne had planned not to marry or have children, and they well understood why he had come to that position. Things had changed greatly since this all started centuries ago.

Johann and Stephan did not know all that Thorne knew of Olivia. They were involved in his plan to use Olivia to free Chance, but Thorne alone had done the scouting in preparation for kidnapping her. Olivia's father, the Prince of Tyrol, would most certainly not agree to a marriage between Thorne and Olivia. The prince was well-known throughout the empire, and should his daughter magically appear—and married to a man known to be at odds with the prince—questions would arise, questions that the prince would not want asked. His divorce could come to light.

Johann and Stephan had watched as Thorne had done all Olivia requested without question. They knew that there were few to whom Thorne would listen without argument, but they knew Thorne had thought of marriage once before; both Johann and Stephan had been against it. They were not against Thorne marrying; they were against Thorne's choice. Thorne had considered it only as it would serve his needs; that was no better than what his father had done, marrying for the usual reasons, which was not the way to consider marriage. There was so much more to consider.

Thorne's last choice made both the valet and the huntsman understand how important it was to consider all. When he asked for their opinions regarding his thoughts to marry, they had told him the truth, but neither man knew if his opinion had any bearing on Thorne's decision to wait.

Stephan had done business with Olivia, although Olivia knew not it was Stephan. Stephan had praised her courage and integrity, and had not Olivia come to help Thorne without a squawk about propriety? She had come and was a far better healer than Father Adolphus, but they could not come to a conclusion as to whether Olivia was the woman for Thorne. They must wait and listen and watch. The consequences were far too great for Thorne to choose wrongly.

The wagons and carriages were packed and waiting to whisk Auria and Grego to Grego's family home in the Duchy of Styria. More than one hundred guests remained at the castle, and they took their good-byes before the family. Margarette and Chance were the first in the family to say farewell as Margarette was only a month before her time. It was a tearful good-bye as Auria and Margarette had grown close over the last two years.

As Auria hugged Olivia, she implored, "Promise me you will come to visit me."

Olivia was touched by the depth of the younger woman's plea. She had little doubt that Auria had concern leaving everyone she knew behind and embarking on a new life. These were thoughts that Olivia could well understand.

"If our paths are meant to cross again, then I will, but I will always have you in my thoughts and prayers."

"I have no misgivings that not only will our paths cross again, but our lives will be entwined."

Olivia had no reply; she merely inclined her head and smiled. Mayhaps Auria had thoughts that Father Adolphus would send Olivia to her in some capacity.

Thorne stepped up to hug his sister good-bye. His chest was heavy with grief for losing her, but he forced himself to smile and be happy for Auria. He had complete faith in Grego that he would make Auria happy, but he knew there would forever be a hole in his life ... and that he had to let her go. He knew it would be hard, but he never could have guessed just how hard it would be.

"I will miss you the most. You have been so good to me,

Thorne, a brother and a father, but now you must care for yourself. You need not walk alone. I believe the one you are meant to spend your life with is under your nose." Auria kissed her brother, but could read no reply in his expression.

Auria's words shocked Thorne. His sister had never endeavored to play the matchmaker in his life, and he had given his full measure to hide his feelings for Olivia, especially to Auria. Thorne could not entertain the romantic musings of a young girl in love. He had been thrust into his service, and he would never ask his son to agree to take the mantle upon his shoulders when he was too young to understand the burden he would bear.

There was a long, tearful good-bye between mother and daughter. Olivia reflected that Auria's departure would most likely be more of a burden for the serene highness than for Auria, although the serene highness had Margarette and her grandchildren left; she was not completely alone.

During the wedding preparations she had heard a few of the guests whisper about Thorne. *Why does he not marry? Why does he show no interest in looking for a wife?* Strangely, the serene highness had made no comment. One would have thought she would be placing every available woman under Thorne's nose, but she showed no interest in finding her son a wife.

The guests had long retired to the courtyard for the midday meal and a quiet afternoon of games; no other special activities had been planned. Olivia could feel Thorne's deep sadness as she walked beside him back into the castle. Olivia had no duties and no desire to spend the afternoon in idle chit-chat. Once Thorne left her side, she started for her room, but as she reached to open the door of her room, her heart told her to go otherwise. She found him sitting in the Chapel of Our Lady with a candle in his hands. Olivia had been drawn here, and now she knew why.

She took the candle from Thorne's hands, lit it, and set it with the other prayers. "She is more than a sister to you."

"Yes. My father died when Auria was very young. She was special to my father, his special little princess. After he died, she called out for him. My mother said that in time she would forget him and stop calling for him, but it broke my heart. She was such a beautiful, happy girl, so when she called for my father, I picked her up and gave her the attention my father would have. She was a child. She should not have to be in mourning. She could not understand."

Thorne stopped. He had never spoken to anyone about

this, not even Chance. Everyone knew that he treated Auria more like a daughter than a sister, but no one had ever asked him why. His family had assumed that he was simply very fond of the delightful child. His true feeling was something Thorne must bear alone. He was not sure he wanted to tell Olivia. She was a stranger—even though she did not feel like a stranger to him. Did he want to say the words to her that he could not say even to his twin?

"I have no plan to marry for reasons of my own, so Auria became the daughter I would never have. I never planned that it should be that way, and now it is as it should be. Little girls grow up and marry. They become wives and mothers, no longer precious daughters, but one cannot help but feel the loss of what can never be again."

Olivia said nothing. There was nothing she could say. Thorne was right: it was as it should be, but a great loss none the same. She sat there with him looking at the candles flickering, each lost in their own thoughts, yet thoughts connected to loss and children. The hours passed, though time seemed to stand still. Finally, Thorne stood and walked from the chapel. Olivia stayed and let him leave with his dignity intact. To give any words, or even acknowledge this time they spent together, would have betrayed the trust Thorne had given her by sharing his heart with her.

He had told her more than simply what he had said. It was his duty to marry, to provide an heir. This duty would have been pressed upon him since the moment of his first breath. Who would care for the people of Carinthia? One did not turn their back on duty just to be a carefree rogue, and Thorne could not simply hand his duty over to Chance; he had a duty of the house into which he had married. Olivia had seen and heard of Thorne's love for his people.

No, there was another concern here, a concern that could not be spoken aloud. And it was not a small concern.

Olivia would rather have thrown something, but she stomped her foot on the floor instead. Thorne was completely insufferable. He was an arrogant, imperious monster! Had she not nursed him back to health? Had she not played her role to the guests completely? Could he not see what she had done for him of her own accord? Olivia stomped her foot again. Thorne had placed a guard on her again.

Olivia had thought that mayhaps Thorne could see her as more than just a game piece, but now Olivia could see that nothing had changed, despite what she had done for him. She would not allow Thorne to use her any longer. She would play his game. She would be a guest in his home, a guest with a shadow. She would demand that he treat her as he would every other guest. He had not used any of the wedding guests for his own needs, and he would not use her either.

She had free rein of the castle, though she was never truly alone, and she had little doubt that her movements were being reported to Thorne, who had returned to the land of the living. His shoulder still could not be tested, but he could be about without question. The guests were leaving the castle; most had already traveled to Vienna to prepare their palaces for the court season, so Thorne's injury was not widely known.

Father Adolphus had sent letters to Thorne, but he had not returned. Olivia did not know what was in the letters, aside from some general thoughts that Thorne shared privately with the family. Olivia needed to leave before Father Adolphus returned to take her to wherever they planned to deposit her. Thorne's mistake would be dealt with—Olivia would be out of sight and out of mind—but Thorne did not seem to understand that her future mattered to her. Thorne had not practiced diligence with her thus far; Olivia saw no reason to trust him with this matter.

But what was she to do? She must be as the walls of the castle so that she would be forgotten, so that Thorne would forget she was of a mind to escape. Olivia stood at the window of her room looking out as her mind churned. She knew that what she would need would come to her. As she watched the gardeners tend to the herb garden, she knew the answer was here, in front of her. This was exactly what she needed.

She dressed carefully for the evening meal, wanting to look much like the princess. She would bide her time, sitting quietly at the meal. She hoped that Thorne would consume a sufficient amount of wine at the meal; she did not want him thinking at his very best. Thorne need only to agree to allow Olivia to do as she wished. Mayhaps he would have misgivings about what she wanted to do, but Olivia had hope that with enough wine Thorne could be persuaded into letting Olivia proceed with her plan. She would blend in with the walls, become as invisible as the servants, and when the time was right, she would disappear, seemingly into air.

The family was in fine spirits for the evening. Two families remained as guests and would be leaving for Vienna in the morn, so this was a farewell celebration. Wine flowed freely as the courses continued to stream from the kitchen. Olivia played the dutiful guest, chatting with and charming the baroness, a cousin to the archduchess. Margarette had given birth the previous night to a healthy son, and more wine flowed as Chance joined the celebration. To Olivia, the meal was overlong, and she was coming to a loss of compliments for the baroness. After eight courses, the celebrants decided to retire to the drawing room.

At the urging of the serene highness, Olivia played the pianoforte as family and guests relaxed and told stories, and Thorne and Chance competed in a board game. The wine at Thorne's castle was excellent; his lands near the base of the mountains had an extensive vineyard, but the wine was also strong. Olivia could not drink a full crystal without her thoughts becoming muddled. She kept an eye on the measure Thorne consumed and felt confident that if she had a word with him this eve, he would agree to her bidding.

Chance returned to his wife as several guests drifted off to sleep in the drawing room and the servants came to assist them up to bed. The serene highness retired as the last guest was assisted up the stair. Olivia arose and made to follow the serene highness, but then turned back towards Thorne and paused. He looked at her, an eyebrow raised.

"Princely Grace, a word, if I may." Olivia remained at the base of the stair, well in sight of Thorne's mother. If the serene highness had a concern with her being alone with Thorne, a servant could be called.

"Sit, Princess, and share your mind." Thorne indicated the chair that Chance had just abandoned, across the game table.

Olivia perched on the edge of the chair. "I thought that mayhaps I should place some of the healing herbs that I am accustomed to using in the herb garden. I could leave instruction for Father Adolphus on the herbs' preparation and usage."

Thorne looked at her with intent. Olivia had concern that she had somehow given away her true thoughts as he sat and sipped his wine, but she could do little except sit and wait for Thorne to answer her. Her temper became inflamed. Why was he just sitting there without answering her? It was not right that she would be sitting alone with him in the near darkness. Thorne could not keep treating her with familiarity before others; there could be no honorable intention between them, and Olivia would not allow any other intention. She struggled to maintain a serene outward appearance, though she had little doubt that he was vexing her for his own amusement.

After the two sat without speaking for far longer than necessary for a simple request, Thorne finally finished his glass of wine. He rose from the chair and went to the window. "It is kind of you to have concern for Father Adolphus's skills, but I have concern that your request has a cause that you are not willing to say."

"I do willingly admit that it is not my custom to be idle." Olivia would not try to make Thorne think her actions were solely unselfish.

"Yes, I remember that you were invariably engaged."

Olivia had no idea to what Thorne was referring. He spoke as if they had known each other for more than the past six months—and far more intimately. "I know not to what you refer."

"When I was watching you, before I took you from your grandparents' estate. You were not the usual princess of leisure. I am sure that you noticed that our wedding guests did not participate in a tiring schedule."

"You were watching me?" Olivia did not relish that thought.

"I had to understand the workings of the estate and your daily activities."

Thorne continued to look out the window. For some reason, he felt he should tell her that he had watched her for several weeks, though for what purpose to his confession, he could not say. Olivia was not a stranger to him anymore, although he never had thought that she would ever consume more than a few days of his life. Mayhaps his confession would vanquish her from his mind. He could not continue to spend every moment aching for her.

"Of course, it is expected that one would observe their prey to ensure a successful hunt." That was much as how Olivia felt, like she was a deer, tracked to be slaughtered. Why would he confess this to her now, but to press upon her why she was here? The reminder that she was little more than an animal to be used as his need arose pained her, but it also reminded her of why she needed to leave. Thorne had no concern for her whatsoever. What little kindness he displayed to her was simply a matter of public graciousness or his own need.

"You may do as you wish without my agreement—except leave, of course." Thorne had no misgivings about giving Olivia a full measure of freedom, except to leave. She was not a fanciful woman.

Eleven

Father Adolphus would not be returning until the Dark Horse was dead; this was how the Cardinal would keep Thorne in check on this manner. Father Adolphus was not being imprisoned, but he was restricted to a monastery in the mountains. Eventually word would get out among the empire of the Papal displeasure with Thorne. There would be murmurings in the archduchess's ear—Olivia's own father being the loudest—that Thorne's family was not fit to keep the duchy intact. Thorne's lack of participation at court made him an easy target for the more ambitious aristocracy. As Thorne read the Cardinal's edict, he knew he must find a way to bring this concern with the Dark Horse to a close before it made him—and his people—vulnerable.

As the morning dawned, Olivia headed out to the herb gardens. She walked through each garden, getting an understanding of which were cooking herbs, which were medicinal herbs, and which were the herbs and flowers used for fragrance. The kitchen garden was well-thought-out, but the rest of the gardens were without reason. Olivia was sure that plants had been added as space allowed without much consideration. She would completely rearrange these areas. It would be less of a concern for her guard and for Thorne if she appeared to be immersed in the gardens.

Olivia headed for the small tool shed near the garden for a shovel and pots, if any were to be gained, having decided to start in the front and work her way back. There had been no pathways to access the herbs, so she would put those in as well. The land was naturally rocky, and Olivia was sure there were piles of rocks somewhere that she could use. She would consult with the gardeners when they arrived.

Thorne watched Olivia in the garden. The sun was rising, and she looked like an angel with the sun glowing in her hair. He turned and finished dressing. Thorne had always enjoyed the very early of the morning; few in the castle were up and about, and he could enjoy some peace. He was due to meet with Johann and Stephan at the stables in a while, though there had been no detection of the Dark Horse. Thorne knew that the Dark Horse had not died from the wound Thorne had imposed on him, and the Dark Horse would make his presence known again soon.

As Thorne headed out the kitchen for the stables, he saw

Olivia wrestling with a root-bound lavender and changed his direction, heading straight for her. He remembered her bloody hands that had given him the chisel to escape. He would never allow her to have bloody hands again. She was a princess, despite her father's rejection; he would not allow her to think of herself as another paid servant of his.

Olivia heard the boots approach and was grateful that the gardeners had arrived, although it was much earlier than she had seen them arrive any other morning. She needed help to rip the lavender free. She would need a gardener to hold the plant up while she freed the stubborn roots that were no doubt entwined in the roots of the adjacent plants. She stopped and swiped the hair from her face and turned to greet the gardeners.

"What are you doing? The gardeners will move the plants for you. You need only to direct them." Thorne looked into her flushed face, the high color of her cheeks making her even more beautiful.

Olivia was surprised to see Thorne out so early in the morning. Her guard was dozing, sitting on the ground with his back against the shed, and Olivia feared that Thorne would see him and become angry with the guard. Olivia preferred to have a guard that felt at ease to fall asleep while watching her.

"Princely Grace, what a lovely surprise to see you this morning. I fear I have not made much progress on the garden as of yet; it will look like a mud pit for several weeks." Fortunately, the guard had woken up and walked out to the front of the shed, looking like he was intently watching her.

Without a word Thorne stormed into the garden and scooped Olivia up in his arms, carrying her out of the garden and depositing her on the stone pathway. Olivia was astounded that Thorne should act so familiar with her in front of the guard; she had not forgotten his ill-mannered behavior of the night before. Before angry words flew from her mouth, Olivia turned away from Thorne and bent to straighten her skirt, but Thorne was of another mind. He grabbed her upper arm and pulled her up and to him until their noses were almost touching.

"You are not a servant, you will not act like a servant, and you will direct the servants to do as you wish. Your mother may have had an unrestrained attitude with you, but I expect you to act like a princess." Thorne's face was a mask of anger as he bit the words out at her.

She slapped him smartly across the face. "When you treat me like a princess, then you may decide if my behavior is befitting a princess." Olivia wrenched her arm from his grasp and turned to walk away, but he grabbed her arm again, with less care.

Thorne stepped into her path. "This is my home, and

you will do as I instruct you."

"I may be a caged animal, but I will not be your trained animal. Concern yourself with other issues and leave me alone. You are right—I am not a servant. They are given more respect than you are capable of showing me." Again Olivia wrenched her arm from his vice grip, turning again to walk away. Again Thorne grabbed her arm.

As Thorne stepped into her path once more, Olivia's hand came up, but Thorne had anticipated this and grabbed her wrist before she could slap him. He pulled her hard against him and trapped her arms behind her. Olivia glared up at Thorne as Thorne glared down at her, neither willing to give in to the other.

Thorne stood looking down into the resolute face that refused to bow to him. He remembered how calm she was when she told him that he may as well just kill her on the spot. Thorne knew Olivia would never back down—there was no purpose in it. She was well aware that her father had already forfeited her life; in truth, it was just a matter of time. If she was not hidden well enough, her father would have her killed as soon as he was able, which was why Thorne could not trust her. She held her life with no value; she would not fear death; she would not shy away from what would harm her.

Mayhaps it was guilt that forced Thorne to have care for

her life that she would not have. Surely she knew he could not tolerate her disobedience, yet she could not acquiesce to his requests. He should have her locked in her room, but then she would truly be a caged bird. Thorne understood that she needed to be free, but her freedom would also be her death. Thorne was not willing to impose any more pain on her than he already had, but he also could not tolerate her refusal to behave properly in his home.

When he heard horses coming from the stables, he turned to look; there were three of them. Something was wrong. He was absolute in his thought that this was Johann and Stephan, but the plan was to meet at the stable—and they had not planned to ride out. Thorne had no choice but to leave this matter with Olivia for now. He must attend to his most pressing issue.

With a heavy sigh Thorne leaned over to rest his forehead on Olivia's head. She turned to look up at him, and they were forehead to forehead, their noses touching. Thorne wanted nothing more than to gather her up in his arms and kiss her until they both forgot the world around them. But now was not the time.

"Have thought on my words, Olivia. I must do what will benefit everyone here at the castle. Meet me with this, and I will endeavor to meet with you as well." His words were softly spoken, without anger.

Thorne tore himself away from Olivia as the men and the horses came about. "Princely Grace, a matter that requires your immediate attention." Stephan dismounted and brought Thorne's horse up from the rear.

Olivia stood with her head slightly cocked, looking at Stephan. "This is my huntsman. He will not harm you. He helped you find herbs." Thorne had noted her intent as she looked at Stephan.

Olivia turned to greet the gardeners as they trudged into the garden. They spoke for a while, and Olivia explained her plan for the garden to the men. The men had little concern about what she was asking; they were tasked with working in the garden—it mattered not what they did. Olivia gave them instructions concerning the plants in front, then she sat down and started to lay out her plan in stones that were being discarded as the men worked.

Her mind was troubled. The huntsman's voice ... she was fully certain that she had heard it before. Most of his face had been covered at the time, and he had been dressed in black leather hunting clothes. He had sought her out in a field and asked her to help him rescue Thorne. He had given her coin to buy her freedom from her father's castle. She knew that voice; it was the Dark Horse.

But Thorne was trying to kill the Dark Horse. In the time they spent together while Thorne's wound was healing, Olivia had tried to ask Thorne why he would want to kill the Dark Horse. Had not the Dark Horse saved his life? But Thorne would not talk about it, and now Olivia knew that Stephan was the Dark Horse ... except that Thorne said he had wounded the Dark Horse when Thorne had been shot ... and Johann and Stephan had been with Thorne that night. No, something was amiss here, and Olivia knew not what it was.

"It is said that the Dark Horse has murdered Olivia on your order." Johann was dismounting by the lake as he informed Thorne of what he had heard late last night down in the village.

Both Johann and Stephan had spent much time recently at public houses, trying to find out what was being said concerning the Dark Horse. Everything had been quiet until a stranger rode into the village. The rumor had come from Galatia, at the far end of the empire and far from Olivia's grandparents' estate. Thorne could think of no reason why this would be discussed in this distant duchy.

"Where would Olivia's body be?"

"On the way to her father." Johann was looking far off into the forest. "The priest is accompanying her body."

The prince would be more than happy to kill his own daughter, but Thorne had no doubt that the prince would come looking for Thorne if it was said that Thorne had killed her. It was all quite convenient for Olivia's father. He would be rid of Olivia, and he could get rid of Thorne as well without sanction from the archduchess. However, Olivia was alive—very much alive—and Thorne was determined that she would remain so. Thorne was surprised that the prince had allowed it to be known he had a daughter, but Thorne also realized that the prince could keep the focus on Thorne's crime, not on Olivia, the daughter he had never acknowledged.

"And why would I wish to have Olivia killed?"

"Revenge against her father for imprisoning you and Chance."

"Tell me all that you have gleaned. We know that this is nonsense; you both just saw Olivia, alive and well. But no one really knows what Olivia looks like. Any dead woman of her age would do."

Johann looked to Stephan, and Stephan nodded. Thorne needed to know everything. Olivia's father would soon be riding to gain Thorne's head. They needed to be ready for that day, so Johann related everything to Thorne. As the two men were talking, Stephan looked at the side of Thorne's face; the mark had faded. Both Johann and Stephan had seen the mark, and their eyes had met when Thorne was mounting his horse. Olivia had slapped Thorne—and slapped him hard.

It made perfect sense why Thorne had been restraining her when the two men rode up on the pair in the garden. Stephan wondered what Thorne had done or said to evoke the woman's temper, but what impressed Stephan was that Thorne had not struck her back or punished her in any way. If a woman was foolish enough to strike Thorne, he would have no pause in striking her back. Stephan had witnessed this himself a time or two. Women sometimes felt that they had a free hand to strike a man without consequences, but Thorne thought otherwise; in these circumstances, he treated women just as he did men.

Again Stephan wondered what Thorne had said or done to upset the princess. She did not seem to be an impetuous woman. Stephan was struck by her strength and strong will, but she kept to herself, requiring and wanting little from others. Stephan could also not believe how serene she was, even though she seemed to be a puppet that all wanted to pull and control. Thorne had without a doubt provoked her.

But what would Thorne do with her now? It would

be unfortunate for Thorne to have her here when the prince showed up to kill Thorne. Either way, Thorne would not escape the prince's wrath, and the prince had an army of trained men to inflict the prince's will. Thorne had never had use for an army; he stayed out of the empire's skirmishes. The Turks had not come to this area; this duchy had maintained peace, even when there was none around them, but there would be no peace when the prince arrived on Thorne's doorstep.

Thorne rode back to the castle with his faithful friends. At some point the prince must have been alerted that Olivia was missing, though no one saw Thorne take Olivia from her grandparents' estate. It was just the scheming of someone to suggest that Thorne had Olivia killed. Thorne well knew scheming—he was a master of it—and Thorne was willing to bet his life that this scheming had been done by Olivia's father. She had been missing for over six months. Thorne could understand why her father supposed that she was dead. How could a delicate princess survive six months on her own? But Olivia was no pampered, fragile princess.

Thorne laughed out loud. Olivia had more strength than most men he knew. Yes, this was the work of her father, and this scheme was a godsend for him. He would be rid of his daughter, he would have revenge on Thorne, and the Dark Horse would be hunted down and killed just for good measure. Then the prince would take over another duchy, which would feed his ambition and greed. The only problem that remained was that Thorne had no intention of allowing the prince's plan to succeed.

Walking back from the stables, Thorne saw that Olivia was nowhere near the gardens, though her guard was asleep next to the shed. He thought mayhaps it would be wise to inform her of her death. Thorne asked the gardeners where Olivia could be found, and they pointed towards the river. Thorne walked to the top of the hill and looked down at the water. Olivia had a wheelbarrow full of rocks and was ready to push it up the hill. Calling for her to stop, Thorne headed down the hill with a purpose. The farther down the hill he traveled, the angrier he became with Olivia. Had he not asked her not to act like a servant a few short hours ago?

When he reached the bottom of the hill, he was ready to wring her beautiful neck. It was obvious that Olivia could not be persuaded to do his bidding. He had no choice but to lock her in her room. He exchanged heated words with her, Olivia insisting that the gardeners were too old to push the rocks up the hill. She was, of course, completely correct, but Olivia should have asked some of the younger men to help with this task. Thorne demanded that Olivia abandon the wheelbarrow and go to her room immediately. Olivia stomped her foot and refused.

Thorne started up the hill, thinking he would drag her behind him if necessary. When he turned back, he realized she was not following. Olivia stood as he had left her, arms crossed over her chest and a scowl on her face.

She had realized that the wheelbarrow was much too heavy for her to handle on her own; she scarcely needed Thorne to make it such a concern, and Olivia had no intention of being locked in her room. It seemed that if she did anything herself, Thorne would have concern with it. She could not be an idle doll that sat and ordered others about. Men could go off and do as they wished, but a woman had to stay still and look pretty. Why could he not just leave her be?

Because it was already believed that she was dead, Olivia was in greater peril than she had been. Thorne had to keep her out of sight of strangers, but he could barely keep her under control. Johann and Stephan had wanted to send her away this very day, but Thorne would not entertain the thought. He tried to convince himself that he was motivated solely by guilt, but deep in his heart he started to question himself. Why could he not just let her go?

"Are you going to accompany me back to the castle, or must I carry you back?"

"Mayhaps I should force you to carry me up the hill. You might be able to work off your ill temper."

"Mayhaps I have a reason for an ill temper."

"Mayhaps because you are burdened by me. My very breath seems to cause you ill temper. You should have just killed me beside the stream. What good is my life if you will not allow me to live it?"

Thorne's tested temper soared. He was fighting to keep her alive, and she had no concern for her life. Yes, if she died, that would give her father cause to take Thorne's life, but Thorne knew his life had been forfeited long ago. There was no reason for her life to be as worthless as his own. Thorne had no desire to die, but he had little concern for the prince killing him. His concern was for her only.

He had no idea how to deal with this woman who would not follow his commands. Few dared to question him, and certainly no woman had stood up to him in such a manner. He was near the point of his temper exploding. He picked up a rock from the ground and hurled it at the trunk of the tree where they were standing. Buzzing filled the air. Thorne knew not where the nest was, but the air around Olivia filled with hornets..

Twelve

She lifted her arms to stave off the onslaught as Thorne grabbed her by the waist and lifted her easily to his shoulder. He continued away from the tree, but the buzzing followed them. Thorne had been stung several times, and by the way she shuddered, he was sure Olivia had been as well. He headed down the rocky hill to the wooden dock, and the buzzing followed.

"Hold your breath. We are going into the water."

Thorne jumped into the river, hoping Olivia had been prepared to be submerged. His grasp on her relaxed somewhat, but he did not let go of her. As he headed back up for air, he pulled her with him. A smaller swarm had followed them, but would not enter the water. Olivia came up for air as her lungs began to betray her, and she nearly took a breath of water.

Breaking the surface, she gulped precious air as Thorne yelled at her, "Go under."

She took a deep breath and went under again, Thorne's

hands still on her waist. She did not know how to swim, but he had pulled her up before; she had little choice but to trust he would not allow her to drown. Just as she thought her lungs would burst, Thorne pulled her to the surface. Olivia gulped air again as Thorne hoisted her partially onto his shoulder. Her weight, little as it was, kept taking him under, but Thorne held firmly. When he came up, he looked around at the riverbanks.

The water rushed far faster than it had appeared to do from the wooden dock. Terrified, it took all Olivia's will not to wrap her arms around Thorne. The trees whirled by, and bile rose in her throat. She shut her eyes, but the dizziness followed her into the dark. Her face felt flushed, and she clamped her throat shut to keep from losing anything in her stomach. She focused on the feeling of the cool water on her face.

As Thorne's face came out of the water, he called to Olivia, "We can ... get ... out ... of the ... water ... hunting ... cabin ... not ... too far."

Olivia's face was out of the water, but Thorne thought her color did not look good. Large, red welts splotched her face, and her eyes were swelling. He took comfort that she was breathing easily. He wished there was somewhere else they could get out of the river, but the water was high and the current swift. The muscles in his arms felt like fire from holding Olivia up, but he doubted she could swim and would not lower her.

Olivia felt as if they had been rushing down the river for hours. Her legs were so numb they hurt, and a thousand points on her body pulsated with sharp pain. Her face felt like dough, and when she tried to open her eyes, she could see only a slight blur through the slits of her swollen eyelids. She felt again like she would empty her stomach, and she concentrated on pushing that feeling away. She felt Thorne moving his arms and legs, felt them moving across the water, not just with the current.

When she felt rocks brush against her boots, Thorne turned and lowered her. Somehow she was against his back.

"Put your arms around my neck."

Olivia tried to do as he asked, but she could not feel her hands any longer. She and Thorne were no longer moving, but the water tore at her and wanted to carry her away. She tried to hold tighter to Thorne but was not sure that she was. She tried to open her eyes, but they would not obey. She felt herself lifted out of the water, her boots scraping along the stones. She thought she felt her hands drag along the stones, but she had so little feeling in them that she could not be sure.

Slowly Thorne crawled out of the water on his hands and knees. Fortunately, Olivia had managed to hang on until he had her weight out of the water and on his back. He was worried that she had lost consciousness. Although his arms screamed with pain and the rocks cut into his hands like shards of glass, he carried her still, looking for somewhere soft to place her. Crawling to a thick patch of grass, he slowly stretched out until he was lying in the grass. Thorne wished he could keep her head from hitting the ground, but he had to roll her off his back. He called to her a few times, but she did not answer.

The world exploded in pain. Olivia tried to open her eyes, but she could not. She knew the time had come for her stomach to win the battle, so she rolled to her side and went through the motions of vomiting. Nothing came up. She felt the warmth of Thorne at her back, holding her, and she just wanted to stay here and be still for a very long time. She thought she felt Thorne place his arm under her head.

"We cannot stay here long. Rest a minute."

The pain exploded again in a thousand places on her body, and Olivia tried to roll away, only making it worse.

"Olivia, we must go to the cabin. You need attended to. Stay still—I must carry you. I shall try not to hurt you."

But the pain came again as he lifted her. She tried not to cry out, but it escaped her and she felt Thorne tense. "Well ... I am well."

Thorne started to walk to the cabin, praying that his arms would not drop her. Her head rested on his collarbone, and he glanced at her face. It was almost unrecognizable. The large, red welts had turned purple, and her face was so very swollen. He was sure she could not open her eyes. Her arms and hands were swollen as well, and he could see stings on her forearms and hands where she had tried to shield herself. He counted thirty stings and then stopped; that was only a small measure of them.

He had taken the brunt of the hornets' fury on his back and could feel each sting with every step. He had a few on his face and arms, but Olivia had been the target of their frenzy far more than he had. Thorne's heart grieved; this was his fault. Had he not lost his temper and thrown the rock, Olivia would be in fine health and cursing the day he was born. He walked on. They were several miles from the hunting camp, but he would not stop until they were somewhere she could be attended to. Olivia was having a severe reaction to the venom.

Adele and Matthias would be at the hunting camp, and Adele would know how to help Olivia. Matthias had been the huntsman before his son, Stephan, had taken over. Matthias and Adele had retired to the hunting camp where they kept the camp in order and provided the castle with fresh and smoked meats and fish. Matthias and Stephan worked closely together to keep track of the wildlife on Thorne's land. Fortunately, they had been well blessed, and the castle hosted a hunt each month for the men of the village.

When Thorne felt he could not take one more step, he looked down at Olivia and forced himself to go on. Matthias must have been out in the woods and heard them coming because he came down the dirt path with a wagon to pick them up. Thorne continued to hold Olivia in his arms in the back of the wagon, tortured by the thought that this was his fault. He should not have completely lost his temper with her. He had not even given her an opportunity to speak on her own behalf. He could not have known about the hornet nest, but he should have kept himself under control—but he had not been able to control himself since he laid eyes on Olivia.

Adele was on the porch of Thorne's cabin when they arrived; Matthias must have told her to prepare for Thorne's arrival. He carried Olivia in and placed her on the chair near the warmed bath. Adele was quietly talking to Olivia as Matthias ushered Thorne out. Matthias prepared a bath for him in the couple's cabin. As Thorne stripped off his clothes, he explained what happened to Matthias, who was on the other side of the hearth, seated at the table. The warm water helped soothe the overworked muscles of his arms, but his back still felt like he was being impaled with sharp knife blades. In truth, Thorne knew sharp knife blades would be less painful.

When Thorne finished his story, Matthias went to a cabinet and removed a small pot and a bottle of brown liquid. He put a small amount from the pot on a plate and took the pot and the bottle to his wife in the other cabin. Thorne stepped out of the bath, dried himself, and put on a fresh pair of trousers. He sat still while Matthias applied the salve to the stings, which was almost as painful as the stings themselves.

Olivia's thoughts made no sense. Where was she? Who was this woman that was bathing her? Olivia knew it was not any of the servants she had met at the castle. Mayhaps it would help if she could see, but her eyes were swollen tightly shut. Her face, her head, her arms, and her hands throbbed with pain. The woman was removing dead hornets from her hair. Olivia stepped from the tub with much help, feeling somewhat better, but still in pain and unable to think properly.

After allowing the salve to dry a small measure, Thorne was putting on his shirt when he heard a horse galloping into camp.

Matthias went to the front window. "Stephan," he said, then came back to the table to await his son.

Stephan came bursting through the door. "The prince is

approaching the castle."

"Now, so soon?"

"Yes, he is well manned. I saw his entourage on the road just outside the village, and I came straight here."

"I will leave Olivia here. We must return and greet our guest."

"No, Thorne, you must stay here as well." Stephan knew this would not go well with Thorne, but he had spent the ride here thinking about the options.

"I will face the prince. I cannot leave Chance to do it."

"Chance is well out of the way. I sent Phillip to the castle to get Chance out of sight. He is headed for the vineyards. I do not trust the prince to tell the two of you apart. I also instructed Phillip to tell the serene highness that you have gone in search of the Dark Horse."

"I cannot hide here like a child."

"What purpose would it serve for the prince to truss you and march you to the archduchess, falsely charged with having his daughter murdered? At this moment the prince holds all the game pieces. No, Thorne, you must wait. I will meet with Johann at the lake. We must put all our efforts into finding the Dark Horse. That is the key to everything else." Stephan hoped that Thorne would see the counsel in his words.

Thorne walked to the window and looked without seeing. Stephan's words were what was in Thorne's heart. He would have no defense against a false charge. He would leave his family in jeopardy if he allowed the prince to have him executed, but it was not in Thorne's nature to run from a fight. It was Johann and Stephan who kept Thorne from reacting according to his nature, who forced him to use the reaction in his head. Thorne could not afford to lose this war with the prince; the consequences were too high. The Dark Horse was the key. They must stop acting like the Dark Horse was an unfortunate situation; they must attack this with the importance it deserved.

"I will stay here tonight. Tomorrow we must get a plan together to flush the Dark Horse out." Thorne turned to Stephan. "You and Johann must stay out of the prince's sight. Elias can handle the prince at the castle."

Stephan had already sent word to Elias through his youngest brother, Phillip, to move weapons into the tunnels under the castle should they have need of them. Although the husband of the housekeeper was elderly, Elias still commanded the respect of the staff. He knew the secrets of the castle, and he knew Thorne's plan to keep the castle safe. There were in fact two sets of tunnels under the castle. Several generations ago, the configuration of the tunnels had changed. The entrance stairs to the main tunnels, where food was stored, was obvious. The other was not as obvious, and many of the servants did not know the second set of tunnels existed.

Matthias took off on horseback for the village where the men would stand with Thorne if needed, but Matthias also wanted to speak with his brothers-in-law. Adele belonged to a very large family living in and around the village, and they may need some fresh faces in dealing with the Dark Horse. Matthias had no doubt that his extended family would be at his side, but he wanted to talk to them and prepare them for what could be a long siege by the prince.

Thorne went into his cabin to check on Olivia. He would need to tell her what was happening with her father, but he had doubt that now was the time. Olivia was dressed in one of Adele's nightdresses that was far too large for her. Adele was attempting to have Olivia drink some tea, but Olivia was not cooperating.

"She is ill from the venom and does not fully understand. She asks for you. She will listen to you." Adele handed Thorne the cup. "Have her drink this. It will help her rest."

Thorne gently scooped Olivia up in his arms and spoke

quietly to her. "Olivia, you need to rest. You are ill." He carried her into the sleeping area while Adele placed pillows and blankets at the head of the bed.

"Her head must stay upright for the swelling to go down. If she lies down, the swelling may increase. She has stings on her neck. I do not want the swelling to increase there."

Thorne set Olivia on the bed and slowly coaxed her to drink the herbal tea. He then situated himself on the bed and gently positioned Olivia so that she was sitting upright with her back and head against him. "I will stay with her and keep her upright."

Adele felt no concern leaving Thorne alone with the girl despite his rakish reputation. He was so concerned and gentle with her, and the girl had calmed as soon as Thorne was with her. Although leaving the two was not as it should be with a young lady, Adele could see Thorne's love for her and knew he would do as she needed. No one would know except the four at the hunting camp. As she was leaving, she looked closely at them on the bed. The girl was now asleep, safely held in Thorne's arms, and Thorne himself looked at peace with her there.

The sun was starting to go down. The day had taken a great toll on Thorne—on his body and his mind. When he felt Olivia's breathing become regular, he knew she was asleep, so he rested his head back and drifted off as well.

Olivia awoke, desperate for something to drink. Panic started to grip her as she realized she could not open her eyes and felt arms holding her. When she heard Thorne's voice, she calmed, but she could not remember how or why she was with him. Her mind could not put it all straight.

"Olivia, all is well. Lie still."

"Drink." Her lips were swollen, her mouth parched; she could barely speak.

"I will get water for you. Stay still."

He placed the cup in her hands, but when her fingers did not grasp it, he brought the cup to her lips and poured a small measure into her mouth. With effort Olivia was able to drink. She had not all feeling, and the task was one of the mind, not by nature.

Water ... they had been in the water ... and the hornets ... yes, she had some recollection now.

"Where are we?"

"At my hunting camp."

"A woman ..."

"Adele, Stephan's mother."

"What time of day is it?"

"Night. Do you have need?" She shook her head. "You are ill from the venom. You need to rest. Go back to sleep."

Feeling the sun on her, Olivia thought it must be morning. She started to move, and Thorne's arms tightened around her slightly. She did not need her sight to know it was Thorne; she could feel that it was he. Although she still could not open her eyes, she felt like they were less swollen; she felt some movement in her face when she tried to open them. Behind her, Thorne stretched.

"It is morning. Shall I help you up?"

"Yes."

As Olivia sat at the edge of the bed, a knock came at the door, and she heard the door open. She could smell food and realized she had not eaten but a bit of bread yesterday morning. She felt Thorne move around her, and then he was gone. She heard him speak with Adele on the other side of the curtain, and then he came back to guide her out of the sleeping area. He left her with Adele to attend to her needs, and then she heard him come back into the cabin. Olivia felt very helpless without her sight, a feeling she detested, though she was grateful for the care.

Adele fixed her a bowl with eggs and ham, but because Olivia's hands were still too swollen to use, Thorne fed her breakfast. She felt like a child, but Thorne did not treat her as such. Adele talked with Thorne a bit, and Olivia knew there was something wrong—she could feel it. She listened to the conversation, which told her nothing except Adele's husband, Matthias, had not yet returned and Thorne expected Stephan to come today. Adele collected the dishes and promised to return soon with more salve and to help Olivia dress—in what, Olivia had no understanding.

"Thorne, what is concerning?"

Thorne did not know how or what to tell Olivia. He could not keep everything from her, but he did not see the need to distress her. "Your father is at my castle."

"My father? Why?"

"It is my understanding that he believes that I have had you killed by the Dark Horse."

"That makes no sense."

"In truth, it does. Your father was given a body of a young woman and was told it was you. He was also told that you were killed by the Dark Horse on my order as revenge for holding Chance and me captive."

"But I am not dead."

"You said your father has never laid eyes on you."

"I cannot recall ever seeing my father at my grandparents' estate, but you watched me—"

"I have doubt your father would have watched you as I did. Had he wanted to see you, he could have just come into the estate."

"Yes."

"Your father has come to the castle to take me to the archduchess to be tried for murder. This is not a matter of your father wanting justice for your death. Your father, I believe, wishes to have me and my family removed from the duchy so that he can take control. This all serves many purposes—he will have revenge for my escape, and he will have gained land and power."

"But can you not just show him that I am alive?"

"He will not believe it is you, and if I reveal you, he will most assuredly kill you. You have been missing for some time. I am sure he is confident that you are dead. No, Olivia, it will not serve his purposes for you to be alive. You cannot allow yourself to be revealed to him. If for some reason your paths cross, you must not tell him who you are."

Her mind was not working as it should, but then Olivia remembered. "He would believe me a servant if he had any recollection of me.”

“He saw you at the castle?”

“Yes, he had thoughts that a father should not have. That is why I was desperate to leave.”

“I see.” Thorne was not pleased to hear this. Had Olivia not been through enough? “All the more reason that your paths should not cross. I have concern that there is not anything you could say or do that would persuade him that you are his daughter. It could place you in a precarious position.” Thorne well knew that he would kill the prince if he touched Olivia.

Olivia tried to take it all in, but her mind could not put all to right. Thorne was very much in danger. Olivia had first-hand knowledge of her father’s army of men. They were well trained and loyal, and they had no concern about killing on demand. Olivia knew that what Thorne had said was true. Either her father would not believe she was his daughter, and he would do something which Olivia could not live with, or he would believe she was his daughter. Either way, Olivia was sure that he would kill her.

“What are you going to do?”

“Find the Dark Horse.”

Olivia had heard Thorne get up and then move into the sleeping area while they were talking. He returned to her and asked her to stand up. She could feel him placing something against her body but was confused as to what. Adele returned, and Thorne informed Adele that he thought that the clothes he had found would fit Olivia. She heard him walk out of the cabin and close the door behind him. And then she heard Adele laugh.

Thirteen

Wearing men's trousers felt odd, but after a while Olivia found the trousers to be quite useful. As she could not yet see, she need not concern herself with tripping on her skirts or her skirts knocking anything over. Stephan came around midmorning, and after a good laugh at Olivia in trousers, the three took off on horseback to meet Johann. Olivia thought that the trousers worked quite nicely for horseback, but the thought did occur to her that mayhaps she should learn how to ride a horse.

She was able to open her eyes just a bit, but to do so made her dizzy, then her stomach was wont to empty. As the three men talked, Olivia held a cool rag to her eyes as she had most of the morning, but the water here at the stream was much cooler than in the smaller stream at the hunting camp.

Thorne was to be the bait. It would be made known that Chance was outraged that Thorne had the prince's daughter murdered and was offering a large sum of money for Thorne's capture. Thorne had to be taken alive, however, or the purse would not be paid.

Chance would also agree to hand the duchy over to the prince in exchange for allowing Chance and his family to leave peacefully. Thorne would be captured by some of Stephan's family with the hope that the Dark Horse would try to steal Thorne from his captors for the purse. All the recent tales of the Dark Horse had one common theme: he had love of coin. The offered purse would be very high. The Dark Horse would notice.

The serene highness had too few hours to prepare for the prince's arrival. She was told that Thorne was off chasing the Dark Horse, but there was no mention of Olivia's whereabouts. Elias explained the purpose of the prince's visit and what she should say concerning the whereabouts of her sons. Chance had gone to visit a friend in Bohemia, and Thorne's exact whereabouts were unknown.

The serene highness told the housekeeper that all trace of Olivia was to be removed from the castle immediately, and then the serene highness informed Margarette of their expected visitor, informing her daughter-in-law that there was to be no mention of Olivia. Should the subject come up, Olivia was a distant family member that had left to return home after the wedding.

The serene highness was sure the staff had been given

instruction concerning Olivia as they were busy preparing for the large contingent about to descend upon the castle. The prince had approximately one hundred men with him, most of whom would be relegated to a field just outside the castle. Only the prince and his counsel would be allowed inside the castle gates.

She would be a gracious host and a loyal and devoted mother, denying that her son could ever do such a thing, which would not be an act. She knew Olivia was alive even if she did not know to where the girl had been secreted. It would be best if the men stayed in the field and did not wander off, Elias informed her, so she would provide well for them; pits were being dug for roasting meat, and there was food for the horses, a stream, and two wells. Casks of mead were being loaded onto wagons. Fortunately, they had put in an abundant stock of drink for the wedding and much was left over. The guests had preferred Thorne's excellent wine.

It was expected that the castle would be searched, but Elias was ready for that. The weapons were hidden but accessible, and the best horses had been moved to the vineyards several hours ago. Olivia's wardrobe had been buried under all the seamstresses' materials. All the serene highness's jewels, art, fine wine, and precious metals or stones were hidden. Although this duchy had not been harassed by the Turks, a plan had been made for that event, so securing valuables was a swift, adept process.

Riders had been dispatched to tell the story to the ears that needed to hear, and replies had been received. Within a week they were ready to start putting their plan in place. Chance had agreed that he would stay hidden at the vineyards during the execution of the plan. If there was need, there were large caves at the base of the mountains within which Chance could hide should the prince decide to "view" the lands. Only one small detail remained, and the three men were at odds as to what to do about that detail ... about Olivia.

Thorne wanted Olivia under lock and key and heavily guarded. Johann wanted to send Olivia to Auria's. But Stephan had wanted to keep Olivia with the three of them. They would keep the closest of eye on her, her presence would not endanger them, and she would be there should they have need of her.

Stephan had additional thoughts about what might be done with Olivia. He had used her to help free Thorne and knew she had strength and courage, and given her beauty, she could be used as a spy. But Stephan knew better than to suggest to Thorne that they use Olivia in the plan. Thorne would sooner cut off his own hand than endanger Olivia. Stephan knew that Thorne had softness in his heart for Olivia, but watching him with her now, Stephan was certain it was more than that. Thorne was in love with Olivia. At the end of this, they may well know if Olivia was indeed the woman for Thorne.

The prince was not pleased that both Thorne and Chance were absent from the castle upon his arrival and were not expected back very soon. The serene highness assured him that, had her sons known of his plan to come to the castle, they both would have been there to greet him. The prince was aghast that the serene highness seemed to be completely uninformed that there was such a dispute among the princes. When he informed the serene highness that he was there to take Thorne into custody for the murder of his daughter, she was in such distress that she collapsed.

The prince ordered a search of the castle while the serene highness was taken to her bedchamber to recover from the shock. The search was done with the houseman, Elias, who was painfully slow due to his advanced age, and the prince had thoughts that the houseman's mind was addled as he was sure that they were shown the same rooms more than once. After the search, which took three days, the prince came to the conclusion that not only were the two princes not in the castle, but Thorne's family was obviously not very wealthy.

The serene highness had recovered enough to join the

prince to dine on the second day. The meal was barely palatable to the prince. The beef was full of fat and gristle, the fish smelled rancid, the vegetables were nothing but mush, and none of the dishes were seasoned—not to mention the wine tasted like vinegar. He had been served only three courses, and no one seemed to question if that was hospitable. The serene highness spent the entire meal praising the skills of the cooking staff. After the meal the prince was entertained by Margarette reading from the Scriptures for two hours until the prince claimed to be tired and retired to bed.

An unending supply of mead flowed freely among the men in the field. The serene highness replaced the young females with men or old women, having sent the younger ones to the village, which did not amuse the men in the field. The prince had asked for servants to cut firewood, so the serene highness had sent the old gardeners to help with this task, noting that there were only two fires roasting meat. On the third day fights broke out among the drunken men in the field.

The prince was determined to wait until Thorne or his brother showed up at the castle. To entertain himself, the prince decided to see the lands under the guise of a hunt. The huntsman, Phillip, who was just a boy, spooked the animals with his loud voice and nearly shot one of the prince's advisors with an arrow. When the prince could no longer tolerate the mindless trek through the forest, up and down the mountain, he commanded the huntsman to take him back to the castle.

They rode for three hours before the boy admitted that he was lost. At only minutes shy of midnight, the group slowly rode into the castle, where there was no one to greet them. The houseman informed the prince that the serene highness had gone to bed for the night and he would arrange for a light meal for them. After bringing them cheese and bread, the houseman retired for the night as well. The prince and his advisors ate the cheese and bread, as they had eaten bread and cheese for their midday meal, and the prince's resolve to wait out his prey wavered.

The prince tolerated his stay at Thorne's castle for only one more day after he received a letter from Chance, full of outrage and all but promising his brother's head on a platter and groveling to the prince for full measure. By the time the prince was ready to leave, he questioned Thorne's ability to have his daughter murdered. The family was obviously poor, their staff was decrepit, the serene highness was a witless twit, and Thorne's twin—his knees shaking in fear—was a coward willing to do anything to please the prince.

But it was of no concern. The duchy of Carinthia was rich with resources. Once the prince had control, he would fill his coffers. The man had escaped from his prison and made a laughingstock of him. The prince could not tolerate such an insult. The dead girl looked nothing like him or his first wife, so he had sent riders to the estate and discovered that she was indeed missing and had been for several months. There had been no request for money, she did not associate with any young men, no young men were missing, and no body had been found. The servants at the estate were at a complete loss as to what had happened to the girl.

Most likely she was dead, but the prince had question as to whether the body that had been brought to him was of his relation. His first wife was pleasant to the eye, but the body of the girl was far from pleasant. The coloring was not what he had expected; both he and his first wife were light of hair, and the body was dark of hair. She was short in stature and very round, which also did not describe him or his first wife. He would have preferred that no one remembered that he had the first wife and daughter, but his first wife had stayed quiet and no one thought she was alive.

Regardless, the prince did not like the idea that one of his men was playing him for the fool. This situation suited his needs perfectly—mayhaps too perfectly—but he had not noted anything amiss among his loyal advisors. It had been Franz, a trusted and loyal advisor, who had brought the news to him about his daughter, and yet questions still worried the prince's mind. He dared not give voice to his questions; his closest men would think him mad or witless, or worse, he would allow the betrayer to know his thoughts before he knew the identity of the Judas.

Thorne was stuck at the hunting camp while arrangements were made with Chance and Adele's family. Olivia was able to open her eyes, but still suffered some dizziness. Thorne feared he would go mad with worry for his mother stuck at the castle alone with the prince. Although his mother had many talents, the prince would be single-minded in his endeavor, and his mother would be questioned relentlessly. His mother knew not where he was and would not be able to give the prince that information, but his mother was not accustomed to being treated with such little respect.

Olivia and Thorne headed out to the dock behind the cabins as Thorne needed to keep busy. He baited the hook and put it in the water. Olivia sat on the bench, intending to read, but the words on the page started to move. After a few moments she put the book down. Reading made the dizziness worse, so Olivia wandered over to the fishing poles and picked one up. Reaching into the bucket, she pulled out a worm and put it on the hook as she thought Thorne had done.

"Put the hook through the worm in two places; otherwise the fish will just steal your bait."

"Oh." Olivia did as instructed, then paused. She was not sure how to cast the line.

Thorne set his pole down and came around Olivia. He put his hand on her forearm and the other around her waist, pulling her back close to him, as he did when they rode together. Thorne brought her arm back and went through the motion of casting, doing it twice more as he talked her through the motion. Thorne stepped back, and Olivia did as he had instructed perfectly.

Thorne went back to his own pole as a sadness overtook him. He had not been fishing for many years, though he had always enjoyed it—far more than Chance. Although Chance had gone with him a few times, more often he had gone with Stephan, and Thorne realized he missed it. He also realized he would forever have only his friend with whom to fish; he would never have a son to teach. He shook his head. These were not the thoughts he wanted to have.

"Thorne!" Olivia had no idea what to do. The line jerked and pulled, and she was sure there was a fish.

Thorne placed himself behind her and told her what to do. The fish swung at the end of the line as Olivia tried to figure out how to get the fish off the hook.

"Hold the pole with this hand and grab the line with your other hand."

Thorne told her how to grasp the fish and take the hook out of its mouth. Olivia did not shriek, nor did she drop the pole or the fish. She did just as Thorne instructed, then she placed the fish in the basket and reached for another worm. As Thorne brought his own fish in, he watched Olivia. She had a smile on her face. She was enjoying herself. The dark clouds of Thorne's thoughts floated away.

When the basket was full, they headed up to the cabins. Thorne carried the basket of fish, and Olivia carried the poles and the bucket of worms as Adele watched them. Taking the fish over to the cleaning table by the confluence of the stream and river, Thorne picked up a fish and started to clean it. Olivia put the poles on the porch of the cabin and set the bucket of worms in the shade, then she wandered over to watch Thorne.

Adele knew Olivia was a princess, but she was not like any princess Adele had ever known. Adele had worked closely with the women in the kitchen of the castle and even worked as a servant when there was need. She watched Olivia move next to Thorne and watched Thorne hand her a knife. He was teaching her how to clean fish. Adele knew the secrets of Thorne's family from when her husband had been huntsman to Thorne's father, Tobias. She also knew her son was now involved.

No, this was no normal princess, but Thorne was no normal prince. No wonder he had fallen in love with this woman. She was what Thorne needed. She was nothing like the woman Thorne had thought to marry before. Adele had been acquainted with that woman when Thorne's family had hosted Grego's family, when Auria had become promised in marriage. No, that woman was not for Thorne. That woman was too much like the serene highness, and Thorne was not like his father—well, not much. Olivia was the woman for Thorne.

Fourteen

They had been riding all morning. Thorne spent two days teaching Olivia how to ride, and she had taken to it quicker than Thorne had thought possible for anyone. He took Olivia up and down hills at full gallop and in and out of trees at breakneck speed. He had her follow him as he made sharp turns and reined in abruptly. Olivia was able to control the horse without a stone of effort. He had even taken her across the river, and she was able to keep the horse calm, although Thorne knew that Olivia herself could not swim. He hoped she would never need to take a horse into deep water, but he thought it best to teach her should he not be there to rescue her and the need arose.

They were several miles away from the hunting camp when the skies grew dark and angry. Thorne steered Olivia to a rocky area where they could wait out the storm. They guided the horses through a tight crevasse between two rock embankments to an area that looked as though a giant had lashed out a handful of rock. A few bushes had sprouted between the rocks, giving the horses a morsel to eat while great drops fell from the sky.

Thorne helped Olivia to dismount, took her by the hand, and guided her to the opposite side of the hollow rock where the rain was less likely to fall upon them. Thorne turned to her, with a thought to speak to her, but all his thoughts stopped as he looked at her. He had never seen her look as beautiful as she did this moment; she looked as she did that day in the field of flowers. Her hair was disheveled with tendrils blowing in the wind, her cheeks were flushed, and her lips blushed. Without thought or plan he gathered her into his arms and gently kissed her on the lips, but one kiss did not satisfy him; it only made him want more.

Thorne was not a man accustomed to trifling with affection. He was honest about his attention to his needs and did not play with childish things such as sweet kisses, but he did want to savor the sweetness of Olivia's kisses. His mind spent plenty of time making love to her every night, but holding her closely and tasting her, smelling her sweet wildflower scent, and caressing her tongue with his was a blissful feeling that he had never known with any other woman.

His arms pulled her closer, and his hands trailed down to the soft curve of her buttocks. The trousers confused his mind, but the feel of her body made him want her closer than their clothing would allow. Gently she pulled her lips from his, and her hands slid down his arms to lightly press against his chest. They both knew that nature would not allow them to continue on this way, and Olivia needed to stop him before he got bolder. Thorne did not try to persuade her otherwise; much as he wanted to continue, he knew that she was wise to stop him.

Thorne had to be content with waiting out the storm with his arms around Olivia as he sat with his back against the rock wall and she sat with her back against his chest. He told her of hunting trips he had taken with his father and when his father had taught him how to track wildlife. He told her of trying to track her when she had run off from the first night he had taken her from the estate. She had laughed that he had been unable to find even a trace of her. She had not tried to obscure her tracks; she merely tried to get away without waking him.

The hours flew by, and Thorne thought back to the time she had cared for his gunshot wound. He never tired of her; he told her things that he thought he had forgotten long ago. He shared memories with her that brought a smile to his face. He had not found another with whom he could speak so easily other than Chance, but Chance was busy with his life with Margarette and their children, as it should be. Thorne had never realized that he was lonely, but now he felt lonely without Olivia.

The rain had brought a chill to the air. Though the sky remained dark, the clouds had gone dry, so they headed back to the hunting camp without diversion. It was late afternoon, although the sky gave the thought it was evening. The rain started again when they were but a mile from the camp, and the drops were large and fell hard. As they rode into the camp, both were soaked to the bone, and Olivia clamped her jaw shut to keep her teeth from chattering.

Thorne dismounted and came around to help Olivia, but instead of giving her feet purchase, he carried her up the stairs and into the cabin. The horses went to the stables without a lead, and Matthias was there to tend to them. A roaring fire burned in the fireplace, and both Thorne and Olivia held their hands out to thaw. Thorne went to pour them a glass of wine and suggested that Olivia change out of her wet clothing.

As Olivia entered the sleeping area, she could hear Thorne on the other side of the curtain. She peeled off the wet clothes, but the stockings she wore under the trousers were plastered to her skin. She felt very naked, listening to Thorne just a few paces away and only a curtain between them. She had but one stocking yet to remove when she felt him standing at the opening of the curtain. She froze, unsure what to do, not wanting to draw more attention to herself.

Thorne knew he should stop himself, yet he was power-less to do so. He walked to the opening of the curtain and hesitated, knowing he should not go in. Had it been any other woman than Olivia, he would give ear to his own good sense. Did he want her? Far more than he had ever lusted after any woman ... and now he wanted to feel her skin against his.

He had hung his shirt to dry by the fire; he reached out his hand and opened the curtain. With a look of slight surprise on her face, she stood there, completely without clothing save for a stocking that was still up over the calf of her left leg. She reached for the quilt on the bed to cover herself, but it would not give up its resting place. She reached for the dry clothing she had laid on the bed, but Thorne was swifter than she.

He pulled her up and to him. She tried to push him away, but Thorne would not be denied this moment. He pulled her tight against him, and she felt her breasts against his chest. He kissed her, not as insistently as he would have liked, but he knew this would not come to the end that he dreamed of every night. His hands slowly glided up and down her back and over her buttocks. He could not get enough of the feel of her. Olivia became urgent in her attempt to free herself from his grasp.

"Just let me hold you, just for a moment," Thorne breathed into her neck by her ear.

Olivia stopped fighting Thorne momentarily, and they stood embracing. Olivia felt like she was touching the real Thorne for the first time. Her hands slid slowly up and down his arms. She wanted the feel of him so that she would never forget. With her breasts pressed tightly to his chest, she felt the beat of her heart, and she felt his heart call to hers. Her skin felt the warmth and the gentleness of his hands, as if a sweet kiss upon her. Slowly Thorne withdrew, not knowing a harder act in all his life, but he knew he must. Olivia turned away and covered herself with her arms, feeling very cold and alone without Thorne's arms around her. Why had she allowed him to hold her for those few blissful moments? Why had she entertained what she would never have? Because she wanted the moment just as much as Thorne had.

Olivia changed and brought her wet clothes out to hang by the fire as Thorne went into the sleeping area to change into dry clothes. They sat before the fire, sipping their wine, each wrestling with their own thoughts. As all traces of light left the sky, the rain paused again, and they walked over to Adele and Matthias's cabin to eat. It did not go without notice that the prince and princess were unusually quiet during the meal. Olivia excused herself after the dishes had been washed and dried. Thorne and Matthias discussed the weather. As the men watched, Olivia walked to her cabin alone, at her insistence.

Olivia awaited the men in the abandoned barn. Stephan had assured her that they would be back by dark, but the sun had gone down several hours ago. Something had gone very wrong; she could feel it. She knew Thorne could take care of himself, but not when he was bound hand and foot. She knew not where they were, lest she would have gone to see what was delaying them. Finally, she heard horses coming, and she ran to the opening in the barn door. There were only two men.

Olivia now thought that she knew about the Dark Horse. She thought she understood why Thorne wanted to kill the Dark Horse, and it had no concern with her father. She had thought back to the stories that she had heard of the Dark Horse. Although all feared the Dark Horse, all the stories were of the Dark Horse rescuing the oppressed or righting those who had been wronged. But the Dark Horse had skills that no mere human would have, was able to do what no man could do. Olivia was sure that it was because the Dark Horse was not a man; he was several men—Thorne, Johann, Stephan, and mayhaps Chance and his valet, Akos.

No one had told her thus; she had reasoned it herself. Olivia had the belief that the Dark Horse was passed down through Thorne's family and Thorne was the head of the Dark Horse collective. She knew, without doubt, that it was Stephan that had come to her in the field when she was at the prince's. Because Thorne and Chance were in prison, Stephan had stepped in to be the Dark Horse. The plan was conceived by

Johann; he was the thinker. The details were decided by Thorne and Stephan; Thorne was the tactician, Stephan the hunter. When this was over, mayhaps she would know if her thoughts were true.

"Where is Thorne?" Although Olivia tried to keep her concern from her voice, she heard it as clearly as Johann and Stephan did.

"It was not a good position for us to go in. He could kill Thorne before we could get to the Dark Horse," said Stephan as Johann gave him a look; he did not want to tell Olivia everything. Her face was a mask of despair as it was.

"Have you thought what to do?"

"We need a distraction." Johann knew they needed to get the Dark Horse away from Thorne. Although the purse specified that Thorne must be taken alive, they had no trust of the Dark Horse.

"But he cannot kill Thorne, or Chance will not pay the purse." Olivia knew she was just grasping for hope.

"We know not what your father is offering." Stephan was pleased Olivia had taken no offense at his words.

"Tell me everything. Tell me about the area where the

Dark Horse is holding Thorne." The three sat on a wooden bench, and Johann and Stephan told Olivia all they had seen.

"The area is surrounded by my family," said Stephan. "Should they move tonight, we will know and they will be tracked. The river is on one side. They will not be able to escape in that direction, nor can we use it to come in. A large rocky hill is to their back. It would take time to come in from that direction."

"And considerable skill," Johann added.

"On the third side is a tributary to the river in a deep gully. Again, that would take a considerable amount of time and skill to keep from detection. They are on a flat patch of grass. There are some trees to keep their position from notice, but it is a well-guarded spot, one that any of us would have chosen." Stephan's mind kept thinking of ways to draw the Dark Horse from his position, but all his thoughts ended in Thorne's possible death.

"You believe my father has a purse for Thorne as well?"

"I am not willing to risk Thorne's life. I doubt your father would have care that Thorne be kept alive. It would suit his purpose better to have Thorne's dead body delivered to him." Johann would bet his own life that the prince would be pleased to have Thorne's dead body and willing to pay for such.

"I have an idea how to distract the Dark Horse, rather it was Thorne's idea a long time ago." Olivia explained the plan to the two men. As the first words came out of her mouth, she knew that neither man was willing to endorse the idea, but Olivia saw no other option. She was not willing to allow her father to kill Thorne—or even to have Thorne killed. Olivia would rather throw herself on top of Thorne to save his life than to stand by and do nothing.

"No, no. Thorne would never allow it!" Johann had turned an unnatural shade of white. He had more than strong thoughts about how Thorne would react to Olivia's idea.

"I agree. There is no point in discussing it." Stephan could not imagine surviving Thorne's wrath if he allowed such an absurd idea.

"Have you any idea of your own?" Olivia was outraged that the men would discount her plan so quickly. She thought that it was the only ploy that would work right now.

Both men were at a loss. They had no plan that would serve their purpose, and time was becoming short. No doubt the Dark Horse would be moving on first thing in the morning. Stephan was of the mind that the Dark Horse would try to keep Thorne alive to gain Chance's purse and then deliver a dead

Thorne to the prince once the coin from Chance was in hand. Why settle for one purse when two could be had?

Stephan was the first to break. He would rather endure Thorne's wrath than allow Thorne to die. Thorne was as close as a brother to him as Johann was. Once the Dark Horse was distracted, they could keep Olivia's involvement in the matter to a small piece, then mayhaps Thorne would not vent his anger on the men—though he most certainly would be furious with Olivia. Stephan had witnessed Thorne's restraint with Olivia, even when Thorne wanted to wring her neck.

Olivia changed her clothes inside a horse stall and practiced what she would say and do. She knew she would have to play the part completely and keep her personal feelings in check. In her life she had always been honest and truthful with no concern for the consequences. Now she must be completely deceitful, no matter the consequences. Her only concern was whether Thorne would understand and play along. Was it not his game she would use?

In an old trunk she found a dirndl many sizes too large, and she had not a shift to wear beneath. The neckline of the blouse fell off her shoulder without coaxing, and a fair measure of cleavage and breast was instantly noticeable. The skirt and apron were made for a much younger girl and came only to her mid-calf. She had found a pair of inside slippers, a couple sizes too large, and she stuffed them with straw. With the shortened skirt and the slippers, a very unladylike length of her leg was showing. Lastly, she pulled the scarf from her hair and tied it like the traveling Roma, with her hair cascading to complete a wanton look.

As she stepped from the stall, both men stared at her, their jaws slack, and she knew she need not ask if her attire was as she planned. Johann was exceptionally uncomfortable. No woman of decent repute would ever be seen wearing such, but Olivia counted on her attire to speak for her instead of words. She had no practice with what she would say to the Dark Horse. As she rode on horseback to the site, she thought back to the nights in the servants' quarters at her father's castle, and she thought of the odd words she had heard uttered. She would say those words—with a conviction she did not have.

She followed the route Stephan had described and soon she saw smoke rise from a fire. She knew not what time it was, but she thought mayhaps close to midnight as she rode into the camp. Both Thorne and the Dark Horse had been dozing, but both were instantly awake upon her arrival. She brought the horse up short and quickly dismounted, trying not to show a care for the amount of leg and thigh she flashed to the men as she made her way to the ground. She let the reins fall loose;

Stephan assured her the horse would not leave her, no matter what.

She looked not at Thorne, as though he was not there, and hurried over to the Dark Horse. "My love, I came as soon as I knew you were near."

She stood very close to the Dark Horse, slowly sliding her hands up his chest to his shoulders, suppressing a shudder. She no more wanted to seduce this man than she would have her own father, but she knew she could not hesitate or be coy. She could see little of his face as a black scarf covered most of it, but Olivia knew this was not the man she had spoken to in the field. This man was not shaped the same, and he was older, almost to his fortieth year.

His eyes were wide with shock, his stance wary. Olivia knew she would have to distract him; thus far, he was not taking her bait. "I have missed you sorely. You have kept yourself from me far too long."

"How did you know I was here?" He spoke at last in an unfamiliar voice.

Now Olivia was sure that her thoughts about the Dark Horse were true. This man was false; that is why Thorne needed to kill him. This Dark Horse was terrorizing the people and casting a shadow on the name of the Dark Horse.

"My body can always tell when you are near. We were made to be together, you know that." Olivia pressed herself against the strange man's body as she tried to remember all that she had witnessed and heard, but her mind was struggling with what she was telling her body to do. Reaching up, she pulled his mouth down to hers and realized he was coming around to think as she wanted him to.

Her hands slid down his back and buttocks and went to the ties of his pants. Her mouth said words that would have made her laugh had she heard them spoken, but they did inflame his passion. She had been listening for any type of sound from Thorne, but he remained quiet. She hoped Stephan and Johann were getting into position. She did everything to keep her thoughts off the feel of the stranger's kisses and his hands that were traveling up the back of her thighs. Olivia wanted nothing more than to push him away from her and run, but she would not leave Thorne to die.

She needed to get the stranger's pants down and see if he had a weapon on his body. Although she had thought of this herself, Johann had instructed her to do such. Just speaking of it made Johann blush and stammer. As she untied his pants, Olivia felt a dagger at his waist, which she gently dropped to the ground as she started to lower his pants. Time was moving so slowly. Olivia wanted Stephan and Johann to come and for this stranger to be removed from touching her in any way.

She pushed him to the ground and climbed on top of him to give the men more time should they need it, but soon she rolled over and pulled him on top of her. His pants were well below his knees as Johann said they must be. Only their underclothes protected her from him, and he was searching for hers. Olivia prayed for deliverance as she made the noises of desire she had heard others make.

Fifteen

He heard the men as they rushed into camp. The Dark Horse looked at Olivia and grabbed her by the neck. "I will kill her." He looked at the three startled men.

"By all means, you will save us coin." Stephan said then went back to cutting the ties from Thorne's ankles as Johann freed his wrists.

The Dark Horse's grip on her tightened, and Olivia struggled for air. Her hand found the dagger, and she prayed she would not give in to the stars that danced around her eyes before she could use it. Grasping the hilt, she raised the dagger, and she felt purchase into the flesh of his shoulder. She forced her arm down, and he screamed as she sliced open his back. There were fewer stars and more darkness in front of her eyes. She said a silent prayer and asked to be forgiven of her sins this eve.

As soon as Thorne was free, he sprung on the Dark Horse just as he saw Olivia's hand go limp. Thorne had never known such white-hot rage as he attacked the man. Stephan and Johann pulled Thorne off the Dark Horse before Thorne could kill the man with his bare hands. Stephan held Thorne at bay until the rage started to clear from Thorne's eyes. Johann was tying the bleeding, half-conscious man by hand and feet then hands to feet.

"See to Olivia," Stephan told Thorne, and then Stephan helped Johann carry the Dark Horse to the awaiting horses.

Johann waited until the man was loaded. "She is the one."

"She would make a good ally to the Dark Horse as well, but Thorne would kill all men that looked, touched, or thought about her."

"But Thorne does not believe he can marry her since her father will not agree."

"We have to keep Thorne from being killed by her father first." Stephan turned to look for Thorne. "Mayhaps we should get him moving."

Thorne went to Olivia's side, fearing he was too late. She was so still and made not a sound. Gently he reached down and scooped her up into his arms. His ear went to her mouth, and he stared at her chest, willing it to rise. When Olivia gave a slight moan, Thorne forgot all and crushed her to him. Johann came to collect Thorne and Olivia; it was time to be on the move.

Olivia stirred and looked up into Thorne's face. "You are free. He heard my prayer."

"You are alive. He heard mine." Thorne rose with Olivia in his arms and whistled for his horse.

He set Olivia on her feet while he mounted, and then he reached for her. There were enough horses—she had no need to ride with him—but Johann helped her up in front of Thorne.

It took some measure of persuasion for the man to talk. His name was Gregory, and he had worked for Olivia's father as a higher-ranking man in the prince's army. Apparently the prince did not pay well, and Gregory had seized upon another route to riches. He even told the men where they could find the coin he had gained as the Dark Horse, which he had not spent. Stephan had been correct. Gregory had planned to get the purse from Chance, then kill Thorne and get the purse from the prince, which was dependent on Thorne's death. The prince did not wish to be blamed for Thorne's death, but he wished for it all the same.

Olivia had been resting as much as she could while the men interrogated Gregory, but as she heard them speak of her father's purse for Thorne's death, she came into the barn to hear better. As Thorne finished questioning Gregory, he turned and noticed Olivia. With a purpose he strode to her, taking her by the upper arm and nearly dragging her from the barn.

"You will never do anything like that again!" Thorne spat at her.

Olivia opened her mouth to speak, but Thorne was not through. "I should thrash both Stephan and Johann for allowing you to do such a thing! Of what were your thoughts?"

Olivia opened her mouth to speak again, but Thorne was still not through. "Do you have any thought of what could have happened to you?"

Olivia was determined that she should get a word out. "It was your idea!"

"My idea?" Thorne grabbed her by the upper arms again and pulled her into his face. "How can you suggest that your behavior was my idea?"

"It was you who said I was favored by the Dark Horse!" Thorne looked down into her rebellious face; she had no idea how precise she was.

"I was trying to save your dignity, not destroy it!"

"I was trying to save your life! Does that not concern

you?”

“Not enough for you to sacrifice yourself!”

“Stephan and Johann were coming. I knew they would not let things get carried away. And I took his dagger. I told you I would be prepared.”

“That you did, but you almost had the life choked out of you!” Thorne could see the purple and blue bruises emerging on her neck, bruises that served to remind him she had been in peril and that it had been his fault—again.

“Promise me, promise me, Olivia, that you will never do anything like that again.”

“I cannot, Thorne. You well know that I will do what I need do. The only one that has any concern for my life is you. My father certainly has no concern, and I have little doubt that my mother has already buried me in her mind as she waits to pass into her own peace. There is no reason to be overly concerned with my life. So many more people would be grieved by your passing.” Olivia could not lie to him. She saw no reason for his concern for her life other than his guilt for taking her from the estate. Thorne must be made to see the reason in the circumstance. His life mattered to many; her life mattered to no one but herself.

“Can you not grant me this one thing?”

"I will grant you that I will not try to be a concern for you. But if you would only see reason and let me be on my way, then you would not need me to grant this to you." Olivia was tired of fighting with Thorne's sense of duty. What was done was done.

He relaxed his hold on her, but just enough to gather her up in his arms. He kissed her gently, then buried his face in her neck. It had been torture for him to sit by and watch the false Dark Horse place a hand on her, but he had forced himself to be quiet. He was well aware that Olivia would not have done anything like that unless she had purpose. Thorne had wanted to kill Gregory for touching Olivia—he had not a care that the man had been planning to kill him—but Stephan's and Johann's presence kept him from it.

"I will take the first guard. We will have to ride with the light," said Stephan.

Thorne and Olivia climbed into the back of a wagon that had some hay left in it. The chill of the night was starting to seep into Olivia's bones, and she shivered. She had changed back into her borrowed shirt and trousers. Thorne wrapped his arms around her, and the two were fast asleep within minutes. Olivia heard a noise and realized that Stephan and Johann had changed the guard. She thought the sun seemed to be peeking over the horizon, but when she put her head down again, Thorne pulled her closer and she fell back asleep.

At first light they headed to the hunting camp. No decision had been made about what to do with Gregory. Before he could come back into the light of day, Thorne needed more proof to offer the prince that the body that had been sent to him was not his daughter's. They stayed the night at the hunting camp and decided to take Olivia and Gregory back to the castle. Thorne would need Gregory's testimony, but until that time he would stay locked up in the castle prison, which was much nicer than the prison at the prince's castle.

Thorne sent a missive to Father Adolphus concerning the Dark Horse. Gregory was ensconced in the prison, and Thorne actually considered putting Olivia there as well—at least he would know where she was. Instead, he placed a new guard on vOlivia, warning him that if Olivia escaped, the guard would be severely punished. Thorne and Johann prepared to leave for Galatia to search for the origin of the body that was sent to the prince.

It was nearly midnight when the guests arrived at the castle. Four carriages carried the entire party, and the clamor in the courtyard woke Thorne, the serene highness, and Olivia. Chance and his family were en route to Auria's in the Duchy of

Styria. Olivia thought to go back to bed until Thorne knocked at her door and told her to dress to meet the guests. Olivia dressed quickly, and as she heard Thorne and the serene highness head down the stair, she joined the family. Mayhaps Thorne thought to explain her presence as the distant cousin as they had for the wedding.

Several men filed in the door, followed by a woman of about Olivia's age who was dressed in mourning clothes. Olivia immediately felt Thorne tense. He had been relaxed as he greeted the men; his object of concern was the woman. The serene highness greeted the woman as she would a long-lost daughter, with great affection. Then the serene highness turned to introduce Olivia, but Thorne stepped up to do the honors.

"Countess, this is our guest, Princess Olivia." Thorne offered no explanation of where Olivia was from, an obvious faux pas in etiquette.

The countess gave Thorne a long, warm hug before turning to Olivia, who had tied her hair back with a scarf as was her routine, except in more formal occasions. The countess reached over and swept Olivia's hair off her shoulder so it hung straight down her back.

"I wish I had the courage to be so provincial." The countess's sweet tone did not match the insult of her words.

Olivia smiled and inclined her head slightly, unsure how to respond, as the serene highness ushered the group into the dining hall. Soup, bread, cheeses, and smoked fish were brought as a light repast for the guests, and Thorne provided wine for everyone. Olivia excused herself to get some water for her wine. If she drank it undiluted, she would likely sleep until noon. As she headed for the kitchen, Thorne blocked her way.

"I will have the servants bring you water. You need not trouble yourself." Thorne was not about to let her by.

"It is no trouble. The servants are busy serving the guests. I do not wish to slow them."

"Olivia, please allow the servants to take care of you. That is why I pay them, to take care of us."

"I do not wish to argue with you tonight, Thorne. I am accustomed to taking care of myself. The servants know I do not mean it as an insult. Please let me do the little things for myself. Give me at least that freedom."

Thorne stepped aside and held the door for her as Olivia filled a small pitcher of water and brought it with her to the table. He held the chair for her as she sat down, and she murmured her thank-you for his kindness, knowing that Thorne was not bothering her because of his kind heart. Mayhaps it was because her guard was in the other room; mayhaps Thorne felt he needed to watch her closer. Olivia sat quietly as the guests chatted; they were obviously well-known to the family but had not attended the wedding. Mayhaps it had been too close to the countess's cause for mourning.

It seemed that Olivia had just gotten into bed when the door of her room was opened and someone entered her bed-chamber. She glanced at the window, but saw no hint of the sunrise. She knew it was Thorne—she could feel it was him—but she had no idea why he would be in her bedchamber. He walked over to the bed, and Olivia sat upright as he sat near her on the bed.

"We will be leaving this morning—Stephan, Johann, and I. I do not know how long we will be gone, but we will not re-turn until we have found out about your father's dead daughter. This all needs put to rest. You will be here when I return. The guards understand that if you are not, they will forfeit their own lives—"

"Thorne, you cannot do that! You cannot make them responsible for me!"

"You do not value your life well. I hope you will value their lives more than your own. I cannot take you with me or else I would. I trust you not out of my sight. When this is all over, then you and I will discuss what your future holds, but until then, you must stay here. You need not concern yourself with entertaining the countess; my mother will take care of that. The gardeners have finished your garden. I care not with what you fill your time. Redecorate the entire castle if you wish. The only thing you cannot do is leave. I have left strict instructions that you may do anything else without my permission. My home is your home."

"Except leave."

"If you do, someone will die. Keep that thought." Thorne leaned over and kissed her lightly on the lips. Olivia did not pull away. He gathered her up in his arms and kissed her deeper. Then he forced himself to leave.

Olivia would not be able to go back to sleep, so she dressed and, with her guard, headed to the Chapel of Our Lady to pray. Thorne had done the one thing she could not abide—threatened to kill another for her actions. She prayed that Thorne's mission went swiftly and successfully. She prayed for her guards, and she prayed for the patience to wait to leave until Thorne returned. The sun was well up when she headed back to the castle.

She ate a quiet breakfast in the kitchen; no one else in

the house was up. Olivia and her guard headed for the stables; she would go for a ride. Olivia loved riding horseback. It was a very freeing experience. She thought back to when she had first been upon a horse with Thorne almost eight months earlier. She had been more afraid of being on the horse than of Thorne.

The air had a bite to it; it would snow soon. She and the guard took a ride around the castle property. Although Olivia knew that Thorne's land went on for miles and miles, she did not try to go that far. They rode to a small lake that would be beautiful in spring, summer, or fall, but now, without the leaves, the lake just looked bleak. She wondered if she dare ride if it snowed. If Thorne was about, she would have asked him. He had been gone only a few hours, but it seemed like an age.

When they returned to the house late morning, Olivia heard voices in the dining hall and headed in that direction. She had a thought as to what she would do for the rest of the day. The serene highness and the guests were enjoying a brunch, so Olivia sat and listened to the conversation. The serene highness and the countess were very close, but they had not seen each other for almost a year. Part of their conversation was stilted and veiled; Olivia thought perhaps it had to do with Thorne. If Olivia was to know what that was, she would have to learn it another time.

"I would have thought that we would have seen Thorne by now." The countess tossed the phrase out as if it was a passing thought.

The serene highness said nothing, but looked distressed. Olivia said nothing; no one had asked for her thoughts.

"Have you seen him this morning?" The countess turned to Olivia.

"I spoke with him briefly, earlier this morning," Olivia replied. It was the serene highness's duty to inform her guests that Thorne had left, but it appeared that the serene highness was reluctant to do so.

"Oh, when did you see him?" Again, the countess made the comment appear as casual discussion, but Olivia knew she was being interrogated by the woman. Why would the serene highness allow this?

"Just before daybreak, just before I went to the chapel for prayer." Olivia matched the countess's casual tone. A game was being played here, and Olivia had no desire to give up any of her game pieces—any morsel of information.

"You have been up and about for some time."

"Yes, after prayer I went for a ride on horseback and have just returned."

"Thorne was always an early riser."

Olivia felt no need to reply, nor did she feel the need to stay any longer. She rose from the table and wished the ladies a good day.

"Have you plans for the day, Olivia?" The serene highness finally entered the conversation.

"I had thoughts to mayhaps redecorate the castle." Olivia stated with a slight smile. The serene highness nearly choked on her breakfast, assuring Olivia that Thorne had indeed told these words to his mother.

As Olivia left the room, she heard the countess say something to the serene highness although Olivia could not hear the words. Olivia was sure that the countess would be demanding to know who Olivia was, and she felt slightly guilty for leaving that to the serene highness, but only slightly. Olivia did indeed wander about the castle looking for something to do. She was most likely stuck indoors and had little with which to occupy herself.

Sixteen

inding herself in an overstuffed chair in a lounging area in the guest wing, Olivia finally allowed herself to admit she was in love with Thorne and had been for quite some time. She had never intended for that to happen. She had spent her life staying away from anyone that could truly break her heart, except her mother.

It had not been difficult. As soon as a nursemaid or tutor heard stories about the prince and his daughter, another position became available in another duchy. They feared that when the day came that the prince would wish to rid himself of the pesky child, they might mayhaps be caught in the rain of arrows that would come crashing down. It would vex her grandparents to have to hire another. Of course, Olivia could have told them that it would most likely be of greater ease just to hire a whole new house staff, the ones that chased the nursemaids and tutors off.

As Olivia got older, so did the servants. The house staff had no fear of being killed by the prince, but her mother began to withdraw with melancholy. Mayhaps the years of isolation had become too much to bear. Mayhaps she knew the day was coming when her father would want his history completely erased. Mayhaps she was already starting to say good-bye to her daughter. Olivia knew all children must grow up and leave home, some never to see their families again. Olivia tried to keep this in mind as the time she spent with her mother became less and less. She was lucky to have what time she did have with her mother.

She tried to think back and figure out when she had fallen in love with Thorne. She thought that it was when they had sat beside the stream, talking, the night he took her from her home. It was not a prudent emotional reaction. She had lost her fear of him by then. It was something about how he sat there and spoke with her. Something about the way he listened to her and did not belittle her thoughts. It was something, even if she did not know what that something was.

But she could walk away from Thorne. She would walk away from Thorne ... but she would hold him in her thought. She would not allow her feelings to change her path. Her father had blotted out her future, but she would not dwell in misery in her present. She would enjoy her life today. Thorne would be back soon, and he would come to understand that it would be best to let her go on her own way. If he did not, then she would go to where Father Adolphus sent her until eyes were off her, then she would slip away. Mayhaps she would go to another country, a place that had never heard of her father, a place her father would not care if she got lost.

The chairs, that was the reason she had come, to look at the chairs. She had the seamstresses make new drapes for this lounge and had wanted the chairs re-covered as well, but time had gotten short. The guests started to arrive, there were other duties to attend to, and the chairs had been overlooked. Now she had time—she had nothing but time. She went in search of the seamstresses to see if there was fabric left over from the drapes.

Olivia had the fabric spread out on the large table, and she started to mark with chalk where she would need to cut for the chairs. The seamstresses had been shocked to find out that Olivia intended to re-cover the chairs herself. Olivia assured the women that she had done it before.

She needed to remember why she was here. She was here so that Niklas would not die. Niklas, who worked in the vineyards and who had a wife and two children.

She had spent her life knowing that someone had the power over her life and death, but she would not do that to another. Her guards had names and families. She would stop looking at them as nameless bodies; she would learn their names and find out about their families. When she thought she would go mad from the monotony of tasks for which she had no heart, she would remember why she was doing them.

At the evening meal Olivia was formally introduced to the four gentlemen that accompanied the countess. Lukas, her older brother, looked much like his sister. Lukas's best friend, Sebastian, was traveling with him, and the other two men were quite a bit older, Father John and Father John Michael, two priests who were traveling to a castle in Croatia. They would be picked up in a few days.

Olivia was seated between the two priests, and with little effort the two priests carried the conversation through all the courses. After the meal, Olivia sat with the priests and worked on her needlework. She was making a coat of arms to place in the inset of each of the chairs that she was refinishing. It was a perfectly normal, boring evening … until the countess set her sights on Olivia.

"Princess, I hope we can spend some time together and get to know one another." The countess had come over and sat in a chair across from Olivia.

"Will you be staying long?" Olivia really did not care, but

she should be polite.

"Our traveling plans have not been finalized. We could spend the afternoon together tomorrow. Just two women chatting and having a good time." Olivia looked at the countess's black dress. Was someone in mourning supposed to be having a good time?

Chance and his valet rode to the old tower, where he knew they were meeting. The stone tower was all that was left of a large estate home built in the fourteenth century. His ancestors had lived there while the castle was being built. A more formidable structure was necessary due to the on-again, off-again skirmishes with neighbors in the region that had destroyed the estate home.

Three horses were tethered outside the round stone structure, but Chance knew that no one was inside; they had hidden themselves at the sound of hooves. Chance well knew where each was hidden; he had been taught by the best, just as Thorne had. Chance and Akos both dismounted before their horses came to a stop, just as the men had. It was a skill, not easily learned, but one that could be of great use.

"Thorne, Johann, Stephan, come. We need to speak." Chance waited but a second but heard no sound nor saw a movement. "Mayhaps you need a display of my tracking skills."

Thorne was the first to emerge, hoping that his brother was not there for the purpose that Thorne suspected. He had thought he had hidden his life well from his brother, but Thorne knew from the tone of Chance's voice that this was not idle speak.

"Brother, have you come to hunt as we have?" Thorne would admit nothing to his brother.

"We all know that hunting is not the reason for this meeting. Akos and I have come to join your cause."

"I know not what you speak."

"The Dark Horse."

"We have not come to meet with the Dark Horse."

"You are the Dark Horse." Chance put up a hand to stop the denial about to pour from his brother's mouth. "I know all, Thorne. I have for some time."

Thorne knew he was trapped. Though he could deny everything, Chance would know he was lying, and Thorne could no more blatantly lie to his brother than he could to Johann or Stephan. Thorne looked to the two men standing with him. All he would say would involve them as well. Johann and Stephan gave a single nod; it was time to share the truth, but in truth,

Johann had known this was coming. He had been watching Chance train Akos for several years.

"How long have you known?"

"Since about a year after Father died. I waited for you to ask me to join you, but you did not. A few years later I thought to confront you, but Johann had joined you and I suspect Stephan had as well. I have doubt that Father's valet helped him, but he would have known, as I am sure Stephan's father knew as well."

Stephan nodded. Chance had figured out far more than he would have guessed. There had been no sign that Chance had known anything. Mayhaps that was more the reason to hear him out now.

"Did you not wonder why I had so many valets?"

Thorne had indeed wondered why his mild-mannered twin was so displeased with so many valets. It seemed that for several years Chance went through a new valet every year ... until two years ago. Akos had come, and the two were inseparable if Chance was not with his wife and child—and therein lay the problem, his wife and child.

"No, I will not allow this! You have a wife and children. I will not allow you to leave Margarette a widow and your children without a father as we were. I have no plan to marry—"

"Yes, another subject about which we should speak, but let us settle the Dark Horse issue first. Thorne, you are far cleverer than our father was; there is safety in our numbers. Had you not brought Stephan into the fold, then we would still be sitting in prison. I have been training Akos for over two years. He understands the risk, and we are ready to join you."

"Does Margarette know about this?"

"Yes, I am here with her blessing. She is fully aware of the risk. I would not be here without her consent."

Thorne looked to Akos. He was as they all were—same height, age, color, and frame. Johann had been the first to mention how alike they both were. Physically they were so very much the same, something Thorne had noted years earlier, and his valet joined him readily. Johann had suggested that they bring Stephan into the fold, but Thorne had already started laying the foundation for that. Both Johann and Chance were right; there was safety in numbers, but this was not his decision alone to make.

Thorne turned to Johann. "And you say?"

"I have known for at least two years that Chance was preparing Akos. Chance is of sound counsel; we are stronger in numbers." Johann feared Thorne would be angry with him for not telling him what Chance was doing, but it was not Johann's place to tell him.

"And you say?" Thorne turned to Stephan.

"It is his birthright as well. Has he not proven he has the talent to be the Dark Horse?" Stephan answered.

"Akos, are you certain that you wish to risk your life?" Thorne did not know this man well, but he knew that Akos was loyal to Chance.

"Yes, my prince, I well know what is asked of me. As you know, I have a wife as well. She does not know—her lips can be loose among the servants—but I am willing to place my life where it need be. I ask only that you will allow my wife to remain at the castle should I die."

"Of course! We would never turn her out." Thorne knew he had agreed without the words leaving his lips. Chance and Akos would join them.

"Now, let us speak of Olivia." Chance was grateful that Thorne had brought up the subject of his marrying; it would be easier to discuss this way.

"Olivia? Of what concern does she have of this?" Thorne could not imagine how Olivia could be involved. He would not allow her to be involved.

"It is my belief that the two of you," Chance looked to

Johann and Stephan, "have come to the same conclusion as I have, but have not spoken of this to Thorne." Both men looked to the other, and Chance knew he was right.

"If you allow Olivia to be sent away, you will lose her forever. A woman must be a wife to you and to the Dark Horse. You will never find another that can be that. As you yourself declared, she is favored by the Dark Horse."

"How can you know that? You were not there!"

"I was when you had words with her about it." Chance saw the shock on the faces of his brother, the valet, and the huntsman. "I have been there more than once. Since none of you detected me, is that not enough to prove I am ready to join you?"

<hr/>

Olivia had no acceptable reason to refuse the countess's offer. She had no doubt she would be heavily queried by the woman, and Olivia felt as though she was walking blindfolded into a lion's den. She had no idea what the serene highness had said about her to the countess. Olivia could only hope that the countess enjoyed talking about herself as much as Olivia suspected.

She dressed simply, as she did most days, even though she now had a wardrobe that was far grander than most who had attended the wedding. Olivia did not want to invite questions by appearing to be someone of status. She left her hair down, pulled back and tied in a scarf, as she usually did, and she arrived in the garden at the precise time, not a minute early or late, as she usually did. The countess was already awaiting her arrival.

The countess rose and came to Olivia, taking both her hands. "How kind of you to come and cheer a poor woman in mourning."

As the ladies took their seats, Olivia expressed her condolences. "I am sorry for your loss. Has it been long?" Olivia thought it odd that she had not heard of the reason for the countess's grief.

"I so miss my Maximillian. Our time together was far too short. I just could not walk about our home and be reminded with everything I saw and touched that he was gone. He died suddenly four months ago. We were only married a few months. It was love at first sight ..."

Olivia allowed the countess to go on about her sorrowful state. Although the countess appeared sincere, Olivia had the feeling that this was a grand performance, and she listened intently, committing all to memory. Olivia made all the proper responses at the proper times. If not other, the countess would have to admit that Olivia had been properly educated in etiquette.

"But let us talk about you. Anja tells me you are a distant cousin." The countess gave Olivia a very sweet smile.

"Yes. Is your family from Carinthia as well?" Olivia would turn the conversation back onto the countess.

"My parents are gone. My brother is all I have left." The countess looked as though she would burst into tears.

Olivia again made all the proper responses and was able to get the countess to talk about herself again. She came from a family rich in wealth, but poor in title. The countess was not an unpleasant woman, although Olivia would not have called her beautiful. Surely titled families that were not wealthy would consider her.

"You never married?" The countess sprung the question on Olivia without warning, as if hoping to catch the princess who was always on guard, off her guard.

A stricken look seized Olivia's face, and she brought her hand to her mouth to stifle a cry. Looking away, she took several deep breaths, trying to control her anguish as tears started to cascade down her cheeks. Finally, when Olivia felt her emotions under control, she turned to the countess. "I ... " she stammered, "I cannot speak of it." Olivia rose from her chair quickly, knocking it to the ground. "Forgive me," she said and ran from the garden.

Seventeen

Katarina was speechless, which was uncharacteristic of her. She had never meant to upset the young princess so. A tragic love story—mayhaps even a scandalous one—haunted the girl, and Anja had been particularly tight-lipped about her. Now it made sense why the princess was allowed to run free and act as though she herself owned the castle. But why did she have a guard? From whom was she being protected?

Katarina would have discovered the story of the princess if she had been able to go to court. Now that she was a countess, she could go, but not until her mourning year was over. Katarina wondered who was the pompous fool that contrived such rules. Had not being married to that buffoon for three months been punishment enough? If Thorne had only married her, this would not be her state. Had she not tried every stratagem she knew to get him to marry her? She had even attempted to trap him by getting with child, but Thorne had not cooperated.

Had not her mother been a woman of talents in Paris?

She had been able to trap a wealthy businessman into marriage, and she had educated her daughter as well. But Auria had become promised in marriage, and Thorne would not think of marriage until his precious Auria had been wed. At least she was gone. Thorne had been far too attached to his sister, and Auria had never taken to Katarina.

At least she had Anja on her side. The serene highness had always loved Katarina and had been in favor of Thorne and Katarina marrying, but Katarina wanted assurances that this Olivia was not going to be a problem. She was young and very beautiful. The countess had been shocked that the princess was not married. Had not both her brother and his friend mentioned her beauty the very night they arrived?

Katarina was twenty now—an old woman to marry—and the count had not left her enough money to live the way Katarina wanted to live. But Thorne had much money. Katarina had seen all the serene highness's jewels; her collection was enormous. And to host half the aristocracy for the summer? Few families could afford such extravagance, but had that not been her plan all along? She had always known she would come back for Thorne once she had gotten rid of the count.

Anja was not pleased when Katarina showed up on her doorstep. Was she not to stay shut up in her home for her year of mourning? Why, Anja herself could barely eat for crying at the loss of her Tobias, but Katarina had said her home only reminded her of her loss, where Anja had found comfort in her home. Even now, Tobias's clothing filled his drawers; she could not bear to part with any of his things. Anja also believed that Katarina was far too interested in Olivia.

Thorne had placed a guard on her; he must have concern that the prince would find her and come after her, and now Katarina was asking question after question about Olivia. Anja was not sure what she thought about Olivia. She had ears for what Elena had said about the princess, that the princess herself had scrubbed and cleaned in the guest wing, which had been such a mess. Had not the princess taken care, the family would have been the embarrassment of the empire.

And horseback riding? It was not right that a woman should ride astride a horse. Some of the servants were forced to do such, but it was not for a gentlewoman. And Olivia did not ride sedately—she rode as a man would—and Thorne had taught her such.

Auria believed that Olivia was perfect for Thorne; he did seem to keep an eye on her at all times. One minute Anja was convinced that Thorne and Olivia were in love; the next minute she talked herself out of the thought. Thorne had made no move towards marriage, but they had spent too much time alone together. Should anyone find out, it would be scandalous. Anja thought mayhaps it would be best to keep Olivia at the castle for a time to see if she was with child. Did she not know her son's reputation?

Thorne had refused to write to Father Adolphus and the Holy See and assure them that the Dark Horse situation had been resolved. Her son was of the thought that the man in the prison was not the true Dark Horse and that all was not settled.

Olivia resigned herself to spending the midday in her room. Fortunately, when she fled in anguish to her room, she had the foresight to pick up her stitching. Olivia knew the countess would ask why she had not married, but Olivia had not resolved how she was going to answer. It was the countess's performance that came to Olivia's mind when the countess did ask, and Olivia was quite certain that the countess was not the only one with a talent for performance. From the look on the countess's face, Olivia believed she was correct.

Thorne was not pleased with anything. For three weeks he and Johann traveled town to village to find from where the dead girl had come, without luck. In that time, there had been no word from Stephan or from Chance, and Thorne wanted to go home. He did not like leaving Olivia and Katarina together. He did not like having Katarina at the castle at all. At least she had not shown until Auria had left; Auria detested the woman.

Thorne had left strict instructions with his mother to keep the two women apart. He did not trust Katarina. Had she not already come to his rooms? Thorne had managed to send her on her way after she sobbed to him about her loneliness, but it was not without difficulty that Thorne was able to remove Katarina from his rooms. She had appeared about a half hour after all had retired for the night and, without knocking, walked boldly into his rooms. Thorne had not crawled into bed as yet, and as soon as she saw him, she had thrown herself into his arms, clothed only in a thin, short nightdress. Thorne had never seen a piece of women's clothing so short that it did not cover even her knees.

She had sobbed and poured her heart out to him for another hour. Thorne put not his arms around her, but she never let go of him. Despite her tears, Thorne felt she was rubbing her barely dressed body against him. When she calmed, she had asked to stay with him, to spend the night. She wanted just to have someone hold her. As Thorne moved closer to the door, it took many words for him to tell her to leave. It was not until he opened the door that she finally understood that he would not allow her to stay.

Thorne had heard that she had married not long after she left his castle; she had been angry that he would not marry her. Thorne had said he would not consider marrying her until after Auria had wed, but when he heard that she had married six months later, he felt that was a sign that marriage was not in his future.

After her performance with the Dark Horse, Thorne did not doubt that Olivia could well handle Katarina, but Olivia should not have to roll in Thorne's dirty laundry. Thorne should be at the castle now, throwing Katarina out, but there was the problem of his mother. She had always favored Katarina, and Thorne had never stopped to wonder how his mother thought of Olivia. The two women did not get on as Katarina and his mother did.

Lukas and Sebastian were everywhere she turned. They attended morning prayer. They were in the stable to go for a morning ride as Olivia had become accustomed to doing if there was not much snow and the footing was true. She had finished covering the chairs and then collected all the books placed haphazardly about the castle. She felt like a military officer with her troops following behind as the men trailed her room to room, collecting the books. It was of good fortune that the two men enjoyed talking about themselves and telling stories of their younger-year exploits.

Olivia had large bookcases made and a step stair to reach

books placed on the highest shelves. She had removed a large tapestry from the wall against which the bookcases were placed. The serene highness was in great distress at the removal of the tapestry (forgetting that the tapestry had been placed only a fortnight before the wedding); it had been made by her grandmother. Olivia explained to the near-crying, hand-wringing serene highness that the sun would, in time, destroy the tapestry, just as the sun destroyed the draperies. Olivia had planned to have a frame made for the tapestry so that it could be hung properly in the dining area.

A two-sided pedestal was made for the large illuminated Book of Proverbs and Book of Psalms that Olivia found, and it would sit in front of the bookcases. She wondered if this artwork of worship had been created by Father Adolphus; it looked to be fairly recently made. Olivia had found the books in a cabinet in the drawing room and could not understand why such beauty would not be displayed. She had spoken to Elena and told the housekeeper that the pages needed to be carefully turned every week or two to keep the ink from fading.

Anja was not at all pleased with what Olivia was doing with the castle. The re-covered chairs looked wonderful, and her stitched coat of arms was beautiful. Anja had to admit that Olivia stitched far better than she or Auria, but Anja was beside herself when Olivia removed the tapestry. In truth, Anja felt like a stranger was taking over her home. Anja knew that someday she would have to step aside as the mistress of the castle when Thorne took a wife, but Olivia was not Thorne's wife. Mayhaps Anja was not as ready to step aside as she thought she was.

Thorne had been very specific in his instructions: She was to allow Olivia to do as she wished. He had said that Olivia could redecorate the entire castle if it suited her and that Olivia could burn down the castle and rebuild it if that suited her better. Thorne had also said that Olivia could spend as much money as she wished. Although she could have spent all the family fortune, as many a woman would have, Olivia had not spent any.

The bookcases had been made by the gardeners, who had little to do in the winter, and these older men appeared to be of great talent. The bookcases featured beautiful, delicate scrolling, and the pedestal had been made with a spiral theme that was a work of art. Olivia had so loved what the gardeners had created that she hugged each man and gave them a kiss on the cheek. The gardeners had absolutely adored Olivia before she hugged them; now they fairly raved about her to all ears. Elena and most of the house staff thought of Olivia as the mistress of the house—a mistress to whom they were completely loyal, heart and soul.

Anja had never given the servants much thought, but

she did not like the servants to be so attached to another. The serene highness had to admit that the cook's food was of more taste since Olivia had found and planted herbs that the cook wanted. It did appear that the girl knew what she was doing; the frame for the tapestry was beautiful. Anja did not want to admit that she had not handled her grandmother's wedding gift properly. It had been placed in a cabinet for twenty-eight years, and when Anja had hung it, she had not done it in a manner to preserve the gift. Anja would have destroyed it.

The five men rendezvoused as they had previously planned. Thorne was not greatly surprised that their search had been fruitless thus far. What about this situation had been easy? It was decided that Thorne and Chance would go to Margarette and escort her back to the castle from Auria and Grego's home. Thorne welcomed the opportunity to see about the welfare of his sister. The three other men would return to the castle in two weeks' time if the information they sought was not found sooner.

Auria fairly glowed. Thorne was not with doubt that she was happy. Margarette was also pleased to see her husband again and looked forward to returning to the castle. Auria was not of good humor that the group would be leaving so soon; she wished to have them visit longer.

As much as possible, Auria injected Olivia into the conversation, and Thorne knew his sister was matchmaking. Auria wanted Thorne to promise he would visit again soon and for a longer time—and to bring Olivia. What had Olivia been doing? Was she lonely without Auria and Margarette there? Had Father Adolphus returned? Auria felt sure that Olivia would not be leaving the castle before Father Adolphus returned. It would be best if Olivia stayed at the castle for as long as possible. Mayhaps Thorne would consider his fondness for her.

Auria and Margarette had spoken of the issue many times. Margarette was a woman of few words, but she wholeheartedly agreed that Thorne and Olivia were more than well suited for each other. A pact was made. Margarette would press with Olivia, and Auria and Chance would press with Thorne. Both had fear that Olivia would be sent away before the two came to their senses.

Thorne walked into a house full of chaos. His mother was in a state over what Olivia had done with her tapestry, though Thorne much preferred the tapestry on the frame and in the dining room. He also thought the book cabinets in the drawing room were not only beautiful, but an excellent addition to the area. He could not understand his mother's concern that the servants adored Olivia. Were the servants lax in their duties? No. Did the servants have a show of disrespect? No. What was the problem with the servants? His mother dissolved into tears.

Katarina felt that Olivia was being intentionally rude to her by ignoring her. Did Olivia refuse to pass pleasantries with her? No. Did Olivia have harsh words with her? No, but Olivia was upsetting the serene highness. Anja had refused to discuss it with Katarina, but Katarina was sure the root of Anja's distress was Olivia. Katarina could not bear to see her dear friend in such a state. Olivia was also playing with the hearts of Lukas and Sebastian, flirting with them both in a wanton way.

Thorne found Olivia reading scripture to the prisoner. "What complaint do you have?" Thorne was sure Olivia could have a list longer than could be heard during the whole of the cold winter season.

"I have no complaint, my prince. I know not what you speak." A true look of innocence was on her beautiful face.

"My mother had complaint of a tapestry."

"I did not move the tapestry to distress her. I told her the sun would fade the piece of art and that it had need to be hung properly. I offered to place it in another area should she wish."

"The tapestry is pleasing as it is now. The book cabinets are beautiful. I would not have thought you had time to have skilled workmen come from Vienna and make them."

"I did not. The gardeners made the book cabinets and pedestal. I believe they are at least as skilled as anyone from Vienna." Olivia was pleased that Thorne thought they had been done by skilled artisans. She would tell the gardeners that Thorne thought such.

"I understand that you have been turning the servants against my mother." Olivia looked at Thorne with an arched eyebrow. The charge was absurd. "Or so she believes."

"I have never had discussions or suggestions about the serene highness concerning the servants. Of this I truly have no idea."

"Katarina says that you are trifling with the affections of her brother and his guest."

"Thorne, I have not tried to upset your mother. I have tried to do as she would wish. I am mindful that this is her home; it is not my home. I have only tried to be fair and kind to the servants. And Lukas and Sebastian have been following me around. I am sure they would be here in the prison if they thought for a moment I was. I have little doubt they are without proper entertainment for men and are using me for sport."

Olivia could not understand how everything could become such a jumbled mess. She had only been attempting to keep herself busy and away from the questions of the guests.

Thorne had not thought that Olivia had been guilty of any of the things the two women had complaint about. It simply was not her nature. Likely it was too many women with too much time on their hands. There was more though; he was of a surety that his mother had never really thought that there would be another woman to take her place as mistress of the castle. His mother had never treated the servants as anything more than servants, and she knew the names of only a few of them. Olivia treated the servants as people; therefore the servants placed her with higher esteem.

Katarina was a completely different matter. Thorne had no doubt that Katarina was jealous. Olivia outshined Katarina in age and beauty—especially in beauty—and Katarina had already laid the foundation of attempting to rekindle a romance with Thorne. As Thorne saw Katarina now, he wondered how he could have thought of marriage with her. Thorne knew that Katarina had one talent and one talent only: she knew how to pleasure a man as a courtesan would. In truth, it had been said that her mother was a courtesan in Paris. Thorne had thought that was just idle gossip, but in the last year he had come to think it may well have been true. Katarina knew how to do things that did not come naturally to women.

On the subject of Lukas and Sebastian, Thorne could not agree with Olivia. Thorne knew that Olivia did not understand how beautiful she was. When Thorne had brought Niklas and Janos together to instruct them on guarding Olivia, he had told them she was beautiful. When Thorne had pointed her out to them, Niklas's jaw dropped. Janos was older and wiser, but Thorne saw the look in the man's eye.

He had warned them not to be fooled by her sweet, pretty face. She had already escaped when bound (Thorne did not admit that she had been bound to him), and she had just been preparing an attempt to escape the castle. His threat of death came mostly from knowledge of Olivia but also from their reactions. They needed to be in fear. Even the prisoner had been sitting there staring at Olivia; Thorne had doubt the man heard the words she was saying, and he did not want to think what was on the man's mind. Thorne became angry beyond reason when he thought that other men had the same thoughts about Olivia as he did.

"I want you to think of this as your home. There is no reason that it cannot be home to both of you. You and my mother are very different, and my mother does not understand you as I do. There has been precious little time without guests about for you and my mother to get to know each other. I have no concern for what Katarina complains, and you do not understand the minds of men. Lukas and Sebastian are not using you for sport; their pursuit of you is no game."

Olivia cared not what Thorne thought concerning the two male guests; they were merely an annoyance to Olivia. She was glad that Thorne had no concern about the countess. Olivia had thoughts that Katarina had marriage plans that concerned Thorne, which made Olivia want to rip the hair from the woman's head. Olivia generally had no difficulty with other women. She had heard servants back at the estate talk about young girls competing for the attentions of a man, but Olivia had no such experience. Her father would never agree to a marriage for her.

Olivia knew that she loved Thorne, and thus she was experiencing jealousy. She did not want Thorne to have a future with Katarina. Olivia was of the thought that Katarina had concern for herself only and would not hesitate to hurt Thorne to get what she desired. Olivia also knew, however, that it was Thorne's mistake to make should he decide such. Olivia preferred to have no knowledge of it.

However, on the topic of the serene highness, Thorne had an absolutely correct thought and a completely wrong notion. Olivia could feel that the serene highness had no affection for her. It was completely true; they were different, but Olivia harbored no foolish notion that the serene highness would like her better if she were to know Olivia. Olivia would never be what the serene highness thought of as an acceptable princess. She could never be a pretty trinket.

Olivia held no ill feelings for the serene highness for being as she was; after all, her own mother was cut from the same cloth. There was too much of life to see, to know, and to experience, and because of this Olivia could never spend her days dressed well, looking for an audience to admire her. Olivia would rather experience scrubbing floors than nothing at all. Mayhaps the two women could come to a polite impasse, but it was of no concern. Olivia planned to leave for another life soon.

Eighteen

While the serene highness spent her mornings writing to her friends throughout the empire, Olivia had already set her plan in motion. Olivia had kept very detailed notes of everyone and anyone she had heard of since coming to the castle, and as the serene highness's letters traversed the country, so did Olivia's. She had kept the identity of a distant, non-titled cousin who would be needing a new position. She had even used Thorne and Auria as references. Olivia was of the thought that no one would actually ask for a reference, given Thorne's and Auria's willingness to provide one.

Olivia now awaited the replies. Thorne could not deny her this; was this not what Father Adolphus was to do with her? Was she not saving Father Adolphus the concern? No one had spoken of when Father Adolphus was to return, and it would be Christmastide soon. Olivia had been gone from the estate since early May. It was time for her to find the life she craved.

Olivia could see no purpose for her staying at the castle

any longer, but she would not run away. Although she often had want, she would not risk Niklas's and Janos's lives. Thorne had no need of her; he had the counterfeit Dark Horse, and he would find from whence the girl had come. Did not the Dark Horse always prevail? No, it would just become harder for her to leave the longer she stayed.

It was of good fortune that it was thought that she was dead. Her father would not come after her; her mother, without doubt, thought she was dead, so Olivia could not go back to her. Staying away would be more valuable to her mother's life. She could travel and live without looking across her shoulder for her father. She could have a life, with a purpose, and she would no longer be a burden to any. Olivia was tired of being a burden; she just wanted to live her life.

The Holy See would not release Father Adolphus. Thorne had written and assured them that the man who called himself the Dark Horse was secured in his prison, but the Holy See wanted this man to come to Rome for trial as his sins were against the church. Thorne was not willing to let Gregory be sent to Vienna or Rome. Gregory had refused to answer concerning the body of the girl that had been presented to the prince as his daughter, but Thorne knew with full certainty that he knew something of this.

Gregory was more afraid of the prince than he was of Thorne, and Thorne had little doubt that the prince had deep tentacles at the Holy See. Thorne felt that Gregory would die before a trial began, and the information that could save Thorne's life would die with him. Thorne, Johann, and Stephan had needed to beat Gregory to get what they did from him. Thorne knew to get more would require more desperate means.

Thorne had not the luxury to settle into his life at home. The prince still had thought that Thorne had killed his daughter. Should the prince have thought that Thorne returned home, he would come with a small army for Thorne. He felt as if he was running from the prince, a thought Thorne loathed, but he could not help his family if his head was separated from his body.

Johann, Stephan, and Akos returned to the castle but had not heard what they sought. The three had spoken of many different routes they could take to get the information. A plan was devised by Johann; without doubt he was the strategist of the group. The plan was sound and would give them the information they sought, but Thorne would like it not.

"We spoke to all the priests as Father Frederico, but none would speak of what we wanted. If the priest who had escorted the body of the girl still had not returned to their village, others would have knowledge. I believe the priest has a great fear of the prince. He would not risk telling another priest. But there is another to whom he would speak the knowledge." Stephan was the one able to present the plan to Thorne. Johann never credited himself with words; his gift was thoughts.

"Who would that be?" Thorne could think of none save the prince himself.

"A Bishop from the Holy See."

"How do we persuade a Bishop to take up our case?"

"We do not." Stephan paused to allow Thorne to come to the only conclusion he could.

"No, no, we cannot." It took Thorne but one moment to understand.

"Hear our thoughts, Thorne."

"The Holy See will not take this with good humor."

"A Bishop in search of evidence of the crimes of the false Dark Horse."

"We would be imprisoned for an entire lifetime," said Thorne.

"*We* will not do it."

"Who?"

"Matthias," said Stephan.

"I cannot ask your father to do this."

"We will make haste and only to the parishes we feel are likely to have knowledge. We will not stay long in any county or duchy. But we will also have a diversion."

"A diversion? What?"

"No, Thorne, who?"

"Who?" Thorne was near mad with Stephan for drawing this plan out.

"You."

"I fail to understand." Thorne was now completely lost.

"You—and Chance, acting as you—will make appearances around the empire. Johann, Akos, and I will make as to be on your trail. We wish to keep the empire focused on you, not on an investigation by the Holy See."

"Will not people talk about one as they would the other?"

"The Bishop will suggest that a priest may have assisted the Dark Horse, and the church wishes to keep that to itself."

"You all have had time to think and speak on this. Give me the night to consider it. If I believe we can be successful, then we will speak with Chance as the sun rises."

Stephan looked to Johann, and the valet nodded. He had anticipated this would be Thorne's decision. Should all not go well, Thorne would insist on taking the blame from the church for the plan. Johann knew that Thorne would come to see the potential success of this plan, but it was Thorne's neck on the chopping block, with the prince as well as with the church.

Olivia had made her presence scarce while Thorne was home. The wildflowers, herbs, plants, bark, and roots that she had put to dry were now ready for use. In the cellar beneath the kitchen, Olivia prepared the vegetation for fragrances and medicinal use. Margarette had taken to spending time with Olivia, who could not remember speaking two words with Margarette afore this, but Margarette sought Olivia out each afternoon. Margarette had no expertise in the use of flowers for fragrances, but she had a strong will to learn.

Olivia made note that the conversation often turned to Thorne. As Olivia turned the discussion away from Thorne, Margarette would steer it back to him. Olivia could not find reason why Margarette would wish to discuss Thorne with her. Mayhaps it was of thought that Olivia was at odds with Thorne as she kept mostly to herself. Olivia could well understand that Thorne's sister-in-law would want Thorne to have ease of mind, but if Thorne was uneasy of mind, Olivia knew she was not the cause.

Thorne was concerned about his mother. The serene highness was apprehensive and overwrought, which was not his mother's usual temperament. She fairly jumped into the air when Thorne entered the room and had the look of one about to burst into tears. In her hands, at all times, was a twisted handkerchief. All his inquiries were for not; his mother insisted that she had no concern. Though clearly something was amiss, the serene highness would not confide in Thorne or Chance.

Katarina took special interest in comforting the serene highness, and Katarina alone seemed capable of heartening the serene highness. Thorne was not pleased that his mother entrusted Katarina so. The serene highness was close to her daughter-in-law, but she rebuffed Margarette's attempts to spend time with her and had no interest in her grandchildren either. It was the habit of the serene highness to spend time after the midday meal with Peter and baby Thomas, but she had not seen them since their arrival from Auria's with Thorne and Chance.

If Thorne thought that he was given to delusions, Chance was well concerned. Chance had no wish to burden Thorne more than was of need, but their mother clearly was not herself. Chance had tried to speak with her several times, but Katarina was always in attendance and the serene highness looked to Katarina to give her the answers to Chance's questions. The household servants—most notably Elena, who had been at the castle when the serene highness had married Tobias and come to the castle—had spoken to both Thorne and Chance about the serene highness's behavior.

Anja had gotten over her concern about Katarina coming to the castle. Katarina had confided that she highly esteemed the serene highness's ability to handle the loss of her husband, and Katarina wanted Anja's guidance. Anja had not given thought that the woman no longer had a mother to whom she could turn, and Katarina had made the subject of Thorne as a concern to be settled. She had a fondness for Thorne, but her heart was with her husband past, Maximillian. She had loved Thorne as a girl, but she had loved Maximillian as a woman. She had no thought for marriage with Thorne any longer.

As her concerns were laid to rest, Anja welcomed an ally. She was lonely with Margarette, Chance, and Thorne gone. She was alone with Olivia, about whom she had grave concerns. Anja had thought it not best to share her concerns about Olivia with Katarina, but they spilled from her heart and her mouth without a thought. At first Anja had been suspicious of Katarina's questions of Olivia, but Katarina explained to her dear, close friend that she felt the unease Anja had with Olivia and wanted to help.

No matter the number of questions, Anja maintained that Olivia was a distant cousin. The serene highness had too much fear of Olivia's father to allow the truth to pass through her lips. Anja had seen when the prince came to the castle that he wanted Carinthia, but Anja said things she had never meant to say. She confided in Katarina that Thorne and Olivia had spent time alone together, time that was not properly supervised, and Anja feared that Olivia was with child.

A rift had started concerning the subject. Katarina had assured the serene highness that, if indeed Olivia was with child, then the situation could be fixed. Anja was horrified. She had no thought how anyone could wish to harm a child—her grandchild, the possible heir. No, no, this could never be done. She could not have imagined one would have such thoughts. Forget not that this would be a grave sin against the church and against God. Her argument was not with the child; her argument would be with Olivia. Anja had started to look at Katarina with new eyes.

Then Anja was not feeling herself. She did not feel ill, she had not a pain, but she was not herself. Her thoughts were often muddled; no matter how hard she tried, she could not make her thoughts flow as they should. She felt like she wanted to jump out of her skin, and she feared everyone and everything. As the sun rose, Anja was of herself, but as the sun moved across the sky, Anja became less and less of herself.

She knew it was not just her thought that she was not of herself. Had not Thorne, Chance, and Margarette spoken to her about their concerns of her? Only Katarina did not badger her with questions for which she had no answer. Katarina consoled her when she was troubled, reminding Anja that her concern about Olivia would make cause for nerves to be as fragile as crystal, and when her thoughts could not be placed together, Katarina was there to remind Anja of what were her thoughts. Anja felt blessed that Katarina was there to be by her side, except upon waking.

It was only then that Anja remembered what Katarina had said about the child. Flashes of memory floated through Anja's mind, but she could not place these pieces of her life. Yesterday, was this? Or had she merely dreamed this? Again, Anja could not have clear knowledge, but in these memories, Katarina was there, always by her side. She knew something was not as it should be, but what, she could not say.

After the evening meal Olivia had taken to playing the pianoforte and then retiring for the night, but she did not go to her room; she went to the Chapel of Our Lady. Father Adolphus was not there to attend to the candles of prayer. Each morn Olivia and Margarette refreshed the candles, and every eve Olivia alone did as well. She would sit and allow her thoughts to come as they did. Although she had been near alone for most of her life, she never felt more alone than she did here at the castle.

Olivia could feel the loathing and suspicion of the serene highness, but for what infraction she could not guess. This had started before the countess had come, but had taken on a fever pitch just a month previous. Olivia attempted to distance herself from the serene highness, so as not to cause her concern, but the serene highness did have concern. Was it not on everyone's lips? What was the concern of the serene highness? Olivia knew it was not she.

Thorne had much concern as well. Of this Olivia thought often. She could do nothing to help Thorne; it was not her family or her home—it was not her concern. But Olivia kept a prayer candle for Thorne lit; it was all she could do to help his concern. Olivia was sure that Katarina had come to claim Thorne as her own again. The serene highness was not of herself, and her father still wanted Thorne's head for her death. Was that not enough to keep one's thoughts swirling?

Christmastide was just days away, and Olivia did not expect to have a response from her letters during the holy season.

There were precious few months before Eastertide, an even higher holy season, and she would have no replies until after then. If she had to wait that long, she would have been at the castle for nigh a year.

Many had been eager to fill Olivia's ears with the story of the countess and Thorne, telling her that they had been very close not too long ago. Katarina had lived here at the castle for over two years. Everyone had expected the two to marry, but just after the engagement of Auria, Katarina packed and left. Thorne did not seem pleased with Katarina's presence at the castle now. Mayhaps he did not want to be near her while she was in mourning. Katarina could not wed at least until her year of mourning was complete—and too quickly after her year would be scandalous—but Olivia had doubt that Katarina had concern about scandalous behavior.

Katarina had watched as Thorne watched Olivia play the pianoforte. It did not increase her humor that Olivia played well; moreover, it made her humor darker. Thorne gazed upon Olivia with eyes full of tenderness and regard. He had never gazed upon her with those eyes. Thorne had only fancied her skill with her body. It would not serve Katarina's plan if Thorne was in love with the princess. The serene highness had suggested that Thorne and Olivia had love for each other; the serene highness had witnessed it.

Nineteen

Katarina's family had been very wealthy, thanks to her father's success in business. He died when Katarina was twelve, and it was said that he died of an unspeakable disease. Her mother had no skill to handle her father's business affairs, and soon more money flowed out than flowed into the family. Lukas tried his hand at the business, and it suffered even more. Their mother died of the same detestable disease, though Katarina and Lukas had been able to keep the cause of their deaths quiet. It was just two years after their parents' death that the two orphaned children knew they must find their means elsewhere. They would marry means.

Katarina had no concern about marrying Thorne for money; she found him quite agreeable as well. He required little of her and allowed her unrestrained freedom. He was generous with his money and gracious of nature. If Lukas was unable to find means, then Katarina would be able to support them both. When Thorne had delayed any thought of marriage, Katarina was more insulted than heartbroken. Finding and marrying Maximillian had been without strain, as had been getting rid of him, but Katarina was not willing to wait to marry again until his wealth was spent. She was not decreasing in age.

Thorne could not sleep as he wrestled with the decision of whether to go through with Johann's plan. He feared not only for Matthias, but for all the others involved. He had already spoken with Chance to glean his thoughts—it was good to have his brother to turn to—but Thorne could not forget Margarette and the children. Chance was in favor of the plan, so Thorne headed to the Chapel of Our Lady. He had not been there since Auria left, but tonight he had need.

She felt him enter the chapel, though his tread made no noise on the stone. Olivia wanted to turn but dared not to make the invitation; she needed to keep Thorne at a distance. Thorne had other thoughts on the subject. He walked to the small front pew and seated himself next to Olivia. Reaching over, he took Olivia's hand from her lap, threaded his fingers through hers, and placed their entwined hands on his thigh. Neither spoke nor looked at each other, but Olivia could feel pain and concern flow from Thorne through her hand, to her heart. She gave direction to her heart to send calm reassurance back to Thorne.

They sat as such for a time that was counted in hours, not minutes. At some point Olivia could feel the pain and concern stop flowing from Thorne, replaced by peace instead. He had left everything behind. The two sat in each other's presence—a slice of her life that Olivia would treasure for all her days—but this time could not last, no matter how much either of them willed it.

"I leave with the sun," he said.

"You will be gone for the start of Christmastide."

"I may well be gone for the full twelve days of Christmastide. I ask for your graciousness and hear my plea."

Olivia looked at Thorne. It was not his nature to ask anything of her; he was in the habit of ordering her. Olivia knew his plea would be something she would not want to do, even more so than to stay at the castle and not be on her way.

"What do you ask?"

"Watch over the serene highness as Margarette will be charged to do as well."

"I distress her."

"Olivia, something truly distresses her, but it is not you. Something is very wrong, although I know not what it could be. I need someone in whom I have full faith to watch over her. There is no one that I trust more than you."

Olivia gave a light laugh. "Tell Janos how much you trust me as he watches my every move this night. I think he would say you have no trust in me."

"You are wrong. Trusting you and knowing your thoughts are not the same. Will you do this for me?"

"Yes, but I have doubt that the countess will allow me or Margarette anywhere near the serene highness."

"Have no trust for Katarina. And she has no authority at the castle. I have made it known that you have full authority, except to leave. The servants will be on your side as Margarette will be as well."

"Your brother goes with you?"

"Yes."

"If my father comes to the castle?"

"Janos and Niklas have been instructed what to do. You will be hidden and safe. But I have doubt your father will do such during the holy season."

"You believe my divorced father will adhere to the precepts of the church?" Olivia did not have as much faith in her father as Thorne, but in truth, Thorne knew her father better than she did.

"Your father, without doubt, is at court. His men will find no kindness if they come here without him. They would be slaughtered at the gates, just as the Turks would be. This castle may not seem the fortress your father's castle is, but the village has many eyes and many hands bearing blades. Should your father leave court to come here during the holy season, it would be noticed. It would be noticed by the archduchess. You need not concern yourself."

"I have no concern for myself, but ... the little ones ..."

"Peter? And Thomas?"

In answer, Olivia could only nod. Her life was nothing, but their lives were valuable to many. "And Margarette and the serene highness."

"There is a plan for all, especially Peter and Thomas."

"The serene highness believes I am with child." Olivia had not meant to say those words to anyone, least of all to Thorne.

"I spoke with her at first light this morn on this subject. I assured her that you are a woman of complete purity, and I would not tolerate words against you by anyone, even her."

"I will do as you ask, Thorne. Will you be safe?" Olivia knew she should not ask, but she could not stop the words spilling from her lips.

Thorne did not answer. Instead, he stood and pulled Olivia to her feet, took her into his arms, and kissed her, slowly, gently. It was a kiss of love, and it could be their last. "Off to rest," Thorne whispered as he held her one last moment.

Olivia left the chapel and headed for her room, tears streaming from her eyes. It was so much easier to keep Thorne at a distance when she could glance over and know that he was well. She would have concern with him gone, but she would not allow him to see her cry. His concern was enough; she would not burden him further. Janos, as usual, followed at a respectable distance. Olivia was sure he had thoughts about her shameless meeting with Thorne and then their kiss. Olivia could not have known that Janos's thoughts were the exact opposite.

Up and ready for the day before the sun rose, Olivia went to the windows of the drawing room to see Thorne off, catching a glimpse of Chance, Thorne, and several others mounting up. Margarette appeared at her side and placed her arm around Olivia's waist, pulling her close. The two women stood side by side and watched the men they loved ride away.

"All will be well. We have each other," Margarette told Olivia.

Lukas and Sebastian also departed, heading to Bohemia to spend Christmastide with relatives of Sebastian. Olivia could not say in good conscience that she was poor in spirit to see them leave. She felt like a mother duck with all her ducklings—

Niklas, Lukas, and Sebastian—following her about. Olivia had hoped the countess would travel with them as well, but she also knew that the countess could not be out during her mourning. In truth, Olivia was of the mind that if the countess could come to this castle, would it be of difference if she went to another?

Olivia had come to understand how difficult it was for Margarette to have her mother-in-law—to whom she had been close—now reject her and replace her with Katarina. But Olivia also knew that now that Margarette had come to know her, the shy woman really enjoyed Olivia's company. Olivia was without doubt that they could be strong allies.

"It will be well," Olivia said with conviction.

The two women made plans to stay where they could observe the serene highness as closely as possible and as much as possible. At mid-morning Olivia suggested that they take the children to see the serene highness in her rooms. Usually no one dared disturb the serene highness there, but Olivia wanted to gauge the woman's state early in the day, and the children would be put to nap after luncheon to prepare for the midnight Christmas Eve Mass. Olivia had little belief that the nap would keep the children awake during the Mass; she would hold Peter as she stood, knelt, and sat during the service.

The serene highness was surprised to see the women and children, but obvious delight shone on her face as well. "I was just thinking of these small ones."

She invited the group into her apartment, where Olivia had never been. It was richly decorated but comfortable as the rest of the castle. Olivia noted that the door to her deceased husband's rooms was open and wondered if she still cried at the loss of her love so many long years ago. The sitting room was large, with plenty of room for little Peter to toddle about and play with the wooden farm animals that one of the servants brought from his room.

The serene highness was of completely normal countenance as she held Thomas and talked to Peter as he played. She seemed delighted to see Margarette and her attitude towards Olivia was the warmest that Olivia had known. The ladies visited until shortly before the midday meal, when Margarette excused herself to nurse Thomas and Olivia took Peter to be fed before freshening up herself. Olivia knew not what had changed the serene highness, but she was this morn as she was when Olivia had come to the castle.

During the meal, Olivia spent time thinking about the change in the serene highness who had become cold to Olivia after Thorne was shot and then colder yet after they returned from the hunting camp. Olivia thought this was because the serene highness felt that she and Thorne had not been properly chaperoned and blamed this on Olivia, but the serene highness was not loathing towards Olivia; this had just started of late. Olivia had thought of the numbers. Had she gotten with child at the hunting camp, this would be known by now as any weight gain would be easily noticed on Olivia's unfashionably slim frame.

The strange behavior of the serene highness had just started in the late fall. When she and Thorne had arrived at the castle with the man acting as the Dark Horse, the serene highness was her usual self. Her odd countenance had started after Katarina's appearance. Although Olivia made all attempt to see this another way, the change had come then. The logical question would be, did Katarina have anything to do with the change in the serene highness, or was this merely coincidental?

Olivia and Margarette spent the afternoon with the serene highness and the countess in the drawing room, the serene highness, Olivia, and Margarette stitching while the countess talked. The serene highness complimented Olivia on her beautiful stitching for the chairs, and she inquired about what Olivia was currently working on. Olivia showed her the floral scene that would become a cover for a footstool in her room and which would match the furnishings in her room.

The topic of covering chairs was explored in depth. Margarette was interested in learning, and Olivia offered to instruct her when the stitching was complete and the footstool ready to be covered. Margarette asked Olivia how it was that she had learned to do such, and Olivia explained that she enjoyed learning all manner of things. The serene highness looked at Olivia intently and opened her mouth for a word; this was an opportunity for Anja to truly get to know Olivia. She looked at Katarina, closed her mouth, and turned away; her interest would encourage more questions from Katarina.

Katarina found the discussion between the two young princesses blasé and wished that she was at court. Without doubt, there would be balls and parties each day of the Christmastide, but she had no choice but to be here, listening to prattle about stitching and recovering furniture. Would it not be of more ease just to have new furniture made? Thorne could well afford to bring craftsman from Vienna to build new furniture, but here was Olivia suggesting that the gardeners make Margarette a footstool as well. Olivia was truly provincial and would never be accepted at court—mayhaps in the stables of the archduchess, but certainly not among the gentry.

Anja felt wonderful, and like herself. It had been so good to spend the morn with her grandchildren. She was so very fond of them and wished the boys were here in the drawing room now. Thorne had spoken to her about what he had heard, that some questioned if Olivia was with child. He had not suggested it was his own mother that had spoken such, but Anja knew that Thorne was aware it had been her. Thorne aptly pointed out to his mother that had Olivia been such, her condition would be made known. And although Thorne admitted to his mother that he had not always lived the life of a monk, he had not known Olivia in a biblical way. Olivia was a woman of integrity.

Anja saw the passion on her son's face as he spoke of the princess. He did love Olivia, and just as she had chosen her own husband, she had allowed her children to choose as well, though Anja never thought they would choose someone she did not take to immediately. In truth, had she ever really gotten to know Olivia? Anja's heart was filled with sorrow. How must this poor girl feel when her own father treated her as though she was some sort of rabid dog? Anja vowed she would look at Olivia with new eyes. She would ask for forgiveness for the lack of graciousness she had shown her, and she would accept Olivia as readily as she accepted Margarette to her family.

It also did not escape Anja's notice that Olivia and Margarette were getting along so very well. Margarette was such a shy girl and did not take to others easily, but she fairly glowed as she talked with Olivia. Anja was happy that Margarette had found someone to whom she could be close now that Auria was gone, and the two young princesses laughed and talked so easily. Anja also remembered what Katarina had said concerning Olivia being with child. The thought haunted Anja, and Anja took that as a sign from God. She must remember the heart, black as night, that had suggested hurting a child.

Katarina had offered to get Anja a goblet of watered wine several times during the afternoon, but Anja had refused and poured her own. Anja thought it odd that Katarina would offer this errand so often, but Anja was having such a glorious day she had no other thought on the matter. After the evening meal, Olivia played the pianoforte, and the ladies sang Christmas hymns. Candles glowed all over the room, and pine needles burned in the fireplace. Although Anja, Margarette, and Olivia missed Thorne and Chance greatly, it was a gay and happy eve to celebrate the birth of the Lord.

At midnight they went to the double chapel, where candles burned on every available surface as well. Everyone from the town had come, nearly filling the chapel. The Mass was very beautiful—majestic but gay, not Father Adolphus' normal solemn service. Margarette and the serene highness took turns holding baby Thomas, and Olivia had Peter firmly in her arms, his little arms around her neck. Anja noticed Olivia occasionally give the child a gentle kiss on the forehead.

Olivia and Margarette directed the servants in the placement of the food in the ballroom. All the servants were helping with the meal; no beds would be made this morn, no carpets beaten, and no floors scrubbed. All manner of meats had been roasting on spits since early morn, and vegetables, potatoes, and pies were cooking and baking in both the outside and inside kitchens. The crowd would be smaller than it had been for the wedding, so fewer people from the town had been brought in to assist with the preparations. The castle would be hosting the people of the town for a joyous Christmas feast.

Anja watched over her grandchildren as Olivia and Margarette handled the preparations for the feast. Olivia was especially good with the servants. She knew them all by name and complimented their efforts, and the servants seemed eager to please her. This day it did not bother Anja; she saw that Olivia truly was gifted with running a household. It was not the way that Anja had been taught, but it was very pleasing. Anja felt so healthy and so much as herself again today; mayhaps what had been the plaque to her health had passed.

Katarina did not emerge from her room until the midday meal and seemed surprised that the three ladies had been down since early morn and working so hard to prepare for the guests. The boys had been taken to their rooms for napping, and the ladies retired to their rooms to change their clothing; the townspeople would start to arrive in less than an hour. As the first guests climbed the steps to the massive front doors, the four ladies were there to greet them and to hand wrappings to the older children of the household servants to be taken to the large dining room.

Twenty

livia played Christmas hymns on the pianoforte for the guests as the serene highness went table to table, talking to all the families. It was obvious to Olivia that the serene highness was well adored among the people of the town. Margarette handed out the small scrap bags with a bottle of wine from the castle's vineyard for the men and a small sachet bag made by Olivia and Margarette for the women.

After the meal, the children ran all over the room, chasing one another, so Margarette and Olivia rounded them up for games. Anja watched as Olivia lead the games, many of which were Olivia's own creation. Small fabric bags filled with sweets were given to the winners ... and to the cleverest, and the tallest, and the youngest, and so forth until every child had miraculously won a bag of sweets.

All the food was consumed, and as the sun started to slip from the sky, families gathered their children and wraps, preparing to go home to their warm beds. The children all had a wonderful time, and all the guests expressed their thanks to Olivia and Margarette, as well as to the serene highness.

The dishes were gathered and scraped and placed in large barrels of water to soak to be cleaned properly in the morn. All the ladies were tired and chose to retire early, though Olivia headed to the chapel as was her usual practice. She would not let her prayer candle for Thorne—nor his for Auria—to extinguish. She stopped and knelt to pray for a minute. She had no knowledge of where Thorne was nor what he was doing, but her heart ached for him more than usual. She prayed for his and all the men's safety and success.

Finally, she headed towards her room. As she approached the door, Janos came to walk level with her. "This Christmastide feast was the best the town has ever known. Thank you and blessed be to you."

Olivia was shocked that this usually quiet, slightly crotchety man had spoken to her and, moreover, was giving her praise. "It is the serene highness you should thank, not me."

"The serene highness has not been well as of late—every eye can see that—although today she seemed as always. Niklas spoke of the time you and Princess Margarette put in planning this celebration. It has great meaning to the people of the town. The Christmastide and Eastertide feasts are greatly anticipated. Mayhaps you are of thought that their words of thanks were mere politeness, but their words are heartfelt." Janos looked down, seeming to struggle with himself, then after a great sigh he continued. "I guard you so that you will not try to escape, but there are many that feel you belong here, at the castle and with the prince. Mayhaps you could have thoughts to change your future plans and stay here. This is meant to be your home."

Standing outside her door, Olivia placed one of her hands on his hand for just a moment. "Thank you for your kind words. I will give thought to what you ask." Olivia turned and went into her room.

Would it be possible? Could she stay here and have a life with Thorne? Olivia would not allow herself to answer that question; it would make her weak and her will faint. The only decision she would make this night was to go to bed, which she did, dreaming of Thorne as she did every night that she remembered her dreams. This night her dream of Thorne was so vivid that she felt she could reach out and touch him, dreaming what her heart cried out for.

The day after Christmas started as the previous two for Anja; she felt well, and she felt herself, though it did not last as it had the previous two days. Shortly after the midday meal, her thoughts became a swirl in her head, and she felt so jittery inside. In truth, the jitters were not just inside her; her hands were shaking ... and Anja was afraid—of what, she could not say.

She had thoughts that, she knew, were important to keep, but she could not bring them to mind. Those thoughts would keep her safe, but still they alluded her. Katarina was at her side, and Olivia and Margarette were in the drawing room as well.

It was Olivia who noticed the difference first. She walked over to the serene highness's chair and knelt next to it so that her face was nearly level with the older princess's. Olivia placed her hand over the serene highness's tightly clenched hands. Despite her attempt to keep her hands from trembling so, Anja could not control the jittering. Olivia could feel the violence of the shaking, and she feared for the serene highness.

"Serene Highness, are you well?"

When Anja looked to the young woman, Olivia saw pure fear on her face. Speaking calmly to the serene highness, Olivia told her that she and Margarette would not leave her, and they would keep her safe. Anja searched the young princess's face. She could not make sense of her words, but she remembered Thorne had spoken of Olivia, though she could not think what her son had said. Margarette came and knelt down as Olivia had on the opposite side of Anja's chair.

"Let her be! Do you not see how you distress her?" Katarina stood in front of the serene highness, facing Olivia's back.

"Please, do not be harsh. Keep your tone of peace. She

needs not another concern," Olivia replied. Anja's body had gone rigid with the anger of Katarina's words and tone.

"Her only concern is you. She loathes you and does not want you in her house any longer. If you have any concern for her, you will leave this house this very day!" Katarina's voice had risen so that she was fairly yelling at Olivia.

Olivia kept her voice calm and light. She knew not how much the serene highness understood of the words, but Olivia could see and feel her reaction to the loud, enraged tones. "I will ask again that you have a mind of the serene highness. You may speak at a normal or quiet volume, and you must not have anger in your voice. Otherwise, I must ask you to go to your room."

Margarette looked at Olivia, amazed by her boldness, but she was of Olivia's mind completely. She would gladly drag the countess out of the room if the need arose.

"How dare you order me about! This is not your home. I am not your servant. It is you that needs to leave. You distress the serene highness. I know Thorne would never allow this!"

Olivia stood. The countess had the greater weight, but Olivia had the regal bearing the countess lacked. Olivia had thought of what was coming, but gave the countess the benefit of graciousness that she would be a lady. This was not to be.

The countess raised both her arms and shoved Olivia with all her anger, the force taking Olivia off her feet, and she found the floor several feet away from where she had been.

Niklas moved across the floor at a speed that shocked even Olivia. Placing himself in front of the countess, with one hand on his blade, he said in a quiet but threatening voice, "Touch the princess not."

The serene highness jumped from her seat and ran from the room with Margarette but a step behind. Olivia picked herself off the floor and turned to face her attacker. Several servants had come at the sound of the commotion.

"I have no wish to have any disagreement with any of the serene highness's guests. We must be of one mind—what is best for the serene highness. I choose to believe that in your concern you mayhaps have forgotten what it is to be a lady, but this will not happen again, lest you will be placed, by word or by hand, in your room until the serene highness has recovered from what ails her." Olivia walked from the room without looking back, her thoughts only on the serene highness.

Margarette and Olivia stayed with the serene highness for the remainder of the day in her private rooms until by evening she was feeling more herself. She wished to remain in her rooms for the evening meal and until it was time to retire to bed. Olivia offered to stay with her through the night, but Anja refused. The serene highness did consent to have her personal maid stay with her, and Olivia instructed the maid to send for her if need be.

It was time to finish the fragrances as the mixtures had been cooked and soaked for several days. Olivia and Margarette had spent much time making the fragrance for Margarette. Olivia felt it should be of roses, but not like the rose water she used now, which was not unpleasant, but it did not speak to Margarette. It was a fragrance that would suit any woman. Olivia always thought of her personal mixture as clean sunshine, but the one for Margarette would be the regal, alluring rose.

As Olivia strained the flowers from the mixture and prepared to pour it into the glass bottles, Margarette plucked a berry from a bowl and prepared to eat it.

"No, Margarette!" Olivia's voice was loud and harsh, and Margarette stopped without thought for the alarm in Olivia's voice.

"That is poisonous." Olivia put the mixture down and grabbed the berry from Margarette's hand. "One berry can kill you."

Margarette had gone white as snow. "Why would you have such?"

"It was not the berry I wanted; it was the leaves. I did not wish to throw these where a horse may try to eat them. I was waiting until the snow was not as great to throw them in the forest."

"Oh dearest Lord, Olivia! Poison! That is the concern! Poison!" Margarette had grabbed Olivia by the shoulders and was trying to tell her something of great importance, but what it was, Olivia did not know.

"Margarette, of what do you speak? I understand not."

"Poison, she is being poisoned!"

The same epiphany came to Olivia. "The serene highness."

"Yes." Margarette needed so much more knowledge. "Is it possible? Is there a poison that can make her tremble inside and muddle her thoughts?"

"I know not of one plant that would do such."

"A mixture."

"I will need to look at my book very carefully and talk to Elena. We must watch the serene highness every moment. But who would do this?" As the words left Olivia's mouth, both women thought of the same person. "But why?" Olivia spoke the words so quietly that she barely heard them herself.

"I know not, but we must find out. And we must save the serene highness," Margarette replied.

Olivia spoke with Elena. A maid must be with the serene highness at all times, day and night. The maid was to make a writing of everything the serene highness had to eat and drink and who had touched the food and drink. The maid was also to note who the serene highness was with at all times, and most importantly, what was the state of the serene highness. If Olivia was not with the serene highness, she was to be summoned if there was a concern. Only the cook or Elena was to touch the food taken to the serene highness.

Olivia had no doubt that the servants would think her mad; her measures to keep the serene highness safe were beyond reason after all. In her mind, though, she saw Margarette with the berry in her hand. One could die ingesting very little poison, if it was the right poison. Olivia had never had much instruction of poisons; she was only instructed on what to avoid. She had some notes in her book concerning what part of what plants were poisonous, but little about the precise action the poison would have upon the body.

Elena knew more than Olivia about poisons, although not a great measure. She had a book similar to Olivia's that Elena's mother had made, and Elena's mother had much knowledge of poisons. Olivia sat in Elena's room reading the book and writing herself notes in a language only she could understand. She studied the book all the morn and all the afternoon. By the evening meal, she had some idea of what the serene highness had been given.

Margarette had spent most of the day with the serene highness while Olivia studied Elena's mother's book. It was a good day for the serene highness; she was of herself, playing with Peter and Thomas in the drawing room after the midday meal. Nothing had been spoken to the serene highness concerning the words exchanged between Katarina and Olivia the day before, and the serene highness did not show a memory of it. Katarina offered to get the older and the younger princess a glass of watered wine, but Margarette refused to allow Katarina to serve the serene highness.

Olivia had thought it best not to tell the serene highness that there was thought of her being poisoned. Margarette had told the serene highness that there was thought that mayhaps she was having a reaction to a food combination or food and drink combination. The words sounded like gibberish in Margarette's ears, but the serene highness seemed to consider the idea. Katarina stated that she had never heard of such and thought it was madness even to suggest it.

As Anja prepared for bed, she thought over the day. Margarette thought that she was being poisoned; of that Anja had no doubt. Her mind first went to Olivia, who had knowledge of plants, roots, herbs, and healing. Olivia must be the one poisoning her ... but she knew in her heart that her thought was not true. Anja told her maid to go to bed for the night, but the maid informed the serene highness that she was to stay with her all night.

As the sun rose, Anja summoned Margarette to her room. Why must a maid stay with her at all times? Margarette told Anja of the measures that Olivia had placed to watch Anja's health. As the morn turned to midday, Anja sat alone in her room, save for her maid, and she thought on what Margarette had told her. Anja's mind gave her the knowledge that Margarette had not. Olivia was not poisoning her; Olivia was trying to save her, but from whom did she need saved? Anja remembered what Katarina had said about the child.

Had this not been a serious concern, Thorne might have enjoyed the sport of the activities. He traveled from town to town, drinking at local inns, getting drunk, starting fights, insulting fellow travelers, being a spectacle for all to see. Chance was doing the same in other towns, but known as Thorne and not himself. In truth, the men with whom he fought were Stephan or a relative of Stephan, and the travelers Chance insulted were Akos or a relative of Stephan. Also in truth, Thorne was not drunk. He wore more liquor on his clothing than he consumed.

Thorne did not hope that his actions would be reported to the prince; he made sure his actions were carried to court, even when his actions were performed by Chance. One would have to believe that Thorne was on a destructive path crisscrossing the empire and embarrassing his mother. At the same time, Bishop Baltier was making inquiries about the recent crimes of the Dark Horse.

Christmastide had come and now was just a week past. Johann had been of the belief that Bishop Baltier should start the search close to Galatia where the word had started about the dead princess, but there was no knowledge to be gleaned. Matthias could not hear or feel a hint of deception from the priests that denied knowledge of the dead girl. Matthias had impressed upon the priests that the matter must be held in confidence; the Holy See had no desire to have the church held in question. Could the Holy See not have control over the angel? Was the Dark Horse truly an angel? Or mayhaps a demon? Was the Holy See allowing this demon to run amuck about the empire?

Johann took the failure of the plan upon his own shoulders. Their search widened into other counties and duchies, but still they could find no word of the dead girl. Cemeteries across the empire were searched for new graves or crypts that had been recently opened, but nothing was found. The thought that all had been a deception crept into the minds of all the men on the mission, but Johann refused to believe it was a deception. Christmastide was over, and the prince would soon come for Thorne.

Twenty One

For a fortnight all was well with the serene highness, but then the bewilderment, anxiety, and fear returned to her. One afternoon Margarette had it as well, and a few days later, several of the servants were the same. Olivia was bewildered. Was this an illness that moved from one to another? No, her heart told her that it was poison, but where was the poison? How could one person be poisoned one day and a different one the following day? Olivia had to find what was contaminated.

Having tossed and turned through the night for her concern about the health of the castle, Olivia was up and dressing for the day as the sun rose. Her mind running in one hundred directions at once, she reached for the scarf on the dresser and toppled the bottle of her fragrance that she and Margarette had just bottled. At morning prayer, Olivia confided in Margarette what she had done to the fragrance bottle in her mindless haste, and after prayer Margarette and Olivia headed to the cellar to fetch another.

As she retrieved a bottle from the shelf, Olivia realized

that the shelf behind the bottles was empty. "Margarette, did you move the bowl of berries?"

"Berries? Oh, that bowl of berries. No, I have not been here since we bottled the fragrances."

"The bowl is missing." Olivia started to remove everything from the shelf. "I had fear that another would eat the berries as you tried to do, so I hid it behind the bottles of my fragrance. I know this is just where I put it."

Margarette could see the panic on Olivia's face. "Mayhaps Elena or someone from the kitchen moved the bowl."

Olivia gathered her skirts in her hands and fairly ran up the stairs. Elena was in the kitchen, as she often was, along with the cook and three other women who were part of the kitchen staff. Olivia's distress was clear to all as she entered the room. Margarette was close behind and nearly ran into Olivia as she came to an abrupt stop.

"There was a bowl of mistletoe berries down in the cellar, high on the shelf, behind some bottles. Has anyone moved the bowl?"

"Olivia, mistletoe berries are poisonous!" Elena could not believe that Olivia would not have this knowledge.

"I am aware. I use a small amount of the leaf in a mixture for rheumatism. I had not the time before the snows to discard the berries properly, but the bowl of berries is gone. Has it been taken by any of you?"

All looked to Olivia, appearing perplexed. Olivia knew the answer would not be found here.

Thorne, Chance, Akos, and Johann waited in the burned-out estate home for Matthias and Stephan to return. Their mission to find out about the body of the dead girl had been completely fruitless. Matthias's family members had returned to the village, but Thorne worried that the prince was watching the castle, awaiting his return home.

Stephan rode out alone. Thorne and Chance would circle about, coming in from the other directions. New snow had fallen during the day, and the horse stepped slowly as the white powder came past its knees. Clouds floated over the slivered moon, but the snow was made bright by what little light came from the sky. When he was a few miles out from the castle, Stephan dismounted and proceeded on his own. He let the reins down, not tethering the horse should he have need.

It was in the first hours of the morn when Stephan came across the men huddled together under the large pine, their snores masking his approach. They had not attempted to hide their tracks, and another group of four or five had branched off from this one; Stephan would deal with them next. His blade cut through the leather as a hot knife through cheese, and the horses slowly started to roam as they wished; they would soon be gone. He then placed two of the rabbits he had taken on his way into their camp near the sleeping men. He could smell the blood of the rabbits, and soon the wolves would too.

Thorne was angry. The castle was surrounded, even though the prince was well aware that Thorne was not there. Thorne felt that the presence of so many men proved the prince was more than watching for him; the prince was preparing to invade. Had they not dispatched group after group of his men as they went from town to town? Chance had done the same, but Chance enjoyed a good fight more than Thorne ever had. Few of the men had actually been killed—only the few that were very foolish—but the prince's men had been willing to fight to the death. The purse must be very high. Most, if not all the men would not be ready to fight again soon. It would take much time for their bones to heal.

He was of the mind to storm the group and slit the necks of every man, but he would stick to Stephan's plan; he would show the prince that their strength was in more than numbers. The huntsman was a master at the game of hunter and prey. Taking first the frozen fish from the leather bag and then the rope, Thorne strung a fish every foot. Thorne slit open the belly of each fish as he threaded the fish on the rope, then slowly lowered the rope over the side of the rock ledge. He heard no stirring from the men below, but the smell of the fish would wake the bear in the cave and bring her out of hibernation. Too bad the prince's men knew not where the nine-foot-tall brown bear had spent the last two winters. Mayhaps they would have chosen a different spot to sleep this night.

Chance had fashioned the arrows before getting into position, and the quiver was full. From his bag, he pulled the dry pine needles wrapped in a scrap and placed them on the dry, flat rock. He then pulled out the flint and blade. He had come here first because the top of this hill afforded full view of the back of the castle. Only a fool would not choose to survey from under the long branches of the tall pine, and only a fool would choose to survey from the most obvious site. With the fire lit, Chance pulled the arrows from the quiver quickly, loading each one before lighting the cloth wrapped on the shaft. His aim was true, into the bed of pine needles. When the quiver was empty, he rose to leave. It was not necessary to look and gauge the success of his arrows; he could hear the screams.

The wooden platforms could not be seen by looking up the mountain, and Thorne and Chance were struggling for their breaths as they ran. It was not the air at the top of this mountain that was truly to blame; their bodies had a lifetime of mountain air. It was the three-hour run to reach the platforms before the sun rose. It was Thorne's idea to build the platforms, and many scoffed at the ideas of the twelve-year-old prince. To Thorne it was readily apparent why the platforms should be built; he could not understand the questions of others. The scoffers had been silenced quickly as Thorne's plan proved to solve a problem that had plagued the castle for decades.

If the wood had voice, it would be groaning with the burden of the snow. It was customary to refresh the platforms after every fall of snow, but Thorne had ordered them not to be touched. He had further ordered that they be girded for a time such as this. None of the platforms had given way; the two camps of men below would receive the full measure of snow. Only the top platform needed to be released; its weight would release the three. By the time the avalanche reached the men, much more snow would be added to the snow of the platforms.

It was possible to survive such an avalanche—both Thorne and Chance had done such—but they had been in-structed by their father. It was Thorne's belief that the prince's top men were in these two camps, which gave the closest view of what transpired on the castle grounds. It was even possible that the prince himself was there. The surrounding springs afforded fresh water, the access was restricted, and abundant sheltering areas made this area the most comfortable. The avalanche would not harm the castle; the planned, controlled avalanches protected the castle. The snow would be deposited into the man-made lake at the base of the mountain.

With the festivities of Christmastide over, the prince attended to business at the court. There was pride to be stroked, characters to mold, and attitudes to be refined. There were cabinet gatherings to attend in which endless prattle about social change and thoughts for the common people spewed forth. The prince was well aware that the nobility had no desire to effect any changes that would make the serving class wiser, richer, or stronger. This was simply a game of the aristocracy—talk of benevolence, talk of compassion, talk, talk, talk.

His mind kept thinking upon the girl that lay in the family crypt. More and more his mind had doubt that the girl was his daughter, but if the girl was not his daughter, why tell him such? The prince loathed the idea that his men would lie to him, but what he feared was the reason they would lie. He had a small group of trusted advisors that had been with him since he assumed the county from his father. These men had been with him through many trials and skirmishes. The prince did not welcome that there was a Judas among them.

But much had not made sense to him. He had been told that the body had been found in Galatia—at the far end of the empire—and his daughter had been at a country estate at the other end of the empire. How would she get that far away? No one at her grandparents' estate could tell him such. He had been told that Thorne took her there for the Dark Horse to kill, but there was no reason for that either.

The prince also had doubts that Thorne would have taken her across the empire. Thorne's problems with the Holy See were not unknown. The Dark Horse was out of control, and the Holy See held Thorne responsible. The duchy of Carinthia had always had a close connection to the Dark Horse; the prince had never been able to reason why. The prince, himself, would like control over the Dark Horse, but the Bishop at the Holy See, the prince's key to the Holy See, had assured the prince that only the Cardinal had say over the Dark Horse. All attempts to sway the Cardinal to the prince's service had failed.

The day was planned for him. Andreas, his advisor that handled his business at court, had secured audiences with those who would serve the prince well, but the prince had no patience for business today. He wanted to see his son. Since the circumstance with his daughter had come about, the prince feared for the life of his son. Andreas had his wife and son well guarded, but the prince still had concern. He sat in a group of about fifteen princes, counts, and barons. He cared little for what they said, and they cared little if he cared. The prince stood, and without courtesies, left the room.

Scheduled to be somewhere every minute, he was not expected home for the day, so the servants were surprised to see him. The prince headed straight to his wife's rooms; his son would be there. The prince was annoyed that no guards stood outside his wife's door, and he vowed to punish the men who were supposed to be guarding his family. Opening the door, he heard his wife laughing and thought she must be playing with their son. When he found her not in the sitting room of her apartment, he continued on into her bedchamber.

Andreas was guarding the prince's wife, naked and on top of her. The prince went to his sleeping son, picked up the child, and left his wife's rooms without a word, the sleeping baby in his arms. The word had spread through the palace that the prince was home, and the guards had returned to their posts.

"Please bring my wife and Andreas, as they are now, to my rooms. Immediately!" The prince continued on to his sitting room.

He called for one of the servants and requested that his son's needs be placed in his rooms. The prince sat down in an overstuffed chair and waited. Soon, his wife and trusted advisor were brought into his rooms in their naked state, firmly under control of the guards. The prince had no need to hurry; he waited as the baby's bed was brought and placed next to his bed, and then he placed his sleeping son in it.

His wife stood naked and sobbing as two guards held her up.

"You will leave my home. Now! I want never to see you again. You will never see your son again."

The prince's wife wailed and sobbed as the guards dragged her down the hall. He would allow her to dress, but other than a cape, she would take nothing with her. He instructed the guards to have a female servant observe his wife dress and make sure that she took no clothing or jewels with her.

"Take Andreas to a prison cell, as he is, and chain him to the wall." The prince saw that the guards were leery of treating this high official as such and was not pleased to see their concern. His house was being taken over from the inside. He had no doubt about that. He would have to prove that he was no fool and that he was still the prince. He had always believed in ruling with an iron fist, and he would do so now.

The prince left his advisor chained to the wall without food or water or clothing for two days. When he went to question him, Andreas was barely conscious. This strong, formidable, commanding leader that had been at the prince's side for so many years had been reduced to a groveling, begging, weeping child. With encouragement, Andreas was ready to tell the prince anything in exchange for his life. Over three days Andreas admitted to all manner of sins against the prince. He had been sleeping with the prince's wife since just days after their marriage and believed that the prince's son was indeed his son. He had slept with the prince's second wife as well. The prince's first wife, Anastasia, had suspected Andreas of stealing from the prince, so Andreas had spoken against her.

It required beating Andreas near to death, but he finally confessed that the body of the girl was not the prince's daughter, relinquishing the name of the family in town from whom he had gotten her. The girl was infected with syphilis, so the family agreed to have the girl strangled for the wage of a year. Andreas knew not where his daughter truly was; in truth, she was missing under mysterious circumstances.

The priest came and gave the prisoner confession and Communion and read the last rites. Still naked and chained, Andreas was loaded into a wagon and taken far outside Vienna into the forest where he was chained to a tree and left. The prince had kept his word; he had not killed Andreas. The prince would allow the wolves, or the bears, or the cold winter wind to kill the Judas.

The prince waited for his other three trusted advisors to come forward and confess their sins. Had they come of their own will, he may have shown them mercy. He had the three chained to the wall in his prison, and all his other men took turns torturing them. Then the prince made it clear to his men that should one deceive him, this torture would rain upon them. His trusted advisors lasted only four days until they were sent to meet Satan.

The wives of the advisors were given to the men to use for their desires. The children of the advisors were sold as servants to the lowest circumstances. A few of the prince's men disappeared over a few nights; they were hunted down and killed slowly. There would be talk of this, but the words would not say that the prince was weak.

At court the prince was aware that words were whispered about his wife's departure. A few asked after Andreas, but the prince gave no reply. The prince knew that the wolves were starting to circle; he had the scent of weakness on him, but he would not let the scheming of others cause his downfall. He would show strength. He would find Thorne and make him pay for escaping his prison. He would take over Carinthia, and he would show that he had the heart of a bear.

Katarina was not pleased with the events of recent. The two princesses had been stuck to the serene highness like a burr to the hem of a dress, and she had been unable to give the serene highness Madam Wu's potion, which was not working as Madam Wu said it would. Katarina had thoughts that mayhaps she was not giving the serene highness the proper amount. Madam Wu had a very heavy accent and was difficult for Katarina to understand. This was not like Maximillian; she had only to give him one dose of that poison.

Katarina was fortunate that Madam Wu would take an audience with her. Although the petite Oriental woman lived in a very expensive mansion, she was known to be extremely temperamental, and no amount of money would change her mind if she asked one to leave or refused to receive one. So Katarina had been afraid to ask the old woman to repeat her instructions and to speak slowly; doing so would have likely resulted in Madam Wu requesting Katarina to leave. Then she would have had nowhere to turn for help except to ask the Dark Horse, and Katarina had heard the Dark Angel would cut out your tongue if the request was unworthy.

It was her mother that had introduced Katarina to Madam Wu. They had gone to the mansion seeking a cure for the syphilis when her father had been diagnosed. Madam Wu informed them that it was too late for the cure; it had to be given just after the disease was contracted. When Katarina's mother was diagnosed, Katarina did not bother to ask Madam Wu; her mother was old and of very little use anymore, now that she had told of all the special potions Madam Wu could make. It was a potion from Madam Wu that Katarina had thoughts of giving Olivia should she be with child. Katarina had seen Madam Wu before leaving Vienna and had gotten the potion for herself, but that had been unnecessary; Katarina was not with child.

Although Thorne had come home, he had not seen Katarina except at the evening meal. From what Katarina could discover from the silly servant girl attending her, the prince had seen his mother twice, he had seen Princess Olivia, and he had met with his brother. He had not come to see Katarina. She had thoughts of going to his rooms during the night, but Princess Olivia had a guard sitting outside her door; the man was always awake and watching, and it appeared that all was being reported to the princess. Whatever Princess Olivia needed to be guarded from had not diminished, but why keep the girl here if someone had want to harm her? Katarina had thoughts to use that argument with Thorne. Why put his family in danger by keeping her here at the castle?

Twenty Two

"He has gone where?" Thorne was obviously agitated at the news as Stephan was sure he would be.

"Johann thinks that the dead girl came from close to the prince's castle. The story that she came from a distance was a ruse." Stephan wished that Johann was here now to handle Thorne; he had much gift for such.

"How could you let him go alone?" Johann's talent lay in thought, not action. Should he have need to protect himself, Johann was the least able to do so.

"A man alone asking questions would not be a concern. It would be less likely that the prince would hear of him."

"We cannot leave him there alone. We must be near should he have need."

Thorne had no desire to leave again soon. They had arrived back at the castle in the last hours before dawn, getting precious few hours of sleep before heading out to make sure that none of the prince's men were still watching the castle. Stephan's plan had worked far better than they had hoped. They had found many dead bodies, but no tracks leading away and no men alive. The snow that fell overnight made it impossible to bring the bodies to the castle, so they buried the dead men in the snow. Beasts would most likely ravage the bodies before they could be retrieved, but there was nothing Thorne could do about that.

He had just met with his mother in her rooms, and she seemed nearly herself, though she seemed bothered. Thorne needed to speak with her alone before he left again. Thorne was not surprised by how much he wanted to see Olivia; he thought of her constantly when he was gone. At the morning meal, he kept stealing looks at her, trying to fill his need for her with the sight of her, but he wanted to hold and kiss her. Thorne knew he could not keep entertaining these thoughts, but he had not found a way to keep his mind from doing such.

"We will leave with the light," Thorne informed Stephan; he had much to do before then.

"Will we take Chance and Akos?"

"I will counsel with them. It will be their decision."

His mother was his first priority, so Thorne headed to

her rooms. She had all her wits about her, but she feared that this illness would come upon her again. Thorne did his best to reassure her, but he could not tell her it would never return; he knew not what it was. He assured his mother that Olivia and Margarette would watch over her and keep her safe for him in his stead. At least his mother was not as resistant to Olivia; mayhaps she was finally beginning to see Olivia for the woman she was.

Next Thorne spoke with Niklas and Janos. Olivia had been behaving; there was no suggestion that she was planning an escape. Of course, with so much snow an escape would be difficult at best, but Thorne knew that he needed to keep a closer eye on her when it seemed least likely for her to escape. Lastly, he went to speak with Olivia. Chance would be talking with Margarette to glean what he could about what had been going on while he was gone.

Olivia was in her room. Thorne knew he should take a chaperone with him, but he could trust no one except Margarette, and Thorne would not intrude on her time with her husband. Thorne knew he needed a chaperone more to keep himself in check than to protect Olivia's honor; he did not doubt that Olivia could protect herself from him; he could never truly hurt her. Thorne knocked upon her door; he would not barge into the room with Niklas there. Olivia answered the door, a surprised look upon her face. Thorne was not sure if she was surprised to see him or surprised that he had knocked.

"A word, Princess."

Olivia started to come out of her room.

"Where ears cannot hear."

Olivia backed up and allowed Thorne to enter. When the door was closed, Thorne said, "My mother seems well."

"I believe she is being poisoned." Olivia saw no reason to pretend other than her true thoughts.

"Poisoned?"

"Yes, it would stand to reason. She would be well and then not, well and then not. Do you know of any illness that would cause such?"

"No." Thorne had the same thought, but he refused to entertain it.

"It was Margarette that reasoned it. We have kept a close eye on her and have watched what she had to eat, but more, to drink."

"Who would do such?" There was only one new to the castle and close to the serene highness, but Thorne could not believe Katarina would do such.

"I will not accuse another without cause. My concern has been with keeping your mother safe."

"I must leave in the morning. I have concern for my mother, but I have comfort that you and Margarette are watching for her. I owe you a debt that I would never be able to repay, even if I gave you all the wealth in this duchy. Think not that I have no thought for all you have done for me and my family, Olivia. I have doubt there is another that would have given so much."

Olivia cocked her head to the side and looked at Thorne with pinched, suspicious eyes. Who was this man, so humble before her? Surely this was some sort of jest or trickery. Mayhaps he thought to get her to admit that she had been planning to run away in the middle of the night, but with the snow as deep as her mid-thigh, escape would not be possible—even Thorne would know such. Mayhaps Thorne was being poisoned as well and the poison caused him to be thoughtful and kind to her.

Thorne saw the look of disbelief on Olivia's face and knew he had not been as kind and thankful to her as he should have been in the past. Even now he could not find the words to tell her how grateful he was to her. He would have been mad with worry for his mother whilst he was gone, but he knew

Olivia would give her own life to save the serene highness. Thorne knew none other, save Johann and Stephan, that would do such. Although the serene highness had not treated Olivia as she should, she readily agreed to protect the serene highness without question.

With no conscious thought, he found himself closing the distance between them and gently taking Olivia into his arms. Looking at her face, he realized his dreams could not conjure her true beauty; even now he could not believe that a mortal was created so perfectly. He wanted to burn every detail of her face into his mind. Slowly his head dipped to kiss her, but he stopped just short of her lips, waiting for her invitation. As she closed her eyes and lifted her face towards his, Thorne gently captured her lips with his.

It was not a hungry kiss, though he had a great hunger for her, but the kiss of a lover of the heart. It was a kiss that told her all the words he could not say. It was a kiss that filled his soul with her; on the cold, worrisome nights this kiss would see him through. It was a kiss that would put his heart to peace should he lose his life before he returned to her. It was the kiss that he dreamed of every night and ached for every waking hour. It was what Thorne needed more than air to breathe, water to drink, or food to eat.

Olivia allowed her hands to slowly slide up his arms,

feeling his strong muscles. Should the Lord take away her sight, her smell, her ears tomorrow, she would know Thorne by the feel of him. Her hands slowly swam through his hair on the collar of his shirt. His hair was as he was—strong, thick, but soft to her hands. Olivia did not make any attempt to stop Thorne; her need for him matched his for her, though she did not know how much she needed to hold him and to feel him and to taste him. In his arms she felt whole, she felt renewed, she felt she could face whatever she had need to endure.

They spent too much time in each other's arms; they should not be alone together this long, and both pulled away as the concern came to them. Thorne stole one last, light kiss before moving away. He tried to make his countenance as it would usually be, but he could not pull his soul from such peacefulness. All would see that he was not himself, all would know why, and Thorne felt guilty for allowing all to know that Olivia had kissed him. It was not his nature to have such thoughts—he cared not what others thought, except where Olivia was concerned.

Thorne met with Chance, who knew at once that this was not the brother he had always known. He recognized the signs; he had once been the man his brother was now, a man wrestling with his heart, but Chance had allowed his heart to win. Thorne could not—not yet. Both brothers had concern about leaving their mother so soon. Margarette was also of the thought that the serene highness was being poisoned. Chance was willing to believe Katarina would do such, but Thorne was not ready to admit to that. Chance was of the thought that he should stay behind with their mother. Thorne agreed that it would be best, but he wanted his brother with him—for what reason, he could not say.

At first light, as Thorne and Stephan prepared to leave, Olivia stood alone at the window. As Stephan mounted, Thorne looked up. He could not see her, but he knew she was there. He gave a final wave and mounted his horse, even while his mount gained speed to keep up with Stephan's. Olivia headed for the Chapel of Our Lady; she would refresh the candles alone this morning. She had told Margarette to spend the time with her husband and promised to give a silent voice to Margarette's prayers as well.

After visiting the chapel, Olivia went to her room and started to make the small roses that would embellish the wedding dress of Pia's sister. Pia wanted to make them herself, but her swollen joints and gnarled fingers would not allow her to fashion the delicate flowers. The balm that Olivia had given her helped greatly with the pain and swelling, but Pia had to admit that she would never be able to stitch again. Olivia had wanted to surprise Pia with the flowers as a thank-you for being her stead for the dress fittings, and because Pia was such a dear woman.

No one had told Katarina that Thorne was leaving again. She found out at the midday meal that he was gone. Katarina surely would have no opportunity to entice Thorne into marrying her if he was not about, and no one would tell her what Thorne was attending to. She would have to wait to ply Thorne with her charms. Until then, there was work to be done. She needed the serene highness fully on her side concerning marrying Thorne. She had need to uncover who was after Olivia, and mayhaps she could be of assistance to them. Katarina also had thought that it might be to her advantage to get Chance and Margarette out of Carinthia as well.

Katarina sat in the drawing room and watched as the serene highness played with her grandchildren. Mayhaps after she and Thorne were married, Katarina could talk the serene highness into moving to Chance and Margarette's castle in Hungary. There would be little use of the woman here. Of fortune, the baby vomited all over Margarette, and the little family retired to their rooms. With Olivia nowhere to be seen, Katarina knew this was her opportunity to talk to the serene highness, who had been so cold to her of late. Katarina knew the cause of the serene highness's concern; she merely needed to convince the serene highness that her concern was not real.

Setting her stitching aside, Katarina walked over to where Anja sat, feeling a wave of coldness emanate from the serene highness. Undeterred, Katarina kneeled down in front of Anja's chair and took the woman's hands in hers.

"Anja, I am so happy you are feeling better. I have been so worried for you. I have been barely able to sleep or eat."

Anja looked down into Katarina's face; the woman did indeed look like she had been of concern, but Anja could not conjure the fondness she once had for the woman. She could not forget the words Katarina had said about the child.

"That is so kind of you, but neglect not yourself for me." Her words sounded stiff and formal, even to Anja herself.

"I fear you are angry with me. Please, Anja, have I done something to upset you?"

Anja looked across the room. She had always been a woman of direct words, but now her tongue found it hard to say the words on her heart. Deep inside she feared Katarina had something to do with her illness, but her mind had argument with her—how could that be? Anja wanted nothing more than her life back as it was at the wedding—laughing, talking, enjoying all. She should show Katarina the error of her ways and forgive her. Was this not her friend?

"You said to me that if Olivia was with child that all could be taken care of."

Anja stopped and weighed her words, but the look on Katarina's face took the words from her tongue. Horror was etched into the woman's face.

"Anja, I know not what you speak! Is that the reason for Princess Olivia's guard? Does she hide from a husband that would harm her and her child?"

"We never discussed if Olivia was with child?"

"No, Anja, never. I was of the thought that the princess was not married."

"She is not."

"I know little of the dear girl except she plays the pianoforte very well. I am confused why anyone would think the princess was with child."

"She is not. I had in my mind that we had a discussion once concerning Olivia and her being with child."

"No, Anja. I swear I recall nothing of the sort."

Anja was more confused than when she had been ill. She remembered the discussion as though it happened but yesterday, but Katarina was without doubt that the discussion had never happened. Anja doubted herself. Did the illness confuse her memory? She knew there was so much that she could not recall, but had the illness put thoughts into her mind that never were? Was she harboring anger against her friend for not?

Anja took Katarina's hands into hers. "Forgive me, my dear friend. The illness must have confused my mind more than I knew. But it is gone, and we must start anew. Please tell me you will forgive me."

Katarina hugged the older woman. "There is nothing to forgive. Let us start anew today."

Katarina was without doubt that her fortune would start changing this very moment. The concern with Anja had been remedied very quickly and without anguish. They would start anew, but Katarina would not let Olivia or Margarette stand in her way this time. She would give the serene highness less of the potion; it would not be pleasing to have the older woman so confused. Katarina need only have Anja slightly addled and trusting her good friend to be at her side.

Anja was relieved that the turmoil that she had suffered had been put to rest. This was her good friend, a woman who had come to seek advice and comfort from her, and Anja had treated her thus. Today Anja would start putting her home and her family back together. Thorne would have the matter with the Dark Horse settled soon, and he would be home. Father

Adolphus would be free to return to the castle, and he would find the place where God wanted Olivia to be. When the snows melted, they all would visit Auria's new home, and life would be as it once was ... except that the small voice inside her kept whispering, *It did happen. Katarina did say that the child could be taken care of. Do not forget. Do not forgive.*

Twenty Three

It continued to snow, and Chance knew that the castle must help to provide for the people of the villages. Chance hated to shift his responsibility for his mother to Margarette for the weeks he would be gone, but his wife assured him it was not a concern. Margarette had changed under Olivia's influence. Margarette had been raised to be meek and quiet, but Olivia had shown her that a woman could be otherwise. Chance was not displeased with the change in his wife, though he knew not that he would have wanted her to change. Margarette was simply being the woman Chance had always known, the woman she was inside.

Near the second week of the second month of the new year, Lukas and Sebastian returned to the castle. The heavy snow made travel slow, and both men had croup by the time they arrived. In truth, neither man looked well at all, their color pallid; one moment they had chilling and shaking, and shortly thereafter they were flush with fever. Olivia feared that both men had a serious lung fever.

Beds were moved to place both men in the same room, and Father Peter Simon was fetched from town. Peppermint and ginger teas were given to the men, as were frequent baths— warm baths when they chilled and cool baths when they were flush. The cook prepared hearty soups for them to eat and hot herb steams to clear their lungs. Servants stayed with the men around the clock to attend to them, and Olivia had the servants wear scarfs over their nose and mouth. Although the countess had thoughts that this was completely unnecessary, Olivia had seen lung fever pass from one person to the next.

The young men's illness just added to an already bur-dened castle. Elena and Elias were so gifted in their ability to run the castle that the guests had no understanding of the other very dark, dangerous cloud hanging over them, but Olivia could not forget. Each day she prepared herself that her father would come with his well-trained army and siege the castle.

The serene highness seemed to have forgotten that the prince wanted Thorne's head for killing his daughter, and now with the serene highness's recent frame of mind, Olivia feared her father's arrival even more. She could not trust the serene highness to handle the prince, and Olivia could not do it her-self.

Although Olivia hated to concern Margarette, she was the only choice Olivia had; she also felt Margarette would be the best person to handle the prince. Margarette was so regal and quiet, almost to the point of timid, but Olivia had learned as she had gotten to know Margarette that she was also very clever, which one must be, Olivia felt, when dealing with her father.

Margarette was honored that Olivia would come to her concerning her father's possible arrival. In all that had transpired in the last few months with Katarina and the serene highness's health, she had not spent much time thinking about whether the prince would come. Margarette had been raised to be quiet and obedient, and to think only of her husband, children, and household, just as her mother had done. Any sort of concern was to be left to men, who would handle any troubling situation.

This way of life had not logic to Margarette however; she was well educated and intelligent, but to what purpose? So she could educate her sons to rule and her daughters to educate their children? Looking at her mother and the serene highness, Margarette knew she did not want to be like them. When she came to the castle and came to know Auria, she caught a glimpse of the woman she wanted to be, but she knew not how. Watching Olivia though, and then later getting to know the

woman, Margarette realized that she had found what she needed, a woman that could teach her how to be the woman she
wanted to be.

The castle was so burdened that it would take only one
snowflake to cause a devastating avalanche. That one snowflake was the countess. Katarina used the young men's illness
as a reason to attempt to take over as mistress of the castle.
She even had the mind to threaten Elena and Elias with being
thrown out of the castle if they did not do as she wished. Olivia
informed Katarina that she had not the authority to do such.
Katarina informed Olivia that she would have Anja throw the
servants out, but no word from the serene highness came forth.

Olivia did all she could to shield the staff from Katarina's
wrath. Every minor infraction was met with a harsh tone and
words that berated the servant, and Katarina would pinch the
young girls on the back of their upper arms. Olivia had never
seen any of the family speak harshly to the staff, and never had
she seen or heard that to punish a servant with pain would be
acceptable.

At Olivia's grandparents' estate, the staff was held with
the highest esteem, and although the serene highness treated
the servants like ... servants, she did not treat them as though
her life was any more valuable than theirs. At the evening meal

when the wedding guests were still at the castle, a young woman that Olivia had not seen afore was retrieving the plates from the table in an improper fashion. After the first course, the serene highness excused herself to tell the cook that the soup had been particularly tasty that eve. In truth, the soup had been very delightful.

Olivia also excused herself to gain a pitcher of water for her wine. As she entered the kitchen, the serene highness was instructing the young woman on the proper way to remove the plates from the table. Her tone was as usual, and her words were not of anger or cruelty. Thorne and Chance were notably kind to the staff, often with words of praise on their tongues.

Olivia and Margarette intervened at every opportunity that presented itself, but the complaints from the staff were becoming a concern. One evening in the drawing room, Olivia and Margarette endeavored to discuss the concern with the serene highness, but the serene highness just looked at the two women as though their words were of a foreign tongue. This was not the first time that the serene highness had responded this way, but it still alarmed the princesses.

Looking much the dutiful sister, Katarina sat at Lukas' bedside, arguing with herself as she stitched. Katarina felt that she was indeed giving Anja the proper amount of the potion.

Anja was not too obviously different from her usual self, but she was having problems remembering, and, of course, her dutiful friend was there to help her remember and to reason things. Katarina knew that both Olivia and Margarette were suspicious that Anja was ill again, but Katarina had counseled Anja to deny any concerns to the princesses. Katarina had Anja convinced that she was as always.

It would be best if it was Anja's idea that Katarina and Thorne marry. Slowly Katarina had been placing this thought in Anja's mind that it would be to Anja's favor if Katarina stayed at the castle indefinitely. Margarette and Chance would, at some time in the future, go to Hungary, and Anja had said that Olivia would be leaving soon, while Katarina assured Anja that she would never leave her. Now she was guiding Anja's thoughts towards the picture of the happy family they would be together if she and Thorne married, as they had almost done before. Katarina had little doubt that Anja would convince herself of this.

Because she only had enough of the other poison—the one she had given to Maximillian—for one, she was unsure to whom she should give it. Lukas was already ill; no one would have concern if he died, and Anja would have a heart for Katarina, all alone in the world, suffering from the loss of her husband and now her brother. Lukas was of little use to her, and if he were dead, she would not need concern herself with sharing wealth with him.

Katarina did so want Princess Olivia out of the castle and out of her and Thorne's life. Thorne was in love with Olivia—truly in love with her, not just the lust he had for Katarina—but that did not concern Katarina overly much. She knew Thorne had an aversion to marrying and to having children, which had never made much sense to Katarina. Thorne by birth was the heir; it was his responsibility to provide the next heir. Although Katarina had not been able to trap Thorne with a child afore, she knew that given the time and opportunity, she would be able to make Thorne so mad with passion he would forget his thoughts.

If Olivia suddenly died, however, that could cause concern, and Anja was sure Olivia would be leaving when the snows were gone. Katarina wished she could get Anja to speak more about Olivia, but the serene highness acted as though she knew little on the subject. Mayhaps this was true, but Katarina would still attempt to get more information from Anja concerning Olivia.

Katarina could not find out why Olivia had a guard. The silly servant girl had loose lips, yet her lips became silent with the mention of Olivia. All the servants looked to Olivia for direction as if she was the mistress of the castle. Katarina was completely befuddled why a guest about whom the serene highness knew little had such power at the castle. Katarina wanted that power. She would one day be mistress of the castle; the servants should start treating her as such.

After three weeks of the lung fever, Lukas and Sebastian had greatly improved. Some had thought that the men needed to be bled, but Olivia would not allow it, insisting that the men needed all their strength and that would get them through. Lukas and Sebastian were moved back to their rooms, and the servants need not stay with them at all times. When the men's fever was gone, their chests began to clear, and they improved at a rapid rate and were able to leave their rooms for meals.

Thorne and Stephan could travel no faster. The snow was deep and wet, the roads a muddy bog, and the horses struggled as they headed for the county of Tyrol; Johann had thoughts that the body came from there. In Zirl they noted armed men guarding the parish church. Thorne knew they were in the right place, but where was Johann? They took a room at the inn and asked for their evening meal in their room. The extra coin for such was a wise investment. The owner's daughter delivered the food and remarked that a man that could have been Stephan's brother had been at the inn just a week afore.

She had seen the man drive west in a Vardo wagon, so

Thorne and Stephan headed west on the route Thorne had taken to Olivia's grandparents' estate. Thorne reasoned that Johann was traveling there; for what purpose, he could not say. In three days, Thorne and Stephan spotted the Vardo wagon, an uncommon type of traveling wagon used by the Roma, but Thorne knew the wagon style was from France and was also used for traveling entertainment troupes. As Thorne had believed, the wagon was slow in progress. The roads were difficult for the horses, but a burden for a wagon. As they passed the wagon, they split, Thorne to one side, Stephan to the other, calling to Johann to stop the wagon that they might have words.

"The girl came from Zirl," Johann said, explaining what Thorne and Stephan had guessed. "We will have testimony."

Thorne and Stephan looked one to the other, not understanding what Johann meant, and followed the valet to the back of the wagon. Johann opened the wagon's wooden doors, and seated inside were a man and a woman, their backs together, their hands tied and one tied to the other.

"The girl's parents," Johann stated. "Now we must get Olivia's mother. She can testify that Olivia is indeed alive."

Thorne had misgivings about Johann's plan to kidnap Olivia's mother. One did not kidnap a gently bred woman. In Thorne's mind, he saw the serene highness tied up as the girl's parents were. Had it not been his head that the prince sought, Thorne would not do such.

As they traveled to the estate, Thorne thought mayhaps the direct approach would be best. They would ask Olivia's mother to travel back to Thorne's castle with them. Surely the woman would be thrilled that her daughter was still alive and wish to reunite with her, though convincing her to travel with them in the winter may be difficult ... and having two people trussed up like criminals would not help them make their case.

Thorne approached the main entrance to the estate, looking not like a prince. He had been riding the empire trying to save his life, not entertaining the gentry in his finest. He was shown into the drawing room and awaited his audience with Olivia's mother, planning to present his plea to her, hoping she would agree to come with them. If not, there was little Thorne could do until dark. He had already kidnapped one woman from this estate; he was ready to do it again, if necessary.

After being introduced to Olivia's mother, Anastasia, Thorne gave a brief description of where her daughter was and why. Thorne explained that the prince still had thought that Thorne had Olivia killed, so he was there to ask her to come with him, to his castle, and then write to the prince that Olivia was alive. Thorne waited for the woman's decision. He had not considered the answer he received.

Anastasia could not believe that the prince was so cold as to send someone to try to get her to believe that Olivia was alive. Was it not enough that she had spent year after year knowing that he could come after her and Olivia? Olivia's life was far more valuable than her father's; she was kind and loving—all the good qualities that the prince was not. Now she was gone, and he remained. Her heart grieved for her daughter; although she had tried to prepare herself for the loss, the pain was still unbearable.

Anastasia turned her grief into anger. "Be gone! Tell the prince that I am tired of him and will no longer be party to his malicious games. Tell him to leave me be! He has taken away the only thing I have left to love. Is that not enough? Be gone! Now!"

Thorne could well believe from where Olivia had inherited her temper. Talking to Anastasia and talking to Olivia could well be the same. He stood and walked out the door of the estate, deciding to bide his time. He was leaving for the castle tonight, and he would have Olivia's mother with him.

Thorne felt it best to use no weapon on Olivia's mother, so the three men entered the estate just as Anastasia was sitting down to her evening meal. A few of the kitchen servants remained in the house while the three men focused on packing for Olivia's mother. Johann pulled out dresses, shoes, and other items and passed them to Stephan, who passed them to Thorne, who placed the items in a trunk. The men worked without making a sound, and no one from the ground floor knew they were there.

Twenty Four

L ukas and Sebastian were able to come to both midday and evening meals and even spent some time each evening in the drawing room talking or playing board games. Everyone commented on how well the men looked. Their color was returning to normal, and their humor was returning as well. It was believed that the young men were well on the road to mending.

One evening, Lukas did not come to dine. He had gone for a rest before the meal, and no one had heard from him since. Olivia and Janos went to check on Lukas, Janos going into the room as Olivia waited outside the door. She heard no voices inside the room and had concern that Janos was in the room too long. Had Lukas taken ill again? But Janos would have come out directly and told Olivia. No, something was wrong.

"He is gone, my princess."

"Gone? Gone to where?"

"He has gone to his peace."

Olivia rushed into the room. Janos must be mistaken. Lukas was well at the midday meal. It took just one look at the man on the bed, however, to know there was no life left in him. Olivia asked Elias to send for Father Peter Simon, and she proceeded to the drawing room to tell the countess and Sebastian the news. Sebastian's color became as white as the snow, and he excused himself to his room. The countess dissolved into tears and fell to the floor, wailing, as the serene highness hurried to the side of her friend to comfort her.

Katarina refused to leave her room for two days, and the serene highness stayed with her all day and until she fell asleep at night. Katarina came to the small funeral service held by Father Peter Simon, sobbing loudly during the entire Mass. Lukas's body was taken to the family crypt until Katarina was ready to travel home. Olivia noted that Father Peter Simon seemed very distressed by the young man's death, but Olivia had no knowledge that the two men were well acquainted.

Katarina was inconsolable. When she finally ventured from her room, she wanted only to stay with Anja in her rooms. When Margarette suggested the two women spend the afternoon together, the countess began to sob and ran from the room. The serene highness was not of herself, day after day, and Olivia reasoned that Katarina was able to poison the serene highness daily now that Anja barely left her rooms. Katarina was still composed enough to order the servants around, and now she had requested that both the serene highness's meals as well as her own be taken in Anja's rooms.

Katarina could not be more pleased with Lukas's death. Anja had been so concerned about her good friend, and now Katarina could truly get to work. It was an easy task to put the potion in Anja's wine in her room, and all Katarina need do was give the serene highness a crystal from time to time during the day. She needed to convince Anja of several things, but she had all day and all eve to put these thoughts into Anja's mind.

First, Katarina needed to convince Anja that she was of herself—or rather, Anja needed to convince everyone else she was her usual. Would not Olivia and Margarette tell Thorne and Chance if they thought something was amiss? Mayhaps Thorne and Chance would think that she was an addled old woman that needed to be locked in her rooms for her own protection. Had not Olivia already tried to do such when the servant had to stay with Anja? No, if Anja had a concern about her mind, she must keep it from her family. Even her good friend Katarina could not stop Thorne from locking her in her rooms.

Being thought of as an addled old woman frightened Anja to near panic, but Katarina gave her wise counsel. Anja could not bear the thought that her sons would lock her away and she would not be able to see her grandchildren. Had not Thorne locked Olivia in her rooms just after the wedding? The servants and guests had suggested such. Thorne had denied it, but now Anja was sure he had. And Anja was sure he would lock her in her rooms too.

Was not Olivia the true concern? Katarina pressed Anja with how Olivia had thrown the castle into upheaval and was trying to take over as mistress. Yes, if Anja had doubts about her mind, it was solely because Olivia concerned her so. No, Olivia was the root of all her concerns; Olivia was evil. And it was Olivia that was not sound of mind.

In truth, Katarina needed not convince Anja of much that Anja had not already thought herself. Many of the things Anja had said to Katarina Anja did not fully believe herself, but with pressing, she did now. Anja had, in truth, done all Katarina's work for her with Anja's own thoughts. Was it not a sign to Katarina that all had been laid out for her already?

Katarina sat in front of the mirror looking at Anja's jewels around her neck. She had not been able to find all Anja's jewels. In fact, these were the least of her collection. Anja claimed that she knew not where the rest of the jewels were, but Katarina did not believe that Anja had spoken truthfully. Katarina also started to doubt that Anja knew so little about Olivia, but Katarina would continue to press Anja. Had not Anja told her about

Anja's fear of Olivia being with child? No, Anja would tell her all; she needed just to press her more.

Olivia needed a few minutes to think, so she snuck away to the guest wing. Thomas was teething, and Margarette had been up with him all night again. Olivia was worried about Margarette; she wasn't eating well, she was up a fair portion of the night with Thomas, and Peter had been a handful recently as well. Chance was still off seeing to the supplies of the towns. The serene highness was spending the day in her rooms again. The countess was running the servants ragged, and Sebastian was no longer a nuisance—he was a considerable concern.

Olivia needed to take control of the household and those in it, but it galled her to do so. This was not her home; these were not her family members nor her guests, but she had made a promise to Thorne and she would not break her word. She had deep concern for the serene highness and Margarette. Olivia had no idea how a household could fall apart so quickly and easily. In truth, though, she did; it was the countess.

Olivia decided to start with the easier concerns first. Chance had taken several of the male servants with him, and Elias had the remaining male servants on watch should the prince's men show up again. Olivia informed Elena that she was to carry on with the household as she normally would with part of the servants away. She was not to concern herself with requests from Katarina or from the serene highness, if the request differed from what the serene highness would normally do. Katarina could learn to live with only a few courses at evening meal, her dresses did not need to be cleaned on the day that she wore them, her room did not need a full cleaning each day, nor could she dictate when the rest of the rooms needed to be cleaned. Olivia felt quite certain that Katarina was making an effort to take over as the mistress of the castle.

Niklas's presence comforted Olivia, as without Lukas about, she felt Sebastian becoming bolder in his romantic intentions towards her. On one occasion he had taken her hand in his, and on another he had reached out and swept her hair over her shoulder. He had started to act as though Niklas was an acceptable chaperone. Olivia needed to let him know that his intentions were not invited. After the midday meal, Olivia asked Elena and Elias to accompany her while she spoke to Sebastian.

Olivia politely explained that she was not able to entertain any suitors. She told Sebastian that it would not be proper for her and him to be alone together and that Niklas was not a chaperone. He only stood there staring at her, and Olivia had doubt that he heard a word she said.

Without warning, Sebastian grabbed Olivia by the shoulders, kissed her, then dropped to his knee. "Olivia, I love you. I want to marry you. I will do anything for you!"

Niklas burst into the room, and he and Elias started to drag the lovesick man from the room. Sebastian still firmly held Olivia's hand, and she was forced to follow along as she and Elena attempted to snatch her hand from his grasp. Had not the situation been so serious, Olivia would have laughed at the scene. The five of them looked like a troupe of traveling jesters. Niklas and Elias escorted Sebastian to his room and had words with him. It was not until Niklas returned that Olivia realized he had left her without a guard for near an hour. She hoped that Sebastian heard the words of the men better than he had heard hers.

Olivia next went in search of Pia. The woman loved children, and though she had not married, she did have several sisters and brothers and talked about her nieces and nephews all the time. Olivia had not wanted to impose on the dear woman, but Margarette needed help, as quickly as possible. Olivia's concern was not as much if Pia would help, it was whether Margarette would let her help. Olivia understood Margarette's thoughts; she was very protective of her children and had no thoughts of leaving the care of her children to others, but Margarette needed a few days of respite. With persuasion, Olivia was able to get Margarette to allow Pia to stay in the nursery and help with the boys for a few days.

With that situation remedied, the last of the concerns were with the serene highness and the countess. Olivia was certain that the serene highness was not herself again, but the signs were less obvious since the serene highness was spending all her days in her rooms with only a rare appearance for a midday meal. The countess was with the serene highness in her rooms from mid-mornings until late at night. Katarina had refused to allow Olivia to enter to see the serene highness for herself, so Olivia was only able to glimpse the woman to know that she was indeed alive.

Olivia knew she must have a discussion with the countess concerning this, but Olivia feared having harsh words in front of the serene highness. It was very late; Olivia had spent much time in the chapel this eve, praying for strength to talk to the countess, for protection for the serene highness, for peace for Margarette, and most of all, for Thorne. Olivia could not find the words for her prayer, so she let her heart speak in the language of pain, concern, need, and love.

It was well after midnight when Olivia headed to her room. The castle was quiet; she had doubt that anyone except Janos and herself were awake, but as she headed down the hallway, a figure headed towards her. Olivia straightened her shoulders. She had no wish to speak with the countess this night, but the opportunity was here in front of her.

"Countess, a word, please."

Katarina looked Olivia straight in the eye, then turned away. She would not even acknowledge the princess's presence with a reply. Olivia hastened her steps until she was fairly running to meet up with the countess before she could slip into her room. Olivia was aware that Katarina was ignoring her; if Olivia allowed this now, then the countess would have no thoughts for Olivia's words. Olivia managed to step in front of the countess's door, preventing her from entering her room. Olivia had thought that the countess was hiding something in the folds of her gown, but the countess had a taste for fuller skirts than Olivia liked; mayhaps it was a trick of the light.

"Countess, we must speak."

"I have no desire to speak with you. Get out of my way." Katarina's words were full of venom, her feelings towards Olivia unmistakable.

"I must speak with you about the serene highness. It is not good for her to be shut up in her rooms without seeing Margarette and her grandchildren."

"I told you, I have nothing to say to you." Katarina pulled

the decanter from the folds of her skirt and cast the contents into Olivia's face.

Olivia's hand flew to her face, and she quickly wiped the wine from her eyes. Taking advantage of the moment, Katarina reached over and grabbed Olivia's hair that had been hanging over her shoulder, pulling on the tail of it. Olivia did not pull away as Katarina expected, but rather stepped towards the countess, pushing her into the wall. Olivia heard Janos coming to her rescue, but this was not his concern.

"Stay back." Olivia said quietly to Janos, her voice calm as though this was a usual occurrence.

The countess was not ready to allow Olivia the upper hand. As she collided with the wall, Katarina lost her hold on Olivia's hair, so she lifted the wine decanter and swung it at Olivia's head. Olivia had thought that Katarina would do such, and she ducked, the force of the swing taking Katarina to the floor. Olivia grabbed the decanter from the countess's hand.

Katarina lay facedown on the floor for but a moment, then she started to push herself upright until a low walking boot on her back stopped her. Katarina tried to roll over, but the pressure became a full weight upon her back. She tried to push up against the foot, thinking her weight would give her the advantage—Olivia's weight was no more than a feather—but she was unable to move.

"Countess, we need to have words."

Katarina growled in response. Again, she tried to move from the weight on her back, but Olivia had not released any of the weight holding the countess down.

"The serene highness will be coming out of her rooms starting tomorrow. If you choose to have argument with me concerning this, I will personally place you in your room and put a guard on you. I have full understanding that you will not act civilly, and I will do what is necessary to keep all in the castle safe and as it should be until the prince returns. It would serve you best to heed my words, countess."

Taking her foot off Katarina's back, Olivia allowed her to rise. "You have no understanding of me. It is you that needs to heed words. You will leave this castle, one route or the other!" Having had the last word, Katarina opened the door to her room, entered, and then slammed the door shut.

Olivia walked to her room. "Thank you, Janos. I want no fists with the countess, but she cannot be allowed to take over this castle. It is not her home, and I have question if she has true concern for those whose home it is."

"You did as you need do. I will always be at the ready for you. This is your home, even if you do not see it as such."

Olivia knew not how to respond, so she inclined her

head and entered her room, the wine decanter still in her hand. Walking closer to the lamp, Olivia inspected the decanter, which had an unusual design etched in the crystal. She had seen that design and this decanter before, but Olivia could not say where. After preparing for bed, she crawled between the covers. As she drifted off to a place where Thorne was always with her, she remembered. Olivia knew where she had seen the decanter and what she need do, but for now her time was meant to be with Thorne, in her dreams.

Twenty Five

Olivia could find no reason to go into the countess's room. She thought upon the dilemma for several days but found no resolution. The countess had heeded Olivia's words, and the serene highness was coming to the midday and evening meals and spending time outside her rooms. Margarette had also appeared well and seemed much more rested. She had allowed Pia to stay for more than just a few nights and help with the children. Although Olivia was pleased that the two women's concerns were abating, it did nothing to help her dilemma, and Olivia was sure the root of the serene highness's problem could be found in the countess's room.

The men's words appeared to have had no effect on Sebastian; he continued to follow her as often as he was able. Olivia needed help. She had no wish to involve others in her plan, but she feared she had no choice. She spoke to Elena first, concerned that the elderly housekeeper would not wish to be part of a deception, but Elena readily agreed. She waited until Janos and Niklas were to change guard, and she spoke with both men. She could not apologize enough to them for involving them in her plan, but both men seemed happy to help. Niklas told Olivia he would do anything for her since she had suggested that he send for his family before the snows became too deep. His wife and children were staying in the guest wing.

She next spoke to Margarette. As their conversation concluded and Olivia went about her way, it occurred to her that Margarette had not been surprised by Olivia's plan; in truth, Margarette had made some suggestions that had been good additions to Olivia's plan. Olivia was of certainty that Margarette had given much time to the same thought before Olivia discussed it with her. Again, Olivia was faced with a circumstance that needed her to beg deception, which was not her nature, and she had to force herself to do such. Olivia felt sure, though, there was no other way to keep the people at the castle safe.

It finally stopped snowing. No one was traveling outdoors unless absolutely necessary because the snow was far too deep. Had it not taken Father Peter Simon almost a full day to travel from town? The countess would not be leaving anytime soon, and Thorne would not be home anytime soon. As she looked up at the moon and stars, Olivia made a vow to Thorne that she would do as she needed until he came home.

Just after the midday meal, Margarette and Pia had brought the children to the drawing room to spend time with the serene highness. The exits from the drawing room were blocked by servants cleaning. Olivia mentioned finding fabric to cover the footstool the gardeners had made for Margarette, which looked more like a piece of art than a piece of furniture. Olivia wanted to get fabric that would accentuate the stool, not take away from its beauty, so she started to wander towards the room where the seamstresses worked, Sebastian following closely behind.

Janos appeared and asked to have a few words with Sebastian. The young man had great reluctance, but Janos could not be deterred. Olivia slipped into the family wing of the castle, and Niklas took up a post in front of Olivia's door to her room. No one would question him standing there, but should anyone come down the hall, Niklas would not allow them anywhere near Olivia's or the countess's door. Elias was stationed at one end of the hallway stair, while Elena was stationed at the other end of the hallway at the bottom of the stair. Hopefully, no one would come up to this floor.

Olivia slipped into Katarina's room and started the search with the cabinets. She looked through everything, careful to return everything she touched to the exact same spot. She knew what she was looking for, but the items could be hidden almost anywhere; Olivia did not dare hope that all the items would be together. After searching for nearly two hours, Olivia found an empty bottle in a shoe and another full bottle in a pashmina. She found the bowl in the back of a drawer and another empty bottle in a pillow cover. She placed the four items into a small fabric bag that she wore under her skirts. Finally, she left the room and slipped into her room where she picked up the fabric she had already selected for the footstool.

Olivia returned to the drawing room, and Margarette and Pia took the sleepy boys up to their rooms for a nap. Margarette returned a short time later with the footstool, and Olivia and Margarette marked the fabric to be cut with chalk. The serene highness had dozed off to sleep in her chair, a habit she just recently seemed to have acquired, and Katarina sat at the window looking out at the sun and snow. Olivia transferred the small fabric bag to the folds of the fabric as the ladies gathered up their supplies for the footstool venture. Margarette took the footstool and fabric to her room. Olivia decided to play the pianoforte.

It was gone—all of it, gone. Katarina tore through her room, throwing her belongings about. The bedcovers were stripped from the bed, and Katarina pulled the heavy mattress from the frame, finding not what she was looking for. There were shoes in the bathing tub, dresses over every inch of the floor, and jewelry all over the bed. She had underestimated Olivia again, having little doubt that it was Olivia that had taken her precious bottles from her room. It must have been today, but Katarina had not noted one item out of place until she could not find the bottles from Madam Wu.

Starting for the door, she had thoughts to storm Olivia's room, but her guard would be there. Katarina left her room—she certainly could not be expected to sleep in such a messy room—and wandered down to the drawing room. Mayhaps this could be useful to her. She had been giving Anja less of the potion, and Anja had started to come around to her way of thinking. Had not Anja said yesterday that she would sorely miss the boys if they had to return to Hungary? Mayhaps she could use this to push Olivia out the door.

She would search Olivia's room on the morrow and find the bottles, then she would tell Anja that Olivia had been poisoning her. And the guard? Anja claimed to not know why Olivia had a guard. What if the guard was to keep Olivia from hurting Anja? Katarina sat in the dark drawing room with a smile on her face. She could be so clever! Yes, Katarina would have the upper hand; she was the one with the clever mind.

Katarina slipped into Olivia's room just moments after the princess and her guard headed for morning prayer, tearing through Olivia's room just as she had through her own, but Katarina did not find the bottles. She was so angry that she took a pair of scissors to several of Olivia's dresses. She would have liked to shred all the woman's clothing, but she heard the servants in the hall and decided to leave. No one could prove she had been in Olivia's room if no one saw her in Olivia's room.

Katarina's hatred for Olivia could not be greater. The only obstacle to her plans was this princess, and Katarina's patience was wearing thin. She had not dreamed that it would take so long for her plans to become real. She had planned that Thorne would welcome her back into his bed as soon as she walked through his door and that Anja would be delirious with glee to have her good friend back. Katarina had waited until Auria was gone; she had no intention of allowing the little girl to stand in her way this time.

This princess had taken everything that should be Katarina's, and on top of that, the woman was young and beautiful. As Katarina stood near Olivia, Olivia so outshined Katarina that she may as well have been a troll. Olivia had been born with a title, but she obviously had no idea how to use what had been given to her. Why was she not at court? Why had she not married well? No, Olivia was not deserving of a title.

And Thorne had fallen in love with Olivia. Why could Thorne not be in love with her? Thorne need not be in love with her, but was not what she could do for his body enough for him to love her? Was that not what was most important to men? Everyone at the castle adored Olivia—Margarette, the servants, and Anja even said that Auria was in awe of Olivia. These people should be loyal to her. Had she not lived there for two years? Was not Olivia a stranger to them?

At least Anja had not become entranced by Olivia, and Katarina only needed Anja. After she was married to Thorne, all others would be beholden to her. She would be the mistress of the castle. Her word would be all that mattered. The servants that held Olivia in high esteem would find themselves thrown out of the castle, Margarette would have to come begging for her favor, and Auria—she would never be allowed to set one foot into the castle again.

Her hatred for Olivia was so great that her hands itched to choke the life out of the woman. She made herself be patient until the princess was gone, but that was not what she truly wanted. She wanted to kill Olivia—with her own hands—but there had been no opportunity for such. She would keep looking, and hoping, and dreaming of the day that she truly rid herself of this horrible annoyance.

When Chance arrived back at the castle two days before Eastertide, both Olivia and Margarette were relieved to see him. The snow was still too great for the people of the town to come for Mass or for the feast, though Father Peter Simon came the day after Easter and said a Mass for those at the castle. Even the prisoner Gregory was brought to Mass. The feast would be held in the spring when the snows had melted.

Margarette explained to Chance all that had transpired while he was gone. Chance was shocked to hear of Lukas's death and the bottles Olivia had found in Katarina's room. He was even more shocked to hear of Katarina's rampage on Olivia's room and wardrobe. He wanted Katarina out of the castle as soon as possible. He was of the thought that Katarina was a danger to many. Chance spoke to his mother, and his mother went so far as to suggest Olivia had cut up her own clothing and blamed the deed on Katarina.

Chance pressed the thought with his mother many times, but she was absolute in her thought that Katarina was without blame and Olivia was the cause of all misdeeds. Chance had concern that his mother was so controlled by Katarina that even she could become a danger to all in the castle.

When Katarina had not found the poison in Olivia's room, she was furious. It would take months to search every room at the castle, but Katarina had spent a considerable amount of time watching where Olivia went and searching any area connected to the woman. It had taken several weeks, but Katarina found it rather easily once she knew where to go. In truth, Katarina had thoughts that Margarette and Chance would never have the potion where young Peter could possibly find it, but then at last, Katarina convinced herself that Margarette indeed had the bottles; it took several more days to find a time to search. It was a busy set of rooms, always someone coming or going or cleaning.

She wished Thorne had returned. Katarina had planned to give a most convincing performance, and she would benefit if both were convinced at the same time. The thought that Olivia was poisoning the serene highness may be a bitter pill for Thorne to swallow, but Katarina had plans that the serene highness would be pressing Thorne as well.

Katarina almost ruined everything when she told the serene highness that Olivia had gone through her room and thrown Katarina's belongings all about. She had counted on Olivia mentioning what had happened in her room, but Olivia kept silent. The serene highness had been alarmed to hear of the destruction of Katarina's room, and she called for Elena, who told of the destruction to Olivia's room and clothing. Anja mused aloud that it was odd that Olivia would do such to her own room, but with quick words Katarina reminded Anja that Olivia was not of sound mind and capable of doing anything.

Anja was distressed by Katarina's sobbing as she entered Anja's rooms.

"Dear woman, what is your concern?" Anja guided Katarina to a chair. She had not seen the countess this distraught since the death of her brother.

"Oh, Anja, I know not how to tell you this." Katarina paused and then sobbed for several moments. She could see the serene highness was upset, but Katarina wanted Anja to be near panic.

Anja feared what Katarina had to say. Had Thorne been killed? If the woman could not control her crying to speak, then the news must be disastrous. Had something happened to Thomas? Peter?

Katarina could see that the serene highness was of the mind that Katarina wanted her to be. "Please forgive me. I have done something horrible, but I felt I had no choice!"

"My dear, I am sure it is not as horrible as you think. You must tell."

"I have had suspicion for some time that Olivia was poisoning you. I feared she would try to kill you! So I searched her room today. Anja, look what I have found!" Katarina held out her hands with the three glass bottles and the small bowl of mistletoe berries.

Katarina had not known what the berries in the bowl were, but since Olivia had hidden the bowl behind the silly fragrances she made, Katarina knew the berries must be important. The young girl that cleaned Katarina's room told her what the berries were and pressed Katarina that the berries were poisonous. Katarina told the young girl that she thought the berries were pretty and had thoughts of drying them to make beads for a necklace.

That evening Katarina brought the young girl a slice of cake with raspberry glaze to thank her for everything she did for Katarina. Tragically, the young girl became ill during the night with complaints of severe stomach cramps and was taken to the town for her mother to care for her. She had not returned to the castle. Katarina had thoughts that mayhaps she had died. In truth, Katarina could not have the young girl telling everyone in the castle that the countess had mistletoe berries and wanted to know about them.

Anja looked at the items in Katarina's hands—a small, empty glass bottle; two larger bottles, one containing a brown, clear liquid; and a small bowl of mistletoe berries. She could not believe it. Anja could not believe that Olivia was, indeed, poisoning her. To what purpose? Anja could think of no reason that Olivia would have to do this. In truth, Anja had never really gotten to know the young princess and had never treated Olivia with great warmth, but why would Olivia pick Anja to poison? And why had Olivia not just killed Anja?

Anja had never seen Olivia act oddly in the presence of others. Olivia, without doubt, had her own way of doing things, but her way had logic and sense. Anja could find no logic or sense in poisoning her. And how had Olivia gotten the poison? Margarette had been with Olivia when she prepared the fragrances and the other herbs and roots. Olivia had labeled everything in her neat handwriting on a parchment tied to the bottle.

Margarette had also been at Olivia's side as they dried flowers and made the sachets for the women's Christmastide gifts. Surely Margarette would have seen Olivia make the bottles of poison. Margarette had told Anja of all, but the serene highness had never seen bottles such as these at the castle.

"Margarette was with Olivia when she was making the fragrances and medicinal elixirs. I should speak with Margarette about this."

"Oh no, Anja, she would tell Olivia, and with Olivia not being sound of mind, we know not what evil she could do. We know not that this is all the poison that Olivia may have. No, Anja, for your sake, I beg you to stay quiet about this until Thorne returns."

Katarina's counsel made no sense to Anja. She should allow Olivia to keep poisoning her?

"Fear not, Anja. I will stay by your side and protect you. You must have faith in me. I would never let anything happen to you or Thorne."

"I should have Olivia locked in her room. She could hurt Peter or Thomas!"

"Chance would never let that happen. I will have words with him and warn him, but we cannot let Olivia know that we know what she has been doing until Thorne returns. It is the only way to keep you safe. Promise me you will speak to no one about this. Olivia could find out!"

Katarina had found these things in Olivia's room. The witness was true. And Katarina vowed to protect Anja from Olivia. Hopefully Thorne would return soon, and Anja would press on her son that Olivia had to leave the castle—and soon.

Twenty Six

ot long after the midday meal, the troop of ragged, weary travelers filed through the massive doors of the castle after a two-week-long trip that should have taken two days. The snow had started to melt in the sunshine, decreasing the deep snow very little while greatly increasing its weight. The journey had taken its toll on all the travelers, and the four ladies and Chance hastened to the hall to meet them.

Thorne entered first, nearly dragging the reluctant Anastasia behind him. Olivia's mother stood for a moment, allowing her eyes to adjust from the strong sunlight. They came to rest first upon Chance, and her forehead creased; Thorne had not told her of his twin. Then her eyes scanned the ladies until she came to Olivia, and a hand flew to her mouth to stifle a cry.

"Olivia!" she exclaimed before slowly slipping towards the floor in a faint as the word left her mouth. Thorne quickly grabbed Olivia's unconscious mother before she fell completely to the floor.

Olivia stood with her hands on her hips, anger etched

into her face. "Thorne!"

"Princess Olivia! Have respect for the prince and address him properly!" All eyes went to Katarina, their expressions scornful and incredulous.

The serene highness had been standing behind Margarette and Chance, but now she pressed forward for a better view. "Stasie?"

Now all eyes went to Anja. She knew Olivia's mother, and she knew Olivia's mother well enough to have an intimate name for her. In all the time that Olivia had been at the castle, the serene highness had never suggested that she knew Olivia's mother. Had Anja and Anastasia been friends or foes?

The two ladies who had once been as close as sisters sat in the serene highness's rooms. Anja's and Anastasia's fathers had been the best of friends. One of the girls would spend several months a year at the other girl's as the families visited often. Although Anja was a few years older, the age difference made no concern; the two were inseparable until Anja married Tobias, and then they lost track of each other as they went their separate ways.

"I knew not that you married the prince. That was not to be."

"The foreign baron was known to have lovers that he flaunted in public and was unwilling to give them up with marriage. He also was unwilling to convert to the Holy Roman Church. My father would not honor the wedding promise." Anastasia looked away. She had not done well with marriage, which was how society measured a woman's worth.

Her problems with marriage had not a thing to do with her as a person, and yet she was looked upon as a failure. Mayhaps it was a good thing that the prince had not made a marriage arrangement for Olivia. Anastasia had no wish for her daughter to endure the public scorn with which she had lived.

"My marriage to the prince did not last long, less than a year." Anastasia knew she would go through it all again; Olivia was well worth it.

"You should have written to me and told me where you were." Anja was heartbroken that her friend had been so close and she never knew.

"It was best not to upset the prince. The less he thought of me or Olivia was another day Olivia would live. That was all that mattered to me."

They sat in reflective silence for a while, with no strain between them. Anastasia had not chosen her path, and she had paid dearly for the path that had been chosen for her. She could see that she had allowed the melancholy to rule her life, but she had a renewed sense of purpose now; she would not allow the melancholy to steal one more day of her life.

Anja had supposed that Anastasia had gone on to a glorious life in another land. She had never thought to ask after her friend. How quickly she had replaced her good friend with her new life with her husband.

"Thank you for caring for my daughter. I will never be able to repay your kindness."

"She is not like you."

Anastasia laughed. "No. So often I would look at her and wonder if indeed she was my daughter, but I believe that if she had been born and bred with another family, Olivia would be the same. Some are meant to see life in a different light."

Anja looked sharply at her friend; she herself had said nearly the same words of Thorne. Chance was a mix of his mother and father, but Thorne fit neither parent.

"Olivia is a blessing in a way I could never be. She has a heart that cares for others easily, and she is willing to take on the burdens of others. I have often wished I could step out of the shell I have been wrapped in all my life, that I could really know those of other stations and still have a sense of my own, that I could see that my station begs me to be a leader and a servant at the same time."

As soon as the Vardo wagon was emptied of the travelers, it was made ready to leave again. Thorne met briefly with Chance, and his brother assured him that all would be well with their mother, though Chance refused to say more, explaining they would talk when Thorne returned. Thorne, Johann, and Stephan had just enough time to bathe, change their clothes, and eat before leaving again. Thorne knocked upon the door of Anastasia's room, and it was answered by Olivia. He wanted to spend some moments with Olivia, but there were none.

Thorne apologized to Anastasia for the fright of seeing her daughter. In truth, Thorne had told her repeatedly that Olivia was alive and that Anastasia would see her soon. He pressed Anastasia for a letter confirming Olivia's life. Chance would see that the letter to the prince left the castle on the morrow, but this letter Thorne would carry with him tonight. As Gregory and the girl's parents were loaded into the Vardo wagon, Thorne was struck with the great foresight Johann had in finding the wagon. The prisoners were concealed and contained within the back of the wagon with the wooden sides and roof. Thorne had no desire to draw attention to their activities.

This would be over soon, but he had to stay alive until it was over.

The next morn Anja sat in the same chair as she had yesterday when she spoke with her old friend, claiming to be ill when Katarina came to her rooms. Many things begged to be considered. Anja did not think Anastasia's presence at the castle was a coincidence. It was a sign, but as to what, she could not say.

Katarina was not pleased that the serene highness had not received her. With Olivia's mother here, Olivia would have an ally—an ally that knew Anja well. No, Anja must be kept from softening towards Olivia. Anja had said that Thorne need only to deliver the prisoner to the Holy See and bring Father Adolphus home; then Thorne's concern would be no more.

Katarina had never found out what Thorne's concern was. In truth, she really had not a care. She just wanted Thorne back at the castle so that she could ply him with her large repertoire of charms, which had always pleasantly surprised Thorne. Given the chance, she knew she could wrap him around her finger. In truth, Thorne had yet to understand how large her repertoire of charms really was.

But she could not lose her hold on Anja now. She was

so very close. Anja was sure that Olivia would leave with her mother, and Katarina would do everything possible to make that very soon. Olivia's mother had not seemed eager to be here, nor to stay, but it would be best if Olivia's mother and Anja were kept apart.

Anja had not the heart to tell her friend that her daughter had tried to poison her. In truth, Anja could never think of a reason why Olivia should want to do such, but Katarina had proof that she had. It mattered not now; Olivia would leave with Anastasia soon, and Anja would be no more able to stay close to her friend now than before. Anja could not act as though Olivia had not tried to harm her, and that knowledge would always stand between her and her friend.

She had allowed herself to lose her good friend once; mayhaps that was what she needed to keep as thought. Had not Katarina been telling her thus? Auria was gone, and someday Chance and Margarette would be as well. But Anja's good friend Katarina would stay here by her side as long as Anja needed her to be. Mayhaps Anja was to embrace the opportunity that was in front of her.

Anja had thought that she should be at peace now that she had spent time sorting her thoughts, but unease remained in her heart. She wanted her life as it was. She had never dreamed that the castle would be such a sea of chaos, but the end was near. Anastasia wrote to the prince yesterday, and the letter left the castle before the ink had dried. Soon Anastasia and Olivia would head home. Anja looked forward to spending time with just her family.

Anja had no doubt that Thorne's feelings for Olivia would fade once she was gone. Then he would be free to re-member why he had loved Katarina, and he would want to marry her again. The household would then be complete, and Anja would truly have peace. She would speak to Thorne as soon as he returned home about sending Anastasia and Olivia away as quickly as possible. She could not be completely sure that Katarina had found all the poisons that Olivia had hidden in her room.

Katarina was bored and tired of wearing drab mourning clothes. According to convention, she had to remain in mourning until the middle of summer. Or did she? Surely no one would expect Katarina and Thorne to wait to marry. Had tongues not wagged about her scandalous presence at the castle for two years without a marriage between her and Thorne? She had made known to all that visited the castle that she and Thorne had been a pairing, and Thorne had not said otherwise.

Would anyone be surprised if Katarina and Thorne married this spring?

Anja had already started talking about marriage between the two, as if she and Thorne were together again. The serene highness wanted her son to settle down and stop running all over the empire. She wanted Thorne to take care of Carinthia seriously and stop talking about Chance taking over if need be. Anja feared her son would die young as his father did. Would not Anja endorse a wedding in the spring?

They could travel the empire throughout the summer and fall, Thorne introducing the new serene highness. Katarina thought that sounded so much more regal than "countess." Then in the winter, Katarina would talk Thorne into taking her to court. There would be endless balls and parties, and of course, Thorne would host a ball to introduce his wife to the archduchess. All would be impressed with their enduring love story. How could two who are so much in love wait to marry? No one would think their early marriage scandalous; it would be thought of as romantic.

Katarina would need a new wardrobe. She had an entire new wardrobe made after she married the count, but that wardrobe was outdated. In truth, she had only worn a fraction of her dresses, but new ones sounded much better. The seamstress here at the castle was very good, but Katarina felt she should bring one here from Vienna. She would need new fabrics anyway from Vienna; they could bring a seamstress back with the cloth as well. Katarina became almost giddy with the thought. She could have a wedding dress made as well, and she and Thorne could have a real ceremony at court in Vienna.

"I do not think it wise to send anyone to Vienna until the snows have melted." They were in the drawing room after the evening meal. Elena had spoken with Olivia earlier and alerted her to the countess's request.

"May I inquire as to why we are sending anyone to Vienna?" Chance looked up from the castle of blocks he was helping his son to make.

"It is none of the princess's concern," Katarina said sweetly with a smile to match.

"I disagree. Thorne has given the princess full authority in his absence, but I have no wish to argue with you. It is, however, my concern." Chance sounded so much like Thorne that Olivia would have thought it was Thorne by the words alone.

"The serene highness thought it would cheer me to have new dresses made." Katarina continued stitching, looking completely unconcerned.

Searching her memory for any discussion of such, Anja could find none, and although Katarina had brought the poison bottles to her, she still was not of herself. Anja reasoned that Olivia had more poison that Katarina had not found. As Katarina went on to tell of this discussion they had concerning her wardrobe, Anja was sure she had no memory of this. As she listened, she became more and more concerned.

According to Katarina, Anja had suggested bringing a seamstress from Vienna. Anja had never done that nor considered that, not even for Auria's wedding for which Thorne decreed that no expense be spared. Had not all said that Auria's dress was beyond compare? Had not they mentioned how beautiful her own dress was? Many had also commented on Olivia's dress, which had been made at the last minute, and yet its beauty was noted.

Katarina also said that the men were to buy cloth by Thorne's name, but Thorne never purchased with credit. He believed that craftsman needed their money in due time, not at the leisure of the gentry. Thorne had many methods of transporting coin without the notice of thieves, so why would Anja instruct Katarina to do otherwise?

Olivia and Chance were of the same mind as Anja. It was far too dangerous to send anyone to Vienna now. Had not

Chance had to take supplies to the towns? The snows had been greater this year than the last several years. No, Thorne would never allow any of the staff to travel unless it was absolutely necessary.

But why had Anja suggested that Katarina and Thorne marry in the spring? Katarina's mourning would not be over, and she was the only family Lukas had left; she should mourn for him too. Anja had remained in mourning well past her year—until Thorne told her that she must put her mourning behind her because it was not fair to Auria. Thorne himself had ordered her mourning clothes be packed and put away. Anja could not possibly turn her back on this dictate; it was not how she was raised, and it was not in her nature. No, Anja could not believe she had said such.

Anja worried that mayhaps she was losing her mind. Mayhaps the poison had destroyed her mind. Fear ran through Anja, and she shivered. She could not trust her mind any longer, but Katarina had assured her that she would stay by her side. Katarina must have seen the change in Anja and knew that her friend would never be able to think as she had always.

Anja said nothing as Katarina told Olivia, Chance, and Margarette all these things that Anja had told her. She was ashamed when she saw the looks on all their faces as Katarina told all. They could not believe that Anja would say such, not the Anja that had always been. Chance and Olivia had stayed the trip to Vienna. They had not needed her word.

If her words were not as her usual, could her conduct be the same? Worried that she might do something to hurt Thomas or Peter, Anja vowed to herself that she would not be alone with the boys, but in truth, would she remember this vow to herself? Anja knew a fear she had never known. Mayhaps Thorne should lock her in her rooms; she could not bear the thought that she would ever hurt her grandsons.

Twenty Seven

Anja sat there, just staring ahead, as Katarina spewed angry, profane epitaphs at an invisible Olivia. Katarina was not aware that Anja was of the same mind as Chance and Olivia concerning travel to Vienna, and all Katarina's anger rained down upon the absent Olivia. Katarina had not said one word about Chance; had she, Anja would have to speak.

But this was not a Katarina that she knew. The words pouring from her mouth were none that a woman—let alone a lady and a princess—should ever say. Anja had never thought of Katarina as having a lowly birth and breeding, but she had to remind herself that Katarina had not the benefit of being raised as Olivia did. Anja had heard Elena make mention of Katarina speaking as a drunkard at the inn, and now Anja understood. Her father had been a businessman; mayhaps she had heard her father saying these words in anger.

Regardless, these words and this behavior did not befit a princess. Anja would have to mentor Katarina in the proper way, the thought making Anja weary in spirit; she had already raised her children, and she wanted not to raise another. Thorne would never allow Katarina to act as such; her behavior was befitting Peter, not an adult. She could not act as such every time she did not get her way. This would not go well with Thorne; it would be a burden to their marriage.

Anja felt well today; she felt herself. Mayhaps the poison had not damaged her. She had stopped drinking all wine and was drinking only this herbal tea that Elena made her. Chance told her that Elena was making a special tea to help restore her, and Anja believed that the tea was working. She had asked the servant to bring her some just as Katarina came to her rooms.

As the servant placed the tea on the table next to the serene highness, Anja asked the girl to take the decanter of wine from her room and pour it out.

"This is such a beautiful decanter. The design is very pleasing," the serving girl said as she fetched the decanter.

"It was my mother's," the serene highness replied.

Katarina bolted across the room. "No!" She snatched the decanter from the serving girl's hands.

"Katarina! What has gotten into your thoughts?" Anja was outraged at Katarina's behavior. This was too much.

Katarina looked at Anja, who was as her usual. Katarina looked at the full decanter, realizing Anja had not had any wine.

Katarina had not bothered to check Anja's frame of mind; she had become accustomed to Anja being under the influence of the potion, and her anger was such this morning that she could not hold her tongue. The words that Katarina had spoken earlier came back to her. Anja had heard all!

She must think of a way to keep the wine because Katarina had precious little of the potion left. Olivia had found all of it, save for the small bottle Katarina kept hidden under her skirts. The thought to switch the liquids in the bottle had not occurred to Katarina until she had given the bottles to Anja, and now the bottles were locked in a drawer; Katarina knew not where. She needed Anja under her control as long as possible, which meant Katarina would have to go to Vienna to get more potion, but that could well be months away.

"This is special to you. It was your mother's. I would not want it broken. I will take it and empty it myself." Katarina headed for the door.

"Nonsense, Katarina, the decanter will be fine. It has been cleaned many times and never broken. Our staff is superb in their duties." Anja would not put up with this nonsense any longer. "Give her the decanter and allow her to be on her way. I wish for you to sit. We must have words."

Having little choice to do anything else, Katarina gave the girl the decanter and took a seat as the serene highness began to lecture her on the proper words and conduct of a lady. Katarina could only listen. After dismissing Katarina, Anja headed for the drawing room. She felt so good today she did not want to be shut up in her rooms.

Anastasia was on the floor playing with Peter. "I hope you do not mind that I have borrowed your grandson for a while." Anastasia had concern that Anja would not be pleased. Her old friend was not the same, and Anastasia was a guest forced upon her.

"One day you will have grandchildren of your own to spoil." Anja took her usual chair.

"No, the prince will never allow Olivia to marry," Anastasia said quietly.

Anja was horrified. The prince had already ruined one life—must he have another? Anja had decided when she saw Anastasia in the drawing room that she would put aside the matter of Olivia poisoning her and be gracious to her old friend. It would seem Olivia had stopped now that her mother was here. Again, Anja was struck by how odd this plan to poison her seemed and how odd it was, given Olivia's nature, but she herself had seen the proof.

"I grieve for Olivia more than myself. She loves children and has always gotten on well and naturally with them." Anastasia felt the melancholy start. "But let us talk of happier things."

Anja thought back to when Olivia had cared for the children at Auria's wedding; she was very good with them. Then again at the Christmastide feast, Anja had enjoyed watching her playing games with the children, and she always was so loving to Peter and Thomas.

The women went on to talk of their parents, people they had known when they were younger, and times they shared as children. Chance enjoyed listening to his mother; she was of herself. Olivia had not removed the poison from the bottles she took from Katarina's room, but Chance had. Olivia and Margarette had waited a few days for the poison to leave the serene highness's body, but it took much longer than they had anticipated.

It was Olivia that reasoned that Katarina was putting the poison in the wine decanter in his mother's rooms. She instructed Elena to have the decanter poured out and refilled every time the serene highness left her rooms, but Katarina was keeping the serene highness in her rooms. Olivia decided she must talk to the countess about such. Margarette had wanted to do it, but Olivia reasoned that Chance and Margarette had never had argument with Katarina, and for the sake of the children, Olivia thought it was best to keep it as such.

Chance was more alarmed than before after listening to Katarina speak of her and Thorne marrying in the spring. Chance knew that Katarina's mind was not sane. Chance was frightened by the idea that his mother was being controlled by a delusional woman. While Chance, Margarette, and Olivia kept a close eye on Katarina, Chance also alerted Niklas and Janos that Katarina—or even his mother—may attempt to hurt Olivia.

Chance knew his mother must be confronted about Katarina, or she may try to stop him from removing Katarina from the castle. Chance did not dare hope that Katarina would leave in peace when asked. He did not want to put his mother through such duress, but he knew there was no other option. However, Chance wanted Thorne to be present when he spoke with his mother. They must be of one mind, and Thorne knew not the state of Katarina's mind.

Chance knew that Thorne's heart was with Olivia. He heard Anastasia tell Olivia that Thorne called out for her when he was asleep. She told Olivia that she still had not believed Thorne when he told her that her daughter was alive, even when she heard him call for her. Anastasia asked Olivia why

Thorne would call for her, but Chance had not stayed to hear Olivia's response.

The girl that told Katarina about the mistletoe berries had told Elena, who knew that Olivia's berries were missing and reasoned that those were the same. When Katarina brought the girl the cake to eat, the girl had not trusted Katarina because Katarina had always been harsh with her, pinching her arm when no one was about. The girl did not eat the cake. Again, she told Elena, who feared for the girl and had some men take her down to the village to her parents. Several days later, Katarina asked if the girl had died.

The entire staff was now alerted to how dangerous Katarina could be. Elena declared that no servant be alone with the countess, and the younger girls were replaced by women. The serene highness's personal maid was to linger in the serene highness's rooms for as long as possible.

Chance brought letters from around the empire and from court, thanking the serene highness for her graciousness. He pressed upon his mother that she should begin to answer the letters now so that her replies would be ready to deliver when the snows melted. The serene highness always attended to her correspondence in a timely fashion. Not only was she guided by convention, but she enjoyed writing to her friends that were scattered about. Chance suggested that mayhaps his mother should not entertain Katarina in the morning, as Katarina would distract her from her writing.

Knowing that Katarina would come looking for the poison, Chance removed the poison and placed some watered liquor in the bottle, then Chance alerted his mother's maid to listen for Katarina saying she had found the bottles of poison. The serene highness locked the bottles in a drawer, and only his mother, the maid, and Chance knew which drawer—and only Chance knew the location of the key, which was around Margarette's neck.

Olivia reasoned that Katarina had a small bottle of poison, one she kept with her at all times, but that bottle would not last long. Elena suggested that Chance tell the serene highness to drink only the tea that Elena gave her. Olivia could not do such, as the serene highness was completely of the mind that Olivia was poisoning her. They could not tell the serene highness about Katarina poisoning her until she was no longer influenced by the poison, so Chance had spoken to his mother and convinced her to drink only the tea.

Olivia and Elena agreed that Katarina did not want to kill the serene highness; she could have done so in a much easier way. No, Katarina wanted to keep the serene highness confused and give the serene highness her thoughts. From what Katarina had said, the serene highness had thoughts that Katarina and Thorne should marry in the spring.

Chance had doubt that Thorne was aware of such. In truth, Chance knew that Thorne was in love with Olivia. Had he not seen evidence of Thorne's love over and over again? Thorne had not been heartbroken when Katarina walked out of the castle on her last visit. His heart was not with Katarina— Thorne had confessed to his twin which part of his body was with Katarina.

And Chance knew he would know if Thorne was in love with Katarina. Was that not the way of twins? Chance never felt any love in Thorne for Katarina; whereas he had felt love for Olivia on the day Thorne brought her to the castle, and Chance had felt that love grow stronger in the time Olivia had been among them.

No, Thorne would never marry another when his heart was with Olivia. Chance had always known that Thorne did not plan to marry and have a family; he knew this long before he became part of the Dark Horse. No, once Thorne met Olivia, all thoughts of marrying another—no matter the reason—were gone. Chance could feel this and tried to explain it to Marga-rette, but words did not exist for the knowledge of twins. Had not Thorne told Chance that he was in love with Margarette before Chance allowed the words to escape his lips?

Chance had never understood his mother's fondness for Katarina, although Chance had to admit that his mother could be counted as vain, and Katarina had fawned and lauded the serene highness, treating her as if she was the archduchess herself. Thorne had become acquainted with Katarina while attending to business in Vienna, and then, not three months later, Katarina showed up at the castle doors as a guest of another. In time that was counted in days, Katarina was at the serene highness's side at every turn.

As the other guests traveled on, Katarina stayed—at the serene highness's insistence. Katarina flowered her words and flattered the serene highness as often as an eye would blink. Chance had been at a loss for thought at the honeyed words that flowed continually from Katarina's tongue, but Chance and Margarette had just arrived from their wedding in Hungary. It was not Chance's concern. In truth, his thoughts were rarely of anything other than his bride.

He did know how close Thorne and Katarina's friendship was, and Thorne admitted that they had been lovers in Vienna. The first words of marriage came from Katarina's mouth; with intent she told all guests to the castle that she and Thorne were in love. Before a year had passed, Katarina was suggesting that a wedding would be in the near future. Thorne took all with good humor.

It bothered Thorne not that Katarina was suggesting marriage. One night when Chance first heard these words, he questioned Thorne. The look on Thorne's face told his brother that he had no knowledge of such, but then Thorne started to consider the advantages of a marriage to Katarina. Chance could not endorse such, though he did not tell Thorne; his twin already knew.

Olivia reasoned that Katarina had this plan long before coming to the castle. Had she not prepared by bringing the poison with her? Katarina had come for the purpose of marrying Thorne, but as Thorne had not married her afore as Katarina wished, Katarina sought to make the serene highness in favor of the marriage and to use her to press Thorne to marry Katarina.

Katarina wanted to use the serene highness to get whatever else she wanted too. Olivia, Chance, and Margarette had all seen the look on the serene highness's face as Katarina talked of her new wardrobe and marriage to Thorne in the spring. Despite Katarina's insistence that the serene highness endorsed all, the look on the serene highness's face told them that she knew not of what Katarina spoke.

Olivia felt that Katarina was becoming too assured that her plan was working to risk talking of marriage with Thorne. Olivia knew in her heart that Thorne had no understanding of this all. Katarina spoke as real what was only in her mind. When had Thorne had time to rekindle this love with Katarina? Olivia believed this showed just how dangerous Katarina could be—mayhaps even dangerous enough to kill her brother.

Olivia kept the thoughts of Katarina killing her brother to herself. She would not speak against another without cause, but Lukas's death had served her too well. She had been able to get almost complete control over the serene highness. She had full access to the serene highness and had also restricted others' access to her. Katarina had time—time to make her thoughts the thoughts of the serene highness—and Lukas's death had gone without question. Except to Olivia.

As the group went into the midday meal, Anja was so happy. She had thoroughly enjoyed talking with Anastasia. Her friend still was quick of wit and told stories that kept everyone spellbound. Anja knew she had been spending too much time with Katarina. She must spend more with Chance and Margarette, and she wanted to spend more time with Anastasia.

Olivia knew not what to tell her mother when she asked her why Thorne had called out for Olivia when he was asleep. What was between Olivia and Thorne? This was her mother; she could not lie to her, and there would be not another who would understand her position more than her mother. Olivia sat down on the bed, opened her mouth, and told her mother all—what was in her heart and what was in her mind—and her mother held her hands and listened to her, Anastasia's heart going out to her daughter.

Twenty Eight

Thorne waited in the small room for the Cardinal. Though he had met the man only once, Thorne had a healthy fear of him. It was by the graciousness of the Cardinal that the Dark Horse existed, and it would be by the graciousness of the Cardinal that Thorne would not have to pay for Gregory's sins. Thorne—and Thorne alone—was responsible for everything the Dark Horse did, even if that Dark Horse was not Thorne. The Cardinal's letters made that perfectly clear.

"Thank you for seeing me, Your Most Reverend Eminence." Thorne stood and then bowed and kissed the ring on the man's hand.

The priest that had greeted Thorne had already told the Cardinal everything that Thorne told him, so the Cardinal gestured for Thorne to follow him down a long, barren hallway. Thorne waited for the man to speak; for all that Thorne had knowledge, he was being escorted to a prison cell. At the end of the hallway was a stair, and the two men walked down the steps that emptied into an indoor winter garden. The Cardinal gestured to a set of benches, and the two men sat facing each other.

"The girl had gone mad with syphilis, and her parents wanted only for her to have peace. If I may, I ask that you have mercy on them." Thorne had wanted to tell this to the Cardinal only; his plea would not be the same if conveyed through another.

"Your plea has been heard. You are of the mind that there are no others that wish to take the mantle of the Dark Horse out of greed?"

"Yes, there have been no others since we captured Gregory."

"I trust that Bishop Baltier will be as discreet as his son, Father Frederico, has been."

Thorne knew not what to say; he did not know that the Cardinal knew of either as Father Adolphus had not known of Father Frederico. "Yes, the Dark Horse has no wish to slander the church."

"Very well. There will be some changes from the church as there have been changes with the Dark Horse." The elderly man paused. Thorne became alarmed.

"Father Adolphus will remain here. Father Peter Simon will replace him. Father David will parish the village, and you will take him back with you. I think you will find that both men have much in common with your expanded group. What they do not know, you will be tasked to teach them."

Thorne thought upon the man's words. The Cardinal knew that the Dark Horse was no longer just Thorne, and Father Peter Simon was of the proper age, height, weight, and coloring. Thorne believed he would find Father David the same as well.

"What do they know?"

"All," the Cardinal said and then paused. "I have personally selected both of these men. Although their hearts belong fully to the church, I believe you will find that both have another side to them. Neither was originally bound for the church. They have skills and talents, although hidden, that you would expect any of your group to have.

"You were wise to expand your group. I wish I could say that I had that wisdom concerning the Dark Horse, but a thought such as that never came to me. Not only will you—and the others—be more protected, you will protect innocents as well.

"You are much like your father, Thorne, although that

side of your father was rarely seen. I worried that you, like your father, would allow yourself to rush in where one should walk gently. I intend not to speak against your father; his training did not encourage him to do otherwise. My intent is to praise your wisdom and ability to restrain your nature, to do what is best. This is what the Dark Horse needs as time goes on—strength with wisdom, not solely strength.

"But you must use this wisdom with which you have been blessed in other areas of your life." The Cardinal could see that Thorne had no understanding. "Think and pray upon my words; you will understand. You must be more than the Dark Horse; others need you."

The Cardinal rose and headed back for the stair. "Now let us speak of the girl."

Thorne had no wish to discuss such. The girl was with the prince; Thorne had no wish to steal a body from a man that wanted him dead. Let the prince do what was right with the girl's body.

"When the prince divorced, he gave up the right to decide his daughter's future. The church has the right to decide that now. You have the blessing of the church to wed the prince's daughter."

Thorne knew not what to say. He had no thoughts of discussing Olivia with the Cardinal. Why would the Cardinal think that he had wish to marry Olivia? But Thorne knew that the blessing from the church would stop the prince. He already had his sights set on Carinthia. Thorne could not provoke him further and expect the prince would not come thundering down on the castle. The prince had made known he was ready; Thorne could not hand him the reason. He had to think of the people of Carinthia and of his family. He knew long ago that the Dark Horse would steal his life from him. And now the Dark Horse had.

**Thorne read the first two letters and then glanced over the rest piled on his desk. Every one of the letters was the same. He threw the one in his hand down on the desk and walked to the window. He had almost come to trust her. He had almost been ready to let Niklas and Janos have their lives back, but as Thorne had warned the guards, he had forgotten that he needed to be most vigilant when it seemed least likely she would escape.

The snow had been too great for the letters, which had originated from all over the empire, to be brought to the castle, so they had been left at the inns and churches for delivery to the castle when the snows melted. As Chance delivered supplies to the towns and cities, they had been given to him. Some of the letters had been addressed to Olivia, but most were sent to Thorne. They would need permission from Thorne to take Olivia into their homes, and they did want to do so; Thorne had at least thirty letters asking for his permission.

Suspicious, Chance had given all the letters to Thorne, including those addressed to Olivia. When Chance mentioned the stack of letters, Thorne spit out a litany of profane words that would have made Satan blush. Chance waited for the eruption he knew would come, and he had little concern for Olivia. If anyone could handle Thorne when his temper erupted, it was she.

Thorne counseled himself to have peace, to have patience. He told himself that there was nothing to be gained by wringing her beautiful neck in front of his family and her mother. There had not been enough time for the prince to reply to Anastasia's letter, so the matter was not settled. How could Olivia have thoughts that she could take off across the empire? Thorne still did not know if the prince would show up at the castle to do harm to Olivia and Anastasia. How could Olivia be safe on her own? How did Olivia think she could keep her father from finding out where she was?

Thorne pounded his fist on the desk, then reminded himself to have thoughts of peace, to have patience. When a knock came upon his door, Thorne opened it and looked at the young man standing there. Sebastian was really only a few years younger than Thorne, but in comparison he seemed so young and naïve. Thorne wondered if the young man had ever had a fight with his fists; he had doubt the young man knew how to use a weapon. Thorne invited Sebastian into his rooms, noting that the young man seemed very nervous.

"I have come to ask for permission to marry Princess Olivia." Thorne opened his mouth to reply, but Sebastian was not finished. "My family is not titled, but we are wealthy and Olivia would want for nothing. I would give her anything her heart desired. I love her, and I will care for her."

It took every measure of his strength not to wring Sebastian's neck. "I cannot give permission for Olivia to marry. I do not have that liberty from her family, but I can tell you that to ask her father for her would surely mean to have your head separated from your shoulders! Do you love her enough to die asking for her?"

"I would gladly give my life for Olivia!"

"But you would gain her not! You would be dead and have gained nothing! It is folly to dream of marrying her. It would be certain death."

"I care not. I do not wish to live if I cannot have Olivia."

Thorne looked at the love-sick young man. Sebastian had no idea what he was saying. He would die for a woman he barely knew? He would rather die than live without Olivia? Thorne could understand that part of the young man's logic. Thorne would rather die than live without Olivia, but there were times in life when one had to accept the fate that had been given to them. Thorne had question if the young man truly understood that Thorne did not mean "death" as a metaphor, that Thorne meant literal death.

"I will kidnap her and run off to another land with her." Sebastian was not of the mind to give up; surely there was a way he and Olivia could be together.

"Sebastian, that would be madness. You must put those thoughts out of your mind. Olivia has a guard. You will not be able to leave here with her."

"She loves me!"

Thorne looked at Sebastian. Was that true? Had Olivia given him the idea that she loved him in an attempt to run away? She knew not of the letters; mayhaps she had decided to go with a different plan. Thorne pictured her beautiful face looking at Sebastian with love in her eyes ... and he lost his temper. It was one thing for her to use his name and family to get a position elsewhere; it was quite another to use this love-sick young man as a means of escape.

"She has told you this? She has told you that she loves you?"

"She needs not to say the words. I can see it in her eyes."

Thorne stomped from the room and headed for the drawing room, where everyone was spending the afternoon and Olivia was playing the pianoforte. Thorne went straight to her, grabbed her upper arm, and pulled her to her feet.

"A word, Princess."

Olivia had little doubt that Thorne was angry about something, no doubt something she had done, or something she had said, or something she was. She held her tongue for now, not wishing to have harsh words in front of everyone. Nearly dragging her by her arm, Thorne headed for the stair. Olivia started to panic. There were only personal rooms on that floor, nowhere that they could go without a chaperone. Olivia had no wish to flaunt convention in front of her mother, nor in front of the serene highness with her mother.

But Thorne gave no impression that he was in the mood for a discussion on convention. As he dragged her up the stair, Olivia tripped over her skirt, and with great effort for patience,

Thorne paused just a moment. He was not completely convinced that Olivia's misstep was not planned.

"Gain your step or I will find another method for you to take the stair."

Olivia stood and gathered her skirts in the hand of her only free arm. Not to his fortune, Sebastian began to descend the stair at this moment. Seeing Olivia struggle to keep up with Thorne, he rushed down the stair, his hand out to her.

"Your assistance in this matter is not welcomed!" Thorne boomed at the young man.

Sebastian had the look of a puppy that had just been kicked. Olivia felt sorry for him, but she dared not speak. Thorne was angry enough. Olivia looked into the drawing room, hoping Margarette would come to her rescue. The serene highness, her mother, and Katarina were all coming to their feet, but Chance sat comfortably in a chair, one hand holding the book he was reading, the other on his wife's arm, staying her from rising. Chance had a smile on his face; indeed, he looked as though he would break out in a laugh at any moment.

A cacophony of voices floated up from the group preparing to mount the stair. Thorne did not hesitate as he reached the last step. The voices floated over and around him, but in his white-hot rage he paid them no mind, rounding the rail and heading straight for his rooms. He glanced back to make sure Olivia was still on her feet and resisted the urge to hoist her over his shoulder to hasten their way.

They were headed to his rooms. There was no other option as they passed Chance and Margarette's rooms. Olivia had never been in his rooms and knew of no escape should she have need. She had never seen Thorne this angry, and his anger gained with every step. Mayhaps Katarina had told him that she was trying to kill his mother, but Olivia knew Thorne would not give thought to that. Olivia and Margarette had already reasoned the serene highness was being poisoned months ago, and Thorne knew it was not Olivia. Had something gone wrong with the Cardinal?

Thorne had seemed of himself at the midday meal. She could see that Thorne was tired, in spirit as well as in body, but he was not angry. No, this was something else. This was something he was of certainty that she had done, and this was no minor infraction as the tapestry had been. Throwing open the door to his rooms, Thorne dragged Olivia into the sitting room and then slammed the door shut.

Striding over to his desk, he grabbed one of the open letters, turned, and descended upon Olivia. As he opened his mouth to speak, the door flew open and his mother, her mother, Katarina, and Sebastian filed into the room. If Thorne had thoughts that he could get no angrier, he was wrong. At the sight of the uninvited guests, his temper went well past exploding.

"Get out! All of you!"

Closest to the door, Anastasia and Sebastian were out before Thorne finished yelling. With thoughts of taking a stand against her son, Anja opened her mouth, but the look on Thorne's face took the words from her tongue; she had never seen her son so angry.

Katarina stepped up with her hands on her hips, and Thorne strode over to her. "Get out! Now!"

Anja grabbed Katarina's arm, and the two women ran from the room. Thorne went to the door and slammed it shut, rattling the doorframe.

Thorne headed back to Olivia and shook the letter in her face. "What thoughts could you have?" he shouted.

Olivia leaned back as Thorne towered over her, shouting in her face. She had not one thought how to answer him as she knew not what he was talking about. She tried to look at the papers in his hands, but he was still shaking them at her.

"What were your thoughts?" Thorne was not satisfied with her silence. He wanted her to answer for what she had done.

Olivia was now angry. How could she answer him when she knew not of what he was speaking? She was not of an ability to know his thoughts! She stood with her hands on her hips and shouted back at him.

"If you wish me to speak, I need to have understanding of what the concern may be!"

"This letter!"

"I have read no letters. I still have no understanding."

"A family from Styria would like permission to give you a position. And a family from Bohemia. And a family from Tyrol. Need I continue? There must be thirty titled families. Am I to believe they decided to write of their own thoughts?"

The letters she had sent ... here were the replies. Olivia had forgotten about the letters. But this was what Thorne wanted—a place to send his unfortunate mistake. How could he have a concern?

"Is that not what Father Adolphus was to do? Find a place for your unfortunate mistake? Your unfortunate mistake saved Father Adolphus the concern."

"It is not your concern."

"It is my life! It is my concern! If one should not be concerned, it is you!"

"You are my responsibility."

"You have kept me prisoner, under guard! What have you done to fix your unfortunate mistake?"

"You are not an unfortunate mistake!"

"No, Thorne, I am merely what you sought to use to fix your unfortunate mistake that put you in my father's prison. Then you used me and my mother to keep your head upon your shoulders. I want not to be your responsibility. I am tired of being someone's responsibility! It has not served me well thus far. I ask only to be left to live my life in peace. Not to be someone's concern that they will push me one way and then another at their will!"

Her words cut into Thorne as a sharp blade. He had used her time and time over as his needs suited him. He was the one that had put the whole set of unfortunate circumstances in motion for his selfish needs. In truth, Olivia had been far more gracious in all of this than he had the right to expect.

Twenty Nine

nja stood outside the closed door, uncertain what to do. Katarina prattled on beside her, but Anja heard not her words. She had not pressed her son about Olivia poisoning her, deciding to hold her tongue for today as the poisoning had stopped. Anja had seen the weary look upon her son's face, and in her mind's eye she saw the twelve-year-old boy that had the weight of the world thrust upon his shoulders. Anja knew far more of what that weight was than Thorne could have guessed. She could do nothing to save him or help him then, and all she could do now to help him was to not place another burden on his shoulders.

She heard the angry voices but could not hear the words. The small voice in her mind told her to let this play out, but the heart of a mother wanted to spare her son another burden. Mayhaps this was what the two inside the room must do before they were separated forever. Anja turned and slowly made her way down the stair. Katarina made no move to follow; she had not noticed Anja leave, and Anja did not care.

"And what of Sebastian?"

"I care not for Sebastian and have made known that his intentions are not welcomed."

"And yet he understands not. He wants to kidnap you and take you to a foreign land where he thinks your father will not find you."

Olivia had not had thoughts that Sebastian would do such, but love could make one do things they normally would not. Olivia well knew this. Of late, she had avoided thoughts of her leaving, which would be much harder than she imagined.

Thorne saw the change in Olivia's thoughts. He wanted not to press further, but he knew she must understand. His anger at her gone now, he searched his mind for what he wanted of this discussion. He should not be in his rooms alone with her, but the damage was well done. He was unable to control his thoughts or anger when it came to Olivia. He had lived his life with strict control, and this one woman had stripped him of all.

"Do you not understand? There will always be a Sebastian wherever you choose to go, or you will be bound and gagged on the ground by the side of the road." Olivia opened her mouth to reply, but Thorne put his palm to her to stay her words. "Yes, you are clever and will do what you need. What do you do when the snows of January are great and the master of the house decides that you must warm his bed? Ultimately, you will die. You will run into the snow and die of it, or of the cold, or the bears, or the wolves. Or you will raise your hand to him."

Thorne need not finish; Olivia well knew his thoughts. She would kill the man and forfeit her life for such, or she would wound him and be put in his prison in which she would be raped at his will and die in the end.

For several minutes, each stood rooted in their own thoughts, which were much the same. Before them stood the one they loved and could not bear to be without, but to be together meant death, now or later. To be separated meant the death of their souls and forever looking over their shoulder for the death of their body. Thorne would die as the Dark Horse, and Olivia would wait for her father to kill her. They could not decide their fates; another had sealed their fates long ago.

Thorne took Olivia into his arms and held her. This moment must last a lifetime. He kissed her slowly, telling her what he dared not give words. Olivia took in as much of Thorne as she had time to do. This part of Thorne would help her endure; it would see her through. She now understood how her mother could give her life over to the melancholy; without this part of Thorne to take with her,

her life may well be the same. They both knew this was a time for good-bye—not only to each other, but to their lives that could have been.

Thorne knew they must part before someone came knocking at the door. He went to the door to call for Niklas, but Niklas was standing just down the hall at the ready.

"Take her to her room and lock her in. She is not to leave without say."

Thorne was not sure if he was having Olivia locked in for her sake or for his own. Thorne too locked himself in his room and did not answer the knocking that came more than once that day. He stood looking out his window, seeing and not seeing, feeling and not feeling. He had not noticed it was dark until he heard the key in the door. Thorne was surprised that his good friend would come into his rooms with the door locked, but Thorne knew Johann would not do it without purpose.

Thorne stood with the letter in his hand. He had read parts of it, and his eyes scanned the rest for what he sought. The prince admitted that Thorne had not had his daughter murdered, that indeed, Olivia was alive. The prince had not been given the full story, but he was well aware that Olivia and Anastasia were at Thorne's castle and that Olivia was quite well.

Chance was well ready, having been planning this for a long time, much longer than anyone would have thought. Even Margarette had not been aware of all Chance had been planning, and he told his dear wife everything. He did not envy his brother who would have to walk into certain death for Olivia. Chance wished he could change that, but only heaven had that power. Chance had faith in Thorne's love for Olivia, though, and faith that his brother would reason what must be done.

"We must have words, Thorne," Johann said as he prepared the prince's bed for the night.

"Shall we speak now?"

"No, at the tower. Midnight."

Thorne knew the nature of the discussion. There would be no time for peace, but there had been no peace for almost a year, since he and Chance had gone to the spring festivities.

Two horses were outside the tower when Thorne arrived, Chance and Johann having beat him there. Thorne dismounted and entered the tower as Chance started a fire in the old stone fireplace.

"Are Stephan and Akos joining us?"

Thorne then heard the wheels of the wagon. Pulling his blade, he took a position at the door, but Chance and Johann did not move. Thorne knew they had heard the wagon as well, but they were not alarmed. One by one the riders in the wagon filed into the tower, and Thorne knew not what to think of this assemblage as Chance and Johann awaited the group to settle themselves. At the end of the line, the driver entered with a woman who was bound and gagged. Now Thorne really was alarmed.

"She was not of a mind to accept my invitation. Mayhaps the prince and princess have had words." Stephan set Olivia down on her feet but made no attempt to remove the cloth binding her hands nor the one stuffed in her mouth.

Chance stood and checked to see if all were in attendance: Johann, Stephan, Akos, Father Peter Simon, Father David, the serene highness, Olivia, and, of course, Thorne. All needed to be here. Thorne stood with a mixture of anger, surprise, and suspicion on his face. Chance was ready to begin.

"A request has been made of the Dark Horse."

Thorne could not imagine why Chance would choose to speak of such in front of his mother and Olivia; they were not part of their group. The look on Chance's face told Thorne that Chance had resolve and would not be stopped. Thorne had little recourse but to follow his lead, to trust his brother that there was good purpose in this meeting.

"What is the request?"

"For Olivia to be killed." Chance looked to the bound and gagged princess who showed neither surprise nor fear. He had expected her to take the news with strength, but he had underestimated her.

Thorne was filled with blind rage, his hands opening wide and closing in fists as he tried to control his temper. "We cannot allow the prince to do this," he barely spit out between clenched teeth.

"The request has not come from the prince," Chance stated quietly.

"Who? Who could want her dead except the prince?" Thorne said a prayer, begging that the request had not been made by his mother.

"Katarina."

The serene highness could not believe what she was hearing. How could Katarina do such? No, there must be a mistake. Anja knew that Katarina was not the woman she had thought her to be, but she could not believe that Katarina would pay an assassin to kill the princess. Anja had been ready to send Olivia away after Katarina told her that Olivia was poisoning her. Mayhaps Katarina was doing this to save her?

Thorne could also not believe Katarina would do such. Yes, she was a conniving woman, but to have another killed? Looking to his mother, he saw the thoughts play across her face. There was more—he knew Chance would not just leave this as such—but Thorne still could not understand why all were here this night. This could have been handled privately with his mother. And did Olivia truly need to know of this?

"It is time for this all to come to an end. You must end this, Thorne. It is no longer an unfortunate circumstance that needs put to right. This is a fire burning out of control, and the time has come to end this." Chance looked to Thorne and saw confusion on his twin's face. Chance knew that there were truths that Thorne did not know or would want to know.

"Send Olivia away. Send her away tonight." The serene highness could see the answer plainly, and Anja was of the thought that she would be at peace with the girl gone.

"Is that what you truly want? To send away the woman who has been protecting your life?" Thorne could not believe his mother had said such. It was clear by his mother's tone that her thoughts were not of protection for Olivia.

"She has been poisoning me! Katarina has been protecting me from Olivia!" The serene highness feared her son could not see the truth for his lust for Olivia. "Katarina brought me the bottles of poison and the mistletoe berries she found in Olivia's room."

"The items were not in Olivia's room. They were in my rooms." Chance turned to his mother; this truth would not come easy for her.

"Your rooms? But why?"

"Olivia has not been poisoning you. Katarina has." Chance now knew that his mother's thoughts were completely controlled by Katarina.

"Olivia took the poisons from Katarina's room but feared that Katarina would simply steal them back. Margarette convinced Olivia to give the poisons to her, and she hid them in my rooms. The poisons disappeared from my rooms just one week ago."

It had been late in the afternoon a week ago that Katarina came to Anja with the evidence. "Katarina would never do anything to hurt me. She is my friend, and she loves Thorne. She always has. She would never do anything to hurt Thorne."

"You are not the first person she has poisoned," Father Peter Simon said quietly.

"How can you say such?" The serene highness set upon the priest with daggers in her voice.

"Her husband was in fine health, then he died. As he lay in agony, he accused her of such. In response, she laughed with mirth. This was witnessed by Maximillian's valet and another servant. The two servants sought to bring a charge against her—the crystal from Maximillian's bedside held more than just wine—but the two servants mysteriously disappeared, never to be heard from again."

"How do you know this? It sounds like lies meant to slander poor Katarina. Lies from someone who has a heart of darkness." The serene highness would not hear such words, even from the priest. Her cold eyes looked at Olivia. The young princess would obviously use her charms on any man, with no concern.

"It was from one with a heart of blackness. One must have a dead heart to murder two innocents at the order of his sister then ask God for absolution on his death bed." Father Peter Simon knew he had violated Lukas's confession.

"The Bishop will not look kindly on what you have said, on what you have done." The serene highness could not believe this priest could stand before her and expect his words to go unpunished. Anja did want this man punished, and then she wanted him to burn for all eternity. Katarina had been so good to her, always at her side, always there to help her when she was ill.

"I will take what is due me on this Earth and in the life with my Lord, but I will not stand aside and allow another life to be taken. I was too late to save Lukas, but I will hold my tongue no longer. Lukas feared she would poison him as well. Foolishly, he told the countess that he had confessed killing the servants for her. I should have spoken then. I take no comfort that a murderer has been murdered."

Anja looked about the room. Her sons believed what this man was saying—she could see it on their faces. How could they believe such lies? Then a small voice from deep in her mind whispered, remembering what had been said about the child. Anja's hands flew to her face, and she tried to rub the thought from her mind as she argued with the small voice ... *No, no, I was ill, I was confused. Katarina knew not about taking care of the child.* But Anja could remember every detail of that discussion; it was clear as day to her.

Anja's mind replayed so many moments in the last couple months, and she looked at those moments with new eyes. *Tell Margarette and Olivia that you are well. Do not let them know you are ill. ... I will always be at your side; if there was a way, I could stay here with you forever. ... When I married the count, I realized how much I loved Thorne. Was not the count's death a sign from God that I should return to Thorne? ... Someday Margarette and Chance will have to go to Hungary, but I shall never leave you. ... The guard is not to protect Olivia! The guard is to protect you from Olivia! ... Olivia is poisoning you. Thorne must have suspect-*

ed it was she, and he placed a guard to protect you from Olivia!

The serene highness fell to her knees and sobbed into her hands. Thorne and Chance ran to their mother's side. Anja had never felt so full of grief, her heart was not this broken when her beloved Tobias died. She had fallen under the spell of a murderess. She had planned that this woman would be her new daughter-in-law. She had dreams of their happy family—Anja, Thorne, and Katarina. She had treated Olivia not as a welcomed guest, but as a loathsome curse. She had tried to push her son into the arms of his doom.

Chance peeled his mother's hands from her face, and, placing a hand under her chin, tilted her face to look at his. "This is not your fault. Olivia and Elena both agreed that, as a man who has had too many crystals of wine will say and do as he is not, so the poison made you say and believe as you would not."

"That is not the full truth. I have always adored Katarina, and I allowed her to stand between me and my family. I never gave Olivia the esteem she deserved. She is not the woman I dreamed would replace me. She is cut from a different cloth than Stasie and I, and I thought that Katarina, being so like me, would make Thorne settle down and leave his adventures behind. Olivia would be of a mind to be by Thorne's side on his adventures." The serene highness looked at her eldest son. "Do you not understand? Your adventures will kill you like they killed your father."

Thorne looked to Chance. She knew. His mother knew he was the Dark Horse, and she did as she thought would save his life. She wanted to find a way to lure him away from his family legacy.

"Thorne is not our father. Our safety is in our number—Thorne, Johann, Stephan, Akos, and myself. The adventure is never of one, but the wits and talents of many. Thorne will not die as our father did. He will never die alone in his duty."

Chance stood and then Thorne. "You must make a decision what you will do with Katarina and Olivia, not because you are the firstborn prince, but because you will have to live with your decision."

Thorne had never shied away from any decision, but this decision he did not want to make. He should send Katarina back to Vienna and allow an investigation of the charges that she killed her husband and brother and poisoned his mother, but Thorne felt complicit in the deed. He should have never allowed himself to question that Katarina was poisoning his mother. He should have listened to Olivia and Chance and Margarette. He was not sure which motivated him more—protecting his pride or his mother's feelings.

He also did not want to make any decision regarding Olivia.

He struggled more with this than any other thing in his life. Things could not continue as they were. He must do what was right and best for Olivia, but would that be what his heart wanted? Thorne looked over at the bound and gagged woman. She had stood there as all had transpired before her, making no noise, not trying to free herself. Only Olivia had the strength and humility to endure so.

"I will send Katarina to Vienna in the morn. Stephan will see to her travel arrangements."

"I should go to Vienna as well. My witness may be needed, but I should speak with the Cardinal first," Father Peter Simon offered.

Thirty

"You will marry Olivia." Chance was unwilling to wait for Thorne to make the correct decision.

"I cannot. Her father would never allow it." Thorne spoke the true concern of his heart.

Thorne had no argument with doing as he willed, but he did not want Olivia to feel her marriage was not legitimate. She had spent her life as a bastard because of her father's decision to divorce, and then her father had not the honor to care for her as an adult. Even as the question of her life and death was made true, her father had never inquired about her well-being. He had only acknowledged that Thorne had not had her murdered.

"Did not the Cardinal give you the blessing to marry her?" The voice of Father Peter Simon broke into Thorne's thoughts.

"What do you know of this?" Thorne looked at the priest with suspicious eyes. How could he know what was said between Thorne and the Cardinal?

"It was my request to the Cardinal. He wrote to me just after Christmastide and told me that Father Adolphus would not be returning and that when a replacement for me had been secured for the village parish, I would replace Father Adolphus. In my reply I made the request."

"Why would you have requested such?" Thorne had not spent much time in the presence of Father Peter Simon. Had his mother made a petition to the priest because Thorne and Olivia had been together without a proper chaperone?

"I asked him to do so," Johann admitted.

"Why?" Thorne had never known his trusted friend to act without a word.

"It is a bold truth to all but you and Olivia that the two of you are to be as one. But it is also a truth that both of you need to see; it is not the path that either of you have been seeking. Chance is of the right thought; it is time. You must embrace your future together, or you must travel your separate paths alone. I have secured a position that would welcome Olivia, one with which I believe Olivia would be agreeable as well, should your paths go in different directions. But you must decide, Thorne."

Chance had asked Johann to write just after he joined

their cause. He knew that Johann would write anyway, but Chance wanted his request to be included. Johann had always taken care of Thorne. They had met when they were children and became friends despite the difference in their dispositions. Johann was the son of their previous seamstress who became ill shortly before their father died. Thorne took Johann as his valet so all could stay at the castle and Johann could care for his dying mother.

Chance knew not that it was the Cardinal that controlled the Dark Horse at the Holy See. He knew only that the church must be closely involved. Johann had been shocked to learn that Chance knew of his intent, but that was Chance's talent. He could see what was not obvious to all. He and Johann were much alike.

On the other side of the mountains, nestled near the base was a small orphanage run by a cloister of nuns. It was not in their duchy, but Chance knew the place well, as did Johann, whose mother had been raised at the orphanage. Chance made several trips a year to deliver supplies there as it was not far from the vineyards that Chance managed. The nuns did not sell the children to be servants; they kept them until they came of age, and the children were educated and taught many different skills.

Chance had gone to the orphanage when he had been

rushed away from the prince to the vineyards and had spoken to the Mother Superior. They would welcome Olivia. Chance told them all concerning her father's divorce and Thorne's kidnapping her. They would welcome Olivia. He told them how wonderful she was with children and how well educated she had been. They would welcome Olivia.

Johann had tears in his eyes when Chance told him of the request, but Chance did not make known he had seen the other man's reaction. The nuns would welcome Olivia, but Chance would not ask them to do such without approval of one high in the church. Then Chance had one last request: he wanted his name to be left out of this to anyone. It would remain between him and Johann only that Chance had been involved.

Each week since Father Adolphus left, Johann gave his confession to Father Peter Simon. Johann confessed all; to him it would be more than a sin to do otherwise. Johann feared his request would not be heard. Who was he but a lowly valet to ask such of a Cardinal? Reluctantly, he asked Father Peter Simon to make the request for him.

Stephan picked Olivia up and headed for the wagon, and Father Peter Simon, Father David, and Akos came to assist the serene highness to the wagon. Johann headed for his horse as well; he could do nothing more here. Chance left the tower without another word; all the words had been said.

Chance rode slowly back to the castle, his body weary. He had not had a moment of peace all afternoon and evening, but this night would not be over for many hours yet. Shortly after his mother, Anastasia, and Katarina retired for the night, he locked the door to Katarina's room, of which Katarina was well aware. Chance could hear her banging on the door and calling out as he walked down the hall to speak with Janos.

He instructed that should anyone attempt to release Katarina from her room, Janos should inform them that Katarina had been locked in her room by Prince Chance and that only he could release her. He also instructed Janos that Stephan would be by to collect the princess for a discussion concerning her future. The princess may not be of a mind to attend willingly, so Janos should not have concern with any method Stephan used to persuade the princess.

All in the castle were aware that Olivia and Thorne had harsh words earlier in the day, but only two—besides Thorne and Olivia—were aware that they had made peace before parting. Niklas had assured Chance that he would keep such knowledge to himself.

After his meeting at the tower, Chance returned to Katarina's room and asked Janos for assistance in escorting the countess to the prison cells. Thorne had only a few prison cells, and though they were rarely used, they were always kept at the ready and were far more comfortable than Olivia's father's.

"I was of the mind that the countess should have been placed in a prison cell after the first time she raised her hand to the princess," Janos informed Chance as they headed for Katarina's door.

"She did more than once?" Chance had only been told of the incident between Katarina and Olivia in the drawing room.

"Yes, one night as the princess went to her room after her nightly prayer, she came across the countess and asked to have words with her. The countess attacked the princess without warning. The princess asked me to stand back, and she put the countess on the floor without a concern and without striking the countess back. If a lady can fight like a lady, the princess did."

Chance laughed. Yes, if any woman could fight like a lady, it would be Olivia, who had kept this incident to herself. After watching Olivia tonight and hearing now the words from Janos, Chance was convinced that Olivia could well be an excellent addition to the Dark Horse. That would come later, though, much later. Mayhaps after they were married, Thorne would not be as protective of her and see the strength Olivia had.

Janos and Chance took a screaming, kicking, spitting Katarina to a prison cell, and Janos was to stay down in the prison tonight. Because Katarina was a countess, Chance would grant her a guard and a light during the night, and Olivia would again be locked in her room. Janos made for the cell farthest from Katarina to spend his time as Chance headed for his rooms. His night was not finished yet. Margarette would want to know everything that had happened, and he would tell her all.

Katarina was screaming out the manner in which she would kill Olivia with her bare hands, certain that this was all Olivia's conniving. She must have seduced Thorne when she was in his rooms and made him believe lies about her. Or mayhaps she had seduced Chance. Katarina need only wait till morn when Anja heard of this. She would come and free her good friend, and Katarina would tell Anja how her son, Chance, had dragged her down here. His behavior was not at all befitting her status as a countess.

Katarina paced the cell. Yes, all this misunderstanding was due to Olivia, who must die. There was no other recourse. Katarina must shelter her castle from this malevolent beast. Katarina stopped pacing, the thought becoming clear in her mind. Olivia must be a demon. Katarina laughed out loud. Were not the signs there all along? Katarina was able to reason all now that she knew the truth.

As a demon Olivia would have talents and skills of which Katarina and her mother did not know. Katarina had no doubt that Olivia had seduced her husband, Thorne, and her brother-in-law, Chance. There was no other answer. She plied them with her expertise of the skin, put them into a trance, and convinced them that Katarina was the one to blame. She had stolen the thoughts of all in the castle except her mother-in-law, the serene highness.

Katarina had shielded the serene highness from Olivia's evil. But how could that be? She must be an angel. Only an angel would have the strength to stop a demon's power. Why had she not reasoned this all afore? It was so clear to her now. She had not reasoned it because Olivia's evil kept the truth from Katarina, but now that she was away from Olivia's evil, she was free to see and know all.

Katarina knew not if there was a particular way that she would need to kill a demon. Katarina had never paid much attention to the droll words of the priests, but as an angel, Katarina was assured that the proper knowledge would come to her. Yes, when the serene highness came to free her in the morning, she would know how to kill Olivia, and she would do it with haste. It was time that Anja took the title of dowager princess.

Katarina was the serene highness. She would speak to her husband, Thorne, after he was released from the spell that Olivia had cast upon him, and she would tell him that she was an angel. Thorne would surely have great love for her if he knew how special his wife was in the eyes of God, and he would worship her and give her whatever her heart desired for saving him and his family. The archduchess would be so humbled that she had been favored with an introduction to an angel.

Thorne stood alone, looking into the dying fire. His life would never be the same no matter what decision he made. He stood as he was, thinking and not thinking, as the stars moved across the night sky. As he rode back to the castle, the first of dawn touched the ground, and Elena and some other servants were in the kitchen. Thorne gave them instructions for the day, then in his room, he sat and wrote a long letter that would travel with Katarina. He placed the letter in the small wooden box that held the bottles and the berries for Stephan, who was giving orders to the stable staff concerning the wagon with which he would be leaving today when Katarina's belongings were packed.

Olivia sat on the stool as the girls used hot towels from the fire to dry her hair. Her clothing was being packed into trunks—she could hear this but not see it. The girls were chattering on about this and that, but nothing of consequence. Olivia had awakened as usual and gone to the chapel for morning prayer, having slept only an hour or two through the night. Last night Stephan brought her back to her room, untied her hands, and removed the cloth from her mouth before leaving her alone and locking her door from the outside.

The door had been still locked this morn, but Olivia heard the key in the lock and when she looked into the hallway, Niklas was there. After prayer, Niklas informed her that she had to return to her room, and she did not argue. A breakfast tray was brought, of which Olivia could eat but a few bites, and then the girls came to bathe her and wash her hair. Now Olivia sat as the ordeal of drying her long hair commenced.

No one had told her anything. She knew not what was happening, but the packing told her she would be leaving the castle soon. Normally the girls fussing about her would make her furious, as would not being told what was to be done with her. Instead, Olivia felt dead inside. A lunch tray was brought, and Olivia was surprised that it was so late in the day. She was unable to eat anything and gave it to the girls.

Her hair was put up using many combs, but Olivia took no real notice. She was dressed in a beautiful gown, though she would have preferred to travel in something less formal and fussy. Niklas escorted her to the family chapel next to the Chapel of Our Lady where Thorne, Chance, Margarette, the serene highness, and her mother were talking in a group at the front of the chapel. As she entered, Margarette rushed to her and took Olivia's hands in hers.

"You look so beautiful. I am so happy for you." Margarette was beaming.

Olivia could not understand what Margarette was talking about, but she noticed everyone was dressed in their finest clothing. Olivia remembered the celebration dinner that was had when the last of the wedding guests had left. Was this to be a celebration prayer before she left? Thorne looked very handsome, very nervous, and very distracted. Olivia's heart almost betrayed her as she felt tears threaten to spill. She felt as if in a dream as Margarette pulled her towards the crowd.

Margarette kissed her on the cheek, then stepped away. Chance next came and kissed her on the cheek. The serene highness stepped up to Olivia, hugging and kissing her. Lastly, her mother came and gave Olivia a long, warm hug. Thorne came through the group and took Olivia by the hand, leading her to the front of the chapel. Father Peter Simon suggested they step into the Chapel of Our Lady for a prayer. Olivia was not sure why they needed to pray before they prayed, but nothing of this day made sense to her.

"Forgive me. I have left my ceremony readings in my room. I will be just a moment." Father Peter Simon hurried from the chapel as quickly as his robes would allow him.

Thorne turned to Olivia. "I am sorry there was not time to make your wedding as grand as Auria's."

The meaning of his words finally resonated in Olivia's mind. Her wedding ... she was not being sent away. This was not some sort of celebration before her departure. She was getting married—no, they were getting married. Panic gripped Olivia. She had seen Thorne's face last night; she had heard his words. Thorne did not want to marry her. It was Chance that had told his brother he must wed. No, no, no, Olivia could not allow this. She wanted not to spend the rest of her life with Thorne when he was forced to marry her. She could not allow his sense of duty to make him feel that he must do this. As Chance had said, this all must end.

"Thorne, listen to my words. You do not have to do this!" Olivia grabbed Thorne's forearms and looked into his face for a sign that he had heard her, truly heard her in his heart.

"Olivia ..."

"No, Thorne, you must listen to me. Do not do this. Your heart is uneasy with this, so listen to your heart. Do not make a mistake you will regret."

Before Thorne could reply, Father Peter Simon hurried into the chapel. "Father, we ask ..." All heads bowed as he prayed.

When the prayer was finished, Father Peter Simon headed for the chapel where the small congregation of guests awaited. Thorne took Olivia by the upper arm and nearly dragged her into the other chapel. Olivia opened her mouth to speak but shut it again as Thorne walked before his family, dragging Olivia behind him. She could not say another word now; she would not embarrass him in front of his family. Olivia fervently prayed that something would bring Thorne to his mind.

Father Peter Simon started the Mass. Olivia stood there as Thorne held her hands, but his eyes were on the priest; she could not will him to look at her. Time was hastening along, scripture was read, prayers were said, and Olivia could think of no way to stop this calamity that was about to destroy both their lives. Father Peter Simon asked Thorne to repeat his words, and Olivia knew that it was time to vow their lives to each other before God. Her eyes were wide and beseeching as she looked at Thorne. She prayed this would end.

Thorne dropped his head. He could not stand before God and make promises that his heart did not feel. Slowly he raised his head and looked at Olivia. He was to repeat the words of the priest, but he could not. He could feel the eyes of his family on him while they waited for him to give the response.

"Olivia, I am sorry ... I cannot. I cannot do this."

Thirty One

tephan came to put Katarina into the Vardo wagon, which had already been loaded with her packed traveling trunks. As he descended the stairs to the cells, he could hear Katarina's voice, but he could not distinguish her words. Nearing her cell, his forehead crinkled in confusion as he understood her words. Janos stepped out of the cell where he had spent the night and motioned Stephan to him.

"She has given herself over to madness. She believes that Olivia is a demon and that she is an angel. She speaks of herself as the serene highness and Thorne as her husband. I trust her not. We should bind her wrists, and you should not dare escort her alone. I am aware that you are very clever, but no one can foresee the thoughts of the mad."

Stephan thought on Janos's words, but only for a moment. "You give wise counsel. I will get Niklas and some rope to prepare to put her in the wagon. Are you prepared to travel to Vienna with me?"

"Who will guard Princess Olivia?"

"Her husband. Thorne and Olivia marry today."

"Thanks be to God." The man crossed himself. "It has been my prayer. I will get my needs for traveling while you get Niklas."

"It has been the prayer of many. We will celebrate when we return."

When all were gathered, the three men entered the cell. Stephan informed the countess that she would be traveling to Vienna today.

Katarina backed away from the men who were under one of Olivia's spells. Olivia still had not given up. Katarina knew that Olivia was aware that she was the angel sent to destroy her.

"I must wait for the dowager princess." Katarina had hoped that the men would listen to reason. "She is coming to take me to my husband. We will hold hands in a circle and the spell over Thorne will be broken."

The men looked one to another. She was truly mad. Her eyes shined unnaturally bright, her movements were spasmodic, and her words were spoken as if speaking a song. They slowly moved forward, Stephan of the mind that she would become hysterical.

As Stephan reached for her wrists, Katarina became a

woman possessed by her madness. Her hands clawed, her teeth bit, her feet kicked, her fists swung. It was a burden for all three to restrain the woman, and none went without scars from this battle. In the end, the woman was bound by her wrists and cloth filled her mouth to keep her from spitting upon them. The men had to carry her to the Vardo wagon; she was not of the mind to do so on her own.

He never meant to reread the letter. What he had gleaned from scanning it was what he had expected from the prince. There was still the original offense to be settled. The prince had no intention of letting Thorne go free. He had seduced the wife of one of the prince's guests. Although the prince made no mention of the escape from his prison, Thorne was without doubt that the escape was truly the offense against the prince.

After the holy season, the prince promised to descend upon Carinthia with his army and the armies of his allies. There would be no escape for Thorne, and should Thorne choose to flee, he would be hunted down, his death would be slow and painful, and the people of Carinthia would pay for his cowardly act. The prince was kind enough to go into detail concerning the manner of Thorne's death and the terror he would rain upon the cities and towns.

Mayhaps Olivia's words from yesterday, spoken to him in his rooms, had set him to introspection—introspection that had begged to be considered yesterday, but which he had refused to entertain. Today it would no longer be denied. Olivia's words ran afresh in his mind, and guilt washed over him. He should be considering a plan against the prince, planning a way to save the people of Carinthia, but he entertained introspection.

Thorne counted himself as dead. He knew that now. His thoughts had changed several years ago, before Katarina came to the castle. It took some thought for him to find when he had allowed his life to end. He had been pursuing a robber known to be on the main thoroughfare through the Duchy of Bohemia. The Dark Horse and the robber had both been astride as they raised their blades during a clear night with a three-quarter moon. As the exchange of blades commenced, Thorne kept the pace slow and endeavored to glean all from his opponent.

The man was not gifted with a blade, and desperation glowed in his eyes. As was Thorne's usual practice, he endeavored to remove the blade from the man. Thorne had wounded the man twice in the arm holding the blade, but the man held fast. Thorne rarely killed—only when there was no other choice. He had not had any thoughts to kill the man, but he had many opportunities. In truth, it would have been easier to kill the man than keep from killing him.

With the third wound near the man's wrist, his opponent finally dropped his blade. The man turned his horse and slapped the rump of the beast; the horse swiftly headed down the road. Thorne gave chase and grabbed the reins of the man's horse with the thought of bringing the horse to a stop.

The man's horse reared, kicking Thorne's horse in the head. As Thorne's horse went down, Thorne brought the man's horse down on top of him and his horse. The man went flying through the air, and the dagger in his hand plunged into Thorne's shoulder. The man's flight was stopped when he went headfirst into a massive boulder at the side of the road. Within seconds, the death of the man was a certainty, despite Thorne's attempt to preserve them all.

The man shook all over, as if lying in the snow, as Thorne sent the man's distressed horse to its peace. Blood trickled from the man's mouth, nose, and large wound to his forehead, and there was no life in his eyes. Thorne stripped his needs from his horse and said a quick prayer for his favored, loyal servant. His wound was not deep, nor had it caused harm to muscle or bone, but his shirt was soaked with blood. Thorne hoisted his needs to his shoulder; he had no choice but to leave the horses in the road, and he headed to rendezvous with Johann.

Death became real to Thorne that night. He knew his

wound would not cause his death, and this was not the first death he had witnessed. There was nothing that should make his thoughts see death with new eyes, but he did. He had known, even before his father died, that the duty of the Dark Horse would greatly increase his time towards death, but death had not been a clear image in his mind. With every step he took, however, his death became very clear to him.

He did not fear death; God would do with him as was His right. He did not fear pain; he knew that it would have an end, just as it had a beginning. That night his thoughts changed from *if* Chance needed to take over the duchy, to *when* Chance would take over the duchy. His life no longer had the meaning or the value that it had afore. His body was passing through time, waiting, as he would for a deer to step out from the trees.

Concerns were awaited to show themselves; Thorne had always searched the concerns out, but he did no longer. Thoughts that he had for Carinthia, ideas that would take many seasons to realize, he no longer sought. He marked off time with his body, his soul no longer relishing life. He counted himself dead even though his heart still beat.

Thorne knew not why these thoughts had changed, nor was he really aware they had. Just as the young do not see the knowledge and wisdom they have gained until they look across their shoulder at what had been, Thorne had not seen where his thoughts had led him. Mayhaps he would have seen thus if he had entertained introspection, but he felt he had no need. He had planned for his future in wisdom; he need only to live his life.

Olivia had, rightfully so, deftly presented to him his selfishness and lack of concern for others. The prince's letters accused Thorne of lacking the ability to care for the people of the duchy and was no less precise than his daughter. Thorne had been selfish and not fit to be the prince. His thoughts to marry Katarina would never have come to his mind had he not been selfish and not fit.

His boredom at the spring festivities had started this set of unfortunate circumstances. There had been a time when championing for his brother was enough; watching Chance excel was a thrill, but his selfishness had ruled him. Now the people of Carinthia were to be used to punish what penalty belonged to Thorne alone. How could he think he was fit to be prince?

Full of anguish, guilt tortured his soul. The one he loved he had treated so carelessly. He put his mother through agony instead of listening to wise counsel and throwing Katarina out of the castle and their lives. He led his closest friends on a wild chase across the empire for a fair portion of a year and caused Chance to endure the prince's prison, and he had frightened, angered, and agitated Anastasia. All he had done for his selfishness.

He never had argument with any in or even around the empire. Had not his home been full for the wedding? Very few of the gentry had not come. Even the countess—the prince's guest that had caught Thorne's eye—and her husband had attended. Not a word had been spoken of the incident; not another guest knew there was a concern by the words or deeds of Thorne or the count or countess.

Chance was right; this had to end. Thorne could see the path for which he had need to walk. He near laughed out loud to himself. Now that he did not wish to count himself dead, his path was of certainty to lead to his actual death. It was not a path for him to walk for himself however; he owed it to Olivia, his mother, Chance, Margarette, Johann, Stephan, Akos, Anastasia, and the people of Carinthia. This he must do to atone for his sins against them.

Thorne dropped his head in prayer, asking not for safety nor for success. He prayed for forgiveness and for the strength and wisdom to set all to right. Yes, it was time for this to end. Then a knock came upon his door.

Stephan walked quietly into the darkened room. Johann had advised him of the events of the day. He had little wish to give Thorne the news, but he would not ask another to do it. Thorne stood next to the window in his sleeping chamber, looking without seeing, and took no notice of the huntsman's presence.

"Princely Grace ..."

Thorne looked at Stephan but showed no emotion or focus on his face. Stephan had thought that Thorne looked dead, although his body was alive. He would give his good friend the news, and he would withstand whatever came from Thorne.

"There is no need for me to travel to Vienna."

Thorne's expression did not change, and Stephan was not sure he heard what he had been told. He wanted to have heart for his friend. Thorne had been through much as late.

"Katarina still had some of the mistletoe berries."

Thorne dropped his head. "I will tell my mother in the morn."

Stephan stood for a while, but Thorne turned to look out the window again. He turned to leave; mayhaps Thorne needed to be without others.

"We leave with the light. You will wear the black."

"Yes, Thorne." Stephan had no understanding of what Thorne had planned, but he would be with his friend.

"There will be three of us." Thorne looked at his good friend, his eyes clear. "Should all not go well, you are to save Olivia. Think not of me—save Olivia. Promise me you will do this for me."

"Yes, Thorne. I would give my life for her as I know you would."

"Thank you, my friend."

Stephan walked out of the darkened room. Although it had been a grave discussion, Stephan had a smile on his face. All would be well; he knew it would be. All would be as it should be.

Chance watched as the three rode out just before dawn, turning the letter over and sliding his finger under the wax seal. Thorne had written not to open the letter unless he did not return. Chance had found it outside his rooms just after Thorne placed it there. He read through the letter the first time, a crease on his forehead. He read the letter again, then laughed. The plan was so simple and brilliantly clever. Should the prince kill Thorne, Chance was to use the plan to save the people of Carinthia. He crumpled the letter and threw it into the fire. Thorne would not fail, whatever he planned to do when he reached the prince. Thorne was clever, and Stephan and Olivia were at his side.

She held the beautiful child in her arms as he looked up at her and smiled. He was a very good baby. He made not a sound as she crept into the room and swept him up in her arms, and now he was just as entranced looking at her as she was looking at him. She could not believe that blood that ran through her veins also ran through his. Bending, she placed a light kiss on his forehead.

Thorne stepped up and rested his hand at the small of her back. She looked up at him, and Thorne placed a light kiss on her lips. She knew what to do. As Thorne gently urged her forward, she knew it was time. The Dark Horse opened the door quietly, and the three walked into the bedchamber. The snoring was like none she had ever heard; it could wake the souls of Hades. Thorne brought a chair across the room for her to sit with the baby in her arms, and the snoring did not cease nor even pause.

Thorne stood beside the bed and announced loudly, "Prince, we must have words."

The prince sat up with shock as Thorne lit the lantern. The prince looked from one face to the next before finally focusing on Thorne.

"You! You! I shall have you cut in half for invading my castle! There will be no reprieve for you this time." The prince struggled with the sheets in an attempt to rise from the bed.

"No need for you to rise. Our business will be brief." Thorne was enjoying the prince's discomfort.

"It will be brief! Your head will be separated from your body as soon as I call my men!"

"Mayhaps you should wonder how it is that I am in your bedchamber and none have come at your shouting."

The prince looked at Thorne dumbfounded as the thought came to him. Then the prince noticed the Dark Horse had a blade in his hand and hovered over the baby.

"If one enters this room or interferes with us, the baby dies." Thorne now had the prince's full attention.

The prince stopped his fight with the bedcovers and sat back, his blustering posture gone. He must protect his son. Otto was all he had left.

Thirty Two

"First of our business is I would like to introduce you to your daughter, Princess Olivia." Thorne looked to the woman holding her half brother in her arms.

The prince leaned forward to look closely at Olivia. "You are very beautiful."

Thorne was struck by the oddity of the prince's words. "Yes, without doubt the most beautiful in all the empire and beyond, I believe."

"I was told you were plain, not one to be used for a marriage bargain." The prince looked away—another lie from a trusted advisor—then back at his daughter with understanding in his eyes. "You helped him escape from my prison."

Olivia nodded. "Yes, with the help of the Dark Horse."

The prince had thoughts that the Dark Horse had been the author of the escape; no mere mortal would be able to escape from his prison.

"So many of the male guests asked for your charms, the new maid in the kitchen. I told them that you were for my use only as my wife was great with child." The prince paused— should he admit to all? "I did notice your great beauty, but I could find no lust for you. I also had the need to keep you from my guests. Now I have the reason why."

"We have come to ask you for your blessing on our marriage." Thorne thought it best to strike while the prince was so reflective.

"I will never give you my blessing." The prince's eyes filled with anger as he spat out the words.

"Understand that Olivia and I will wed. I have the blessing of the Cardinal. The church will not hear your argument. But as you have not been gracious to your daughter, I give you the opportunity now. I will not hide that my wife is your daughter. You must decide how you wish to be thought of throughout the empire. If you give us your blessing, Olivia's mother will remain with us and be known as a relative of her mother's family that raised Olivia."

"She is well?" His voice was so quiet that Thorne almost thought he dreamed the question.

"Yes, she is well."

"Good. I am glad."

The prince took a moment to think. He had thrown Anastasia and his daughter from his home because he had been advised that the child was not his. He had been very fond of Anastasia, mayhaps even in love with her, but now he had little doubt that this was a lie as well. He would not marry again. His ambition was ebbing from his veins, but he had no desire for Otto to be the son of a fool. Thorne was offering him an olive branch, and a very gracious one at that. If he accepted, would he find the peace he now wanted?

"I will give my blessing, but from afar."

Thorne looked at Olivia for her approval; she gave a nod, and he smiled at her in return. This was why they had come. Thorne could not marry Olivia with her father as a dark cloud forever hanging above them, and he had not wanted to marry Olivia in a scandalous way that would taint her; she deserved much better. Her wedding would now be as grand as Auria's, even if her father did not attend.

"Very well. My last demand is that you do not touch what is mine. You will never seek to hurt Olivia, her mother, my family, or our children. You will stay away from Carinthia and not try to take it away from my family."

The prince did not wish to agree to this. It would make him look weak, make him vulnerable to wolves that would seek to take what was his. But he would also be thought of as having an alliance with Thorne and the houses into which his sister and brother had married. Many throughout the empire suspected a connection between Thorne's house and the Dark Horse. It may be thought that the connection extended to him as well. Mayhaps this would be best for Otto. He would not allow his son's birthright to be taken from him. No, he would do whatever necessary to protect Otto and his birthright.

"This agreement must be known only to those in this room."

"I will agree." Thorne looked to Olivia, who nodded her agreement, then he looked to the Dark Horse.

"Know, prince, that I will enforce this agreement for all generations. Your descendants will pay should they break it." The Dark Horse still held the blade close to the baby as he spoke.

The prince nodded. He was aware that the Dark Horse would indeed make sure that the agreement was upheld. He would have to instruct his son and have his son instruct his children as well, but at least the wolves would not hear of this and think him weak.

"Our business here is complete. If anyone interferes with our leaving, your son will die. Never doubt that." Thorne looked to the prince, who was not the angry tyrant he had been when they entered the room. He was now a man with understanding, and Thorne felt no fear from him.

Olivia stood with the baby in her arms and walked to her father's bedside, gazing down at her brother's sweet face again. She leaned and kissed the child's forehead and whispered, "Be well, my little brother," then she handed the baby to the prince. Both Thorne and Olivia had expected that the prince would not be well versed in holding a babe, but the prince took his son readily with a practiced hand.

When he looked up into his daughter's face, his eyes told her, *He is all I have.*

They had come on three horses, but Thorne helped Olivia to mount, then pulled himself up behind her. She gave not a sign of the emotional turmoil that Thorne knew was churning in her heart. When he put his arms around her, she relaxed against him.

Olivia turned towards Thorne. "The baby, would you have …"

"No, and I would not have killed you either." Thorne looked off, unable to face Olivia. He was not proud of all he needed to do. "The Dark Horse has killed, when absolutely necessary, but more often than not, one would disappear, and the story would be that one was killed by the Dark Horse. It is valuable to have people believe that the Dark Horse kills easily." Olivia had just witnessed such. "And I have never cut the tongue from any, but the story lives on, and prudence is practiced in what is asked of the Dark Horse."

Olivia snuggled into Thorne; she needed his warmth and strength right now. Thorne had not dared to hope that his plan would work. It was almost certain death, but Thorne would not ask another, though he had been truly bewildered by the prince. Thorne had not expected the prince to agree to his requests, certainly not all. There was something different about the prince, something Thorne had not been prepared for, something that had nothing to do with Thorne and why he was there, and Thorne was grateful for it.

Thorne's brave words to the prince had been a ruse. Had the prince not agreed to his demands, then Olivia would have gone to live at the orphanage. He would never see her again, but it was the only way he could keep her and his family safe. Thorne almost laughed out loud; he would have to find another way to help the orphanage, a task he would give to his mother. It might help put her heart in the proper place to help plan Olivia's wedding. His mother would come to know and love Olivia in time; she needed time to heal her spirit and mind. A letter would go out to ask Auria to come; she would be good medicine for his mother, and Auria would be thrilled to help plan Olivia's wedding.

Thorne thought a moment about the power of the Dark Horse. There would be those, from time to time, that would seek to steal that power. Gregory had not been the first, and he would not be the last. Had not his own father been lured into a trap by those seeking to steal that power? It mattered not how civilized people were; superstition lived on. Some superstitions fade, others change, but the power of superstition held people firmly.

Thorne straightened the cuffs on his jacket and decided to wait for his wife in the other room. Picking up the silk-lined box, he headed for her dressing room where the maid was placing the delicate diamond combs in her hair. Thorne stepped behind his wife and placed the diamond and emerald necklace around her neck. Dipping his head, he kissed her on the shoulder.

Thorne poured himself a crystal of wine and stood looking out the palace windows. People were arriving for the ball. They would be heavily scrutinized this night. The empire was completely entranced with the story of Thorne and Olivia, and Thorne believed it was the reason the archduchess had insisted they come for this Christmastide ball. In truth, Thorne had to admit that the story did have slivers of truth in it.

It was said that Thorne was to marry the prince's daughter, a promise that had been made by Thorne's father when Thorne was a child. It was known, of course only in whispers, that Thorne was quite a rake, and he delayed the promised wedding over and over again. This displeased the prince greatly.

One day Thorne saw a beautiful woman in a field picking wildflowers and fell in love upon the sight of her. Thorne kidnapped the woman and took her back to his castle. Most of the nobility of the empire had seen the woman while attending Auria's wedding, and many of the ladies had their own tales of Thorne and Olivia from the summer. Olivia had never been told that she was the prince's daughter, nor had she been told that she was to wed Thorne.

The prince had been alerted that his daughter was missing. No one had seen the woman for months, and everyone believed she had befallen a tragic accident—everyone except the prince, who heard that Thorne was keeping a young woman against her will at his castle and that he was in love with the woman and wanted to marry her. Rumors were whispered in the prince's ear that Thorne had murdered his daughter so that he could marry his true love.

The prince embarked on a quest to bring Thorne to justice for the sake of his grief for his murdered daughter. A grand chase was had as Thorne barely stayed one step ahead of the angry prince. As the springtime blossoms filled the countryside, Thorne could wait no longer. He rode to her home and forced her family to come with him to his castle to give permission for the two to wed. It was then that the truth was revealed: the woman Thorne had fallen in love with, kidnapped, and held at his castle was the same woman he was promised to marry, the prince's daughter.

And so it was as it should have been. Thorne married the prince's daughter and his own true love. The prince, however, still harbored anger at his son-in-law for the public embarrassment and calamity, but Thorne was so entranced with his wife that he gave up his rakish ways and now was a man of respectability. Of course, when the two princes were in the same room, it was said that it was best to keep one to one side of the room and the other to the other side of the room.

Olivia had not wanted to come to the ball, Thorne had not wanted to come without her, and Thorne could not just ignore the invitation from the archduchess. Olivia insisted that the reason she did not want to come was that she would look out of place with her bulging abdomen. Thorne had to laugh quietly to himself. Olivia was having twins. No one could look at the size of her and not know—save one, Olivia. She insisted she looked so great because of her natural slimness, but Thorne lay each night with his arms around his wife, holding his children. There was too much kicking for just one.

www.ingramcontent.com/pod-product-compliance
Lightning Source LLC
Chambersburg PA
CBHW020501260626
47156CB00006B/1820